I0551582

HUNTED BY WOLVES

BLOODLINE · BOOK 2

RHEA WATSON

Copyright 2021 Rhea Watson

Published by Rhea Watson, Amazon Edition. All rights reserved.

License Notes

Thank you for downloading this ebook. This book remains the copyrighted property of the author and may not be redistributed to others for commercial or non-commercial purposes.

This is a work of fiction. Any similarities to persons or situations is unintentional and coincidental. References or mention of trademarks are not intended to infringe on trademark status. Any trademarks referenced or used is done so with full acknowledgement of trademarked status and their respective owners. The use of any mentioned trademarks is not sponsored or authorized by the trademark owner.

If you enjoyed this book, please encourage your friends to purchase their own copy. Do not support book pirating websites. They're gross and usually just want your credit card info.

Thank you for your support.

Paperback ISBN: 978-1-989261-13-2

Cover Art: Amanda @ Smoking Hot Covers
Proofreader: One Love Editing

CONTENT WARNING

The Bloodline trilogy is a fated mates reverse harem romance that features steamy content, coarse language, and graphic violence, some of which may not be suitable for all readers. I trust and respect you to know your limits.

A reminder that books 1 and 2 in the trilogy end in cliffhangers. You've been warned, pretties.

CONTENTS

1

LYSSA

Wet warmth dragged across my face. Up my cheeks. Over my forehead. Around and between my slightly parted lips. Extra-special interest in my nostrils. I groaned, waking to a world of soft light behind my closed lids. A gentle huff brushed my skin, familiar in a way, like a packmate snoozing beside me, their breath even and deep with sleep.

More wet.

More warmth.

A more persistent exhale.

Was someone... licking me?

I peeled my well-rested lids open—and found Kira's reflection staring back.

Only it wasn't a reflection. My brows furrowed. No hazy shimmer of water. Nothing out of focus. Just intense blue eyes, bright and intelligent and *focused*. Her fur, grey at the tips and darkening to black at the base. A dark muzzle. Black-tipped ears. Full fluffy mane leading down her neck to her shoulders.

Sprawled on my back in a bed of cushiony grass, I reached for her—with my hands. Not *her* nose like I'd done in the past, poking at the spring or the lake, watching the water ripple and the reflection wobble.

Fur.

Warm, soft, thick *fur*. I flinched back when my fingers grazed her snout.

"K-Kira?"

The enormous wolf snorted, misting my face with a much cooler damp, and then did a happy little jump, her enormous paws pounding the earth on either side of my head. The internet called them tippy-tappies; I'd learned that this past month.

It signaled excitement in dogs.

I blinked up at her as she wiggled and huffed, the apprehension in my belly melting away to *love*. Tears welling, I shot up and grabbed her around the neck, burying my face in her fur, hugging as hard as I could. She nosed at my shoulders, at the marks left by Ewan and Lucian, grunting and whining and nuzzling.

Until she stilled.

The hairs on the back of my neck shot up.

Slowly, I let go. Kira whipped around immediately, hackles raised, a massive wall of black and dark grey blocking whatever she had scented approaching from behind. Although her alertness prickled down my spine, I stole a few precious seconds to take in where we found ourselves.

An orchard.

Rows and rows of trees, their canopies lush and green, their trunks thick and hearty. Wicker baskets full of... *apples* at their base.

Strange. I'd always thought apple harvests happened in the fall; I'd stolen more than my fair share when the pack passed by one in the past. The smell in the air, the morning dew on the thick grass, the pinkish-orange sunrise creeping above the horizon—I could have sworn this orchard was in the throes of summer. The air was much warmer than...

Than... *home*.

This wasn't home.

This wasn't my territory. Redwood Grove's orchards were dead, a wasteland to the south where nothing grew. Even my wolf pack plodded through without stopping, the intensity of game tripling further north.

A low growl rumbled from Kira.

Hesitantly, I touched my face. While still damp from her tongue, nothing seemed out of place. Broken. Swollen. Deformed. I'd hit the ground in the cave pretty hard, an intense heaviness coursing through me back then like cement in my veins. Now, I felt... good? Refreshed. *Whole*, in a way that I didn't understand.

Still naked. A quick check of the rest showed everything was as it should be. My nipples hardened when Kira growled again, tension rising like the hairs on my arms, like the little bumps on my exposed skin.

The river.

It had tricked me.

It was supposed to smell horrible, but it smelled like honey and glittered like diamonds.

A *lie*.

And I fell for it.

Kira unleashed a snarl and a snap of her sharp teeth this time, and I whipped around, hopping up and crouching at her side. Her tail stood so erect it quivered, ears perked, hackles high. Lips peeled back, she stared down a figure drifting through the nearby trees, creeping toward us like a shadow through the morning fog...

She solidified into a breathtaking woman as soon as the first rays of amber sunlight hit her.

Wow.

I'd thought Ewan had angelic beauty, but he paled in comparison to *her*. I gulped, holding my position at Kira's side as the wolf soared over me, massive and intimidating with her next warning growl.

But she didn't scare this woman with honey-blonde hair and eyes like gold. She seemed... young. Younger than me, maybe. Late teens, early twenties? A few inches taller than me if we stood toe to toe, draped in a white gown belted with a thin silver band. Bare feet. Glittering rings on her dainty fingers. A deer pelt around her slim shoulders.

Kira lurched forward—but didn't charge.

We always charged.

I frowned. That had been a bluff—and the stranger called it. Didn't even flinch. Barely even slowed. With a gentle smile, this beautiful creature finally paused beside a nearby tree, maybe ten feet out from me and Kira—from some naked woman and a wolf the size of a black bear—then offered her hand. Palm up and open and empty.

Always the brave one, Kira trotted over, slow and steady but oddly confident in her posture as she approached this ethereal beauty. Still as stone, I watched on, transfixed, unable to look away...

Worried, suddenly, that this was another trap.

Another *lie*.

Kira stopped a few feet off, then leaned forward, sniffing cautiously at the woman's small, outstretched hand.

"What's her name?" the beauty asked, her voice high and clear like Christmas bells. None of our tension, our caution, touched her. She sounded so at ease, that melodious tone a little too similar to the one that had called my name.

Murmured it on the wind.

Cried out to me from the forest.

"Kira," I said without thinking, distracted, sifting through memories and trying to match her to that frantic whisper in the cave.

"Hello, Kira." Her melody softened, like she was speaking to a pup and not a full-grown wolf, an alpha in the making. She tipped her head to the side, smiling, golden eyes locked on Kira's, honeyed waves spilling over her shoulders and fluttering in the breeze. "My name is Idunn."

After another wary sniff, Kira shoved her face into that tiny hand.

My eyebrows shot up, surprise fisting around my heart.

Kira then dropped to her belly and wiggled closer, tail darting back and forth, very much a puppy in the way she greeted this Idunn.

Who stroked her face. Her snout. Her ears.

Every touch—I felt.

Knuckles whispering over my cheeks, in my hair, around the shell of my ear. I swatted at the phantom touch, still on my haunches, still ready to run or fight.

But then Idunn lifted her golden gaze to mine, and I turned to stone again, heavy and frozen, trapped in her eyes.

"You know," she mused, "shifters don't name their inner animals."

I sucked in a harsh breath, trying and failing to so much as twitch my fingers, our eyes locked, mine starting to water.

"She's a part of you," Idunn said gently, and when those beautiful golden orbs dropped to Kira again, I slumped to the side onto my thigh, my hip, then my elbow stabbing into the grass for balance. "Well, I suppose she's more than that." I refused to so much as glance up, refused to look anywhere but Kira's wagging tail—just in case she trapped me again. "She's *you*, Lyssa."

Fear and relief mottled in my belly.

Yeah, that was the voice.

She had called to me over the last few weeks, begging me to come home.

Why?

"Are you an angel?"

Her good-natured chuckle had my head snapping up, and I found her seated cross-legged with Kira's enormous head on her lap. Deer pelt on the ground beside them, her shoulders were bare beneath silver pads bedazzled—another new word courtesy of Rosa—with sapphires.

Sapphires so blue… like Kira's eyes.

"No, sweet girl, I'm not an angel."

I mirrored her position, legs crossed, elbows planted on my thighs, chin on my fists as I watched her fawn over Kira.

And Kira just lapped up the attention, going so far as to expose her belly, tongue lolled to the side, eyes closed.

"Am I dead?"

Did the water poison me? Was this Heaven? Had Reed and Nikki been right all along? My mates had mentioned shifters and stars once, that we lived forever *there*, but I wasn't a star.

I was… here.

Normal.

Still *me*, just in an orchard.

"No, little wolf, you're not dead." Idunn pressed a tender kiss to Kira's snout as she stroked the wolf's belly in broad, circling strokes. "You're chosen."

I felt her peck, her hands on my tummy—but I felt those *words* harder.

"F-for what?"

Her smile widened, but just as she glanced up, maybe to trap me again in her golden gaze, a snarl ripped over the orchard. Then a grunt, a growl, a *bang*, crashing like thunder and clouding up the horizon. I pushed onto my knees, heart hammering, searching for the source, for the reason the darkening sky was at war with itself.

Only to realize... those were my mates.

"Lyssa?"

Lucian. His voice tickled my ear, rumbly and soft, smooth like velvet and warm as afternoon sunshine. But he wasn't... here.

Trembling, I turned to Idunn for answers, but she had already slipped under the safety of the nearby tree, hiding in the canopy's shade and settling there against its trunk, knees hugged to her chest like she was about to ride out the incoming storm. Kira, meanwhile, was up and on the move again, padding toward me, picking up speed with every step—

She jumped.

I braced.

And she dove straight into me, plunging into my chest, filling me up...

The orchard faded away.

The black returned.

"Lyssa?" And Lucian's whisper *cracked* like lightning splitting a tree. "Little mate, please wake up..."

2

EWAN

"Are you sure you don't want us to stay?"

I offered Ethan Perry a lopsided grin, too tired at this point to flash a whole one. "No, no, go. It's late." Almost four in the morning, actually. Beyond the beanpole blond warlock standing on the porch at the front door, his missus loaded little baby Aster into the back of their SUV, the pup still dead to the world. In fact, that tiny witch had slept through this whole nightmare, never once out of Rosa's sight, snoozing away as our pack went up in flames. "I think we're fine... Right?"

"From what we can glean in the ether, she seems okay." Ethan's brown gaze soared upward, almost like he could see through the house to Lyssa's bedroom—to my mate, also dead to the world, limp and lifeless in her bed. "No curses, no magical injury... She's just lost somewhere."

I pinched the bridge of my nose with a frustrated growl. "Fantastic."

"She's strong," Ethan assured me, his tone gentle but raspy, the night taking a toll on all of us. He and his wife had raced over the second I called almost three hours ago, the pair shooting out of bed to help Lyssa. Eyes rimmed with dark circles, he looked just as fucking beat as I felt. "Give her time. I'm sure she'll find her way back. Remember... Everyone who drank from the river before that we know of died." The warlock clapped me on the shoulder, our weary gazes briefly tangled as he added, "This is really promising, even if it doesn't feel that way."

This time, I managed a full smile, thin and heartless as it was, and we said our final goodbyes—for now. If shit hit the fan, he was on fucking speed dial. Ethan had already offered to come back as needed; I'd accepted in a heartbeat, even with Lucian grumbling under his breath about warlock trickery and whatever other bullshit he brought from across the pond.

My inner wolf huffed, frantically pacing around my chest, determined to get back to our mate *now*. The fucker was nowhere near as exhausted as me, alert and hyperfocused on *her*, and it would have been easier to just let him out instead of fighting to keep him in.

But he'd go straight for Soren's throat.

And... that solved nothing.

Apparently.

So, I knuckled at the middle of my chest as I watched Ethan crunch down the gravel driveway, hop in the SUV, and peel away from the house, his shift over.

Bourbon and violet tickled my nostrils as I slowly shuffled around, Jocelyn's natural musk mingled with the liquor she had decided to drown herself in tonight. The fox shifter tiptoed off the stairs across the foyer, swathed in an enormous grey knit, her sweatpants stained and a far cry from the put-together executive assistant she presented to everyone else.

"Are you sure *I* should go?" Arms folded, she side-eyed the foyer staircase behind her. I nodded, so not in the mood

9

to argue tonight. Usually her oomph and snark amused me; now, I just needed her to do what she was told.

"You too, vixen. Good night." I gestured out the open door. "Obviously I'll be taking a sick day tomorrow..." *Fuck's sake.* "*Today*, I guess. Cancel everything and reschedule the—"

"Stop." She raised a hand, meandering right into my personal space with her brows knit and her nose crinkled. Judgy little fox. "Seriously, don't talk about work right now. I got you—but I can stay. Let you guys sleep. I would never let anything happen to your mate."

I gritted my teeth at the wobble in her words, the loss of her own mate ancient history yet fresh as ever given the circumstances. Despite living at the far western edge of the Redwood Grove village, holed up in her private chalet and nursing old heartaches, Jocelyn had blown open this very door in record time after my panicked text, ready to save my mate no matter the cost.

She knew how it felt to lose your fated.

The fear.

The gut-wrenching panic.

The *agony*—and we hadn't even lost Lyssa. She was still here, technically, breathing, maybe even sleeping.

Jocelyn's fated had been dead for years.

I shouldn't have even involved her, but I trusted no one else, no one but her and the Perry coven, to help as my precarious forever threatened to turn to ash.

"I know," I said softly, mustering up a more genuine smile as her eyes watered. "I'd trust Lyssa to you in a second, but *we* have to do this."

Me, Lucian, and mother*fucking* Soren—who had let this happen to our she-wolf in the first place. Outside assistance made a world of difference, especially if there was accursed old magic at play in my mountain range, but at the end of the day, we were responsible for Lyssa. No one else. *Us.*

As soon as Jocelyn shuffled out, I closed the door gently behind her, then slumped into it with a sigh that quickly morphed into a long, frustrated groan. Head hanging, I battled back the memories of the other night, the all-too-vivid flashbacks of the horseshit that spilled out of my mouth after we found Lyssa in the clearing, having just beaten back four Hawthorne invaders all by herself.

Bikers and gangsters and thieves. Sadists. Killers. I knew that fucking pack—because I'd been raised by one just like them. Most of the Quinn wolves were either in a human prison, dead, or in hiding, enemies everywhere, our days of running the Toronto shifter drug trade a distant, painful memory. Still, no matter how fancy a suit I wore, no matter how much *legal* cash I pulled every day, I was still a Quinn in my bones.

Violent. Dangerous. Underhanded. *Killer*.

You couldn't shake that shit.

Legacies were forever.

The Hawthorne pack, our eastern rivals who seemed ready to really test us now, had a legacy steeped in blood and violence.

And Lyssa, our mate, our girl, the future mother of our fucking bloodline and queen of all she surveyed, squared off with a handful of them *alone*—

I'd lost it.

I hadn't meant to.

Hell, I'd barely noticed the venom pouring out unchecked, my inner wolf snarling, raging, yelping in panic.

Just a blur of fear and anger, fists and fury, claws and teeth and *violence* as we three alphas turned on each other, spurred by the visceral turmoil in our pack bond.

I'd fucked up.

Hurt her.

And it was too late to take it all back.

The last thing I had said to her before this Gull River disaster... Hateful. Cruel.

Above all else, a blatant lie.

Yeah, we needed pups ASAP. It was the only true way to cement pack ties and claim this enormous territory. Put down roots. Forge a new legacy.

But we needed *her* more than anything. Our fated should stand above the rest, above bloodline and territory, and I'd ground her into the mud—all because I was terrified.

Fucking coward.

Your father's son.

I snarled and shoved off the door, stalking for the stairs and fighting the flood of memories. My father's son—*fuck* the inner voices. I was his boy by blood and nothing more.

No pup of mine would ever find me with a needle in my arm and a lethal dose of wolfsbane in my veins—all because I couldn't face the consequences of my own fucking actions.

Taking the stairs three at a time, I sprinted up and around the corner, down the hall to the western wing of the house that was finally starting to smell like all of us and not just Lyssa...

Then stopped dead in my tracks, eyes narrowed as Soren sniffed at her open bedroom door.

"What the hell are you doing?"

"I think she's waking up," the blond alpha remarked, squinting into her room, a breath away from crossing the threshold. *Nope.* Fuck no. I ripped him backward by his T-shirt, the stitching torn open, and slammed him into the wall.

"Stay the fuck out," I snarled, *right* in his face, skin humming at the closeness. "You've done enough."

Soren's furious baby blues met my gaze fleetingly, but then he forced them down and away, jaw clenched like he was fighting his dominant urges. Good. He'd fucked up, and

12

we all knew it. He hadn't a goddamn leg to stand on if he tried to pull rank here.

"*Good*," I hissed, on the verge of adding *boy*—but that one word was enough. The alpha in him snapped, and Soren shoved back, snarling, his eyes all amber and danger now, seconds from shifting. The heat of it burned in my chest, our bond stronger, his guilt and fear and regret churning through the connection as we pushed and wrestled away from the bedroom door.

He should have known better.

Explore the mountain range, sure. Humans did it all the time; we made a mint off the seasonal ski slopes, the year-round hiking trails, the climbers with their little metal picks. But to let her bound around *inside*, unsupervised, was the height of fucking stupidity.

I wanted to kick him out.

Boot him from the pack and call it a day.

But we needed a majority vote to expel a fellow alpha; we'd put that in the fucking charter we signed last year when all this had started.

Lucian had said no. Pissed as he was, he couldn't do it—couldn't banish Soren from our territory, land that his ancestors had worked way before either of us showed up, and cut him off from his fated mate.

Furious as we *both* were, that was just too cruel.

Soren might have carried her home, kicked down our doors well after midnight baying for help, eyes wild with panic, but he had no right to access her fucking safe space now—

"Lyssa?" We both stilled at Lucian's murmur. The grizzled alpha hadn't left her bedside since we laid her in it, naked and unconscious. Not even when Rosa and Ethan did whatever magical nonsense necessary to cleanse the air and poke the ether. Right there, planted, rooted in place, Lucian had barely moved, barely spoken, until now.

Which had to mean—

"Little mate, please wake up."

A deep breath and a feminine groan followed. I shoved Soren into the wall one last time, then cracked him across the face with my elbow as I whirled around and charged into her room.

With that fucking blond right at my heels.

Teeth bared, I turned back to clock him again, repay him for the cheap shot he took at me the other night, but then Lucian inhaled sharply. Relief didn't trickle through our bond. No, shock plucked at the strings stretching between all of us—then *fear*.

Soren forgotten, I raced across the biggest suite in the house, over to the four-poster bed beside the balcony's french doors, the space all white linens and gossamer curtains. Stumbling to a halt just behind Lucian's hulking figure, I was about to ask—then she rolled over.

And opened her eyes.

No more greyish-blue marbles.

Gold blazed up at me, rich and warm like it was fresh out the forge.

My inner wolf fell silent.

I just stared, shell-shocked.

Nestled under the sheets, our mate *seemed* fine, no bruises or marks or scars except those Lucian and I had left on her shoulders…

She smiled. Sleepily. Groggily. Adorably. Smiled and rubbed at her lashes, knuckling the crust out of the corners.

"H-hi," Lyssa croaked. Her voice sounded the same. All in all, she *looked* the same. But her eyes.

Fuck.

Fuck.

Something was so, so, so *fucking* wrong. My fingers twitched toward my pants pocket, toward the phone—my lifeline—I'd use to order Ethan back here immediately.

"Lyssa?" Lucian recovered first, sweeping her bronzy-brown hair from her forehead, his tone gentle but cautious. She blinked up at him, then me, then lifted her head like she was searching for Soren.

Who had also marked her.

Who we couldn't banish after *that*—in theory.

"Yeah?" she rasped back, voice still a little scratchy. Actually, my mouth suddenly felt like a fucking desert too, but I pushed through, folding up my dress shirt sleeves that had been torn down from my elbows during the squabble.

"How… are you feeling?" I asked slowly.

"Okay, I guess." Wincing, our mate sat up and scratched at her head, sighing like she'd just had the best sleep of her life. "Tired. Bit stiff."

The linens fell away, and my caveman brain went straight for her tits.

Which also looked… the same.

Nipples like distracting pinkish-brown pearls.

A floorboard creaked, and the second I caught a whiff of Soren's scent creeping up behind me, I swiveled around to bare my teeth, Lucian up and snarling. We prowled toward him, more than capable of throwing his spoiled ass off the balcony, glaring through our wolf eyes, the promise of violence in the air—

"*Stop.*"

The windows rattled, Lyssa's command strong and certain, almost *final* in the way it quieted the fight. She-wolves could subdue their pups with just a look; Lyssa did it now with a single word—a word that triggered a mini earthquake throughout the house. Lucian and I swapped panicked glances, finally looping Soren into the silent conversation. My fellow alpha eyed the windows even after they stopped trembling, and I slowly looked back when Lyssa cleared her throat.

"It's not his fault," she insisted, her golden eyes heavy, her hands in loose fists—but her curled fingers couldn't hide the way they still shook. Something had just happened. Something way outside our realm of expertise. Something *magic*, just like the gold bouncing from alpha to alpha, desperate and exhausted and pleading all at once. "Don't punish him for... me."

"He should have—"

Lucian nudged me in passing, strolling back to his bedside post again. Teeth gritted, I bowed my head to collect my thoughts and subdue my emotions. Hardest thing about solidifying the pack bond was coming to terms with *everyone's* feelings hitting you at once. In time, we'd find a balance. The sensations would be whispers, not roars, amplified only in a crisis.

Mind you, if this wasn't a crisis, I had no *fucking* idea what would be.

Even worse, Lyssa's feelings were muted now. Lucian's resignation. Soren's guilt. My frustration. All that shit simmered along the invisible ropes binding us, but my mate, the she-wolf bonded forever through my bite and her scratch —she felt distant.

Difficult to read, body language included.

I perched on the far corner of the bed with a sigh, fluffing my hair, then folded over to bury my head in my hands.

Why couldn't things just go *smoothly*?

We'd had maybe a few days of peace since finding her, and now this?

"Lyssa, I'm so sorry."

"It's not your fault," she repeated. With her permission, Soren finally marched across the room and clambered onto the bed opposite Lucian, probably still on alert for another attack from either of us. Dark rings circled his eyes too, the toll this night had taken on him obvious, but that did *nothing* to soften my rage. Lyssa, meanwhile, fidgeted with her fingers, refusing to look any of us in the eye as she said, "The water I drank smelled like... honey. And apples. Like that cider we tried... And it looked fine, I swear. I was thirsty. It was there. I didn't really think—I just drank. Then I couldn't move, and then..."

We three stilled, collective breath held when she tapered off. Not only had her eyes turned to fucking gold, the irises molten, but they seemed to have aged a full century. Wisdom sparked in her dreamy look, our mate suddenly a million miles away. Experience. Heft. *Time*. Lyssa was the youngest here, but the gold... It gave her an unnerving edge, like some immortal—like one of the fair folk with their terrifying electric gazes.

Was that it?

Was Gull River a fae trap?

"Then I woke up here," Lyssa finished a few moments later, quiet, thoughtful. Soren, meanwhile, had a frown so deep those forehead lines might become permanent.

He didn't buy it for a second.

Disbelief buzzed in our bond, and when he stole a peek at Lucian, the oldest among us actually nodded like they were on the same page.

Stupid alpha pack bond bullshit.

Made it so much harder to hate him when I could *feel* him.

A tense quiet blanketed the suite. No one mentioned her eyes. We didn't stare. Didn't even allude that something was off.

How... How did you tell someone that?

How did you manage the fallout?

17

"I'm going to shower." Throwing back the blankets, Lyssa crawled out of bed, sounding more herself. Lucian lurched forward to brace her, as if he expected her to stumble and fall, but she breezed by, surefooted as always, and locked herself in the connected bathroom without another word.

Gnawing at the insides of my cheeks, I faced Soren head-on, demanding an explanation with nothing more than a lift of my brows.

And the promise of bloodshed simmering through our bond.

Soren shrugged it off, unfazed by my threat, and shook his head.

"The water smelled like it always does," he whispered with a cautious glance at the bathroom door. "It smelled like shit and garbage and sulfur. Like, it looked *fouled*, like a sewage drain or—"

"For fuck's *sake*," I snarled, launching off the bed. "I'll be back in a bit."

Not looking back, I headed for the door and straight out of the house, stripping down along the way, shifting on the porch and bounding for the nearby woods. There was only one truth.

Honey or garbage.

One or the other—but not both.

Time to take a pilgrimage to Gull *fucking* River and make my own conclusions.

3

LYSSA

Folded over against the bathroom door, I sucked down a shuddering breath, eyes closed and stinging with unshed tears. Out there, whispers—I couldn't make out the exact words, but my mates *had* to be talking about me.

About how I drank from Gull River.

About how the windows shook.

Coming to in bed, Lucian by my side, his voice soft and rich, I'd thought it was all a bad dream. Idunn. The orchard. Kira licking my face.

Then the windows rumbled like the surge of adrenaline in my blood shot out and hit them.

And...

Something was wrong. So, so, so very *wrong*. I bet any shifter could feel it the second they stepped in this house, the thick and smothering wrongness in the air. Tension from my mates twisted and twined throughout my body, all three distinct and strong and compounding with *my* emotions so that everything tightened like a snare. My arms, legs, back, belly—all rock-hard and cramping.

I'd lied.

I *didn't* feel fine. Not okay. Not *just* tired.

It went so much deeper than that.

At the sound of footsteps stomping out of my bedroom—Ewan, probably, given the fast, frantic pace and the click-click-click of his fancy shoes—I finally straightened and wiped under my eyes. Not a tear shed yet. I could do this.

Everything's fine.

In a few days, we'd all forget this had ever happened —right?

Kira huffed a snort. I glared up at my forehead. Why was she so... calm?

Usually we were on the same page about everything: food, mates, pleasure, pain, and the hunt. So aligned. So in sync. *She's you, Lyssa.*

Grimacing, I stuffed a finger in my ear and wiggled like that would shake Idunn's voice out, then crossed to the mirror and—

Oh.

Oh *no.*

It wasn't just her voice I needed to ditch.

Her *eyes* stared back at me from my own reflection, golden and burning. My heart dropped, my belly looped, the cramps worsening by the second. No. No, no, no, no, *no*. I pinched and tugged at my cheeks. Smooshed my lips. Pulled a few hairs from my eyebrows. Closed my eyes super-duper tight, clenched hard, and then opened them as wide as I could, glaring into the mirror, shivering almost violently when the gold was still *there*.

"No," I whispered.

Gull River had changed my eyes.

Or...

Maybe it wasn't a dream.

Maybe this Idunn was like Lady Fate, some divine being here to mess with mortals.

I...

Swallowing hard, I pressed a hand to my shuddering chest, over my hammering heart. Was she inside me now? Did Kira have a bunkmate?

Lucian, Ewan, Soren—they must have seen the gold. It wasn't like my eyes were brown before and now they were just a lighter, brighter, more vibrant shade. No, this was a *change*.

And they hadn't said anything.

They...

Were they afraid?

Freak.

I shook my head, eyes welling, the gold glistening.

Just a freak.

"N-no."

A monster, all over again.

I wasn't—

Never have a family to call your own. Not human. Not shifter. Not anything.

All the old feelings came screaming back. Worthlessness. Otherness. Just when I thought I'd found my *home*...

Sniffling, shaking, I staggered to the standalone shower and frantically turned it on. The powerful stream struck tile, loud and crashing, hopefully drowning out this meltdown.

This *was* my home, those alphas out there my mates. Maybe they could kick me out, reject me for once *again* being different, but until then, I'd stay. Fight. Some stupid river didn't get to decide that for me.

Demon-child, destructive and wanton. Sinful and filthy.

Sure, that all sounded so strong, so brave.

Big talk for a little wolf with knives in her heart, stabbing deeper and harder with every strangled breath.

As the shower warmed, I stumbled back to the sink, gripping the marble countertop with one hand and

21

wrenching on the faucet with the other. Freezing water hissed out, and I scooped it onto my face, over and over again, splashing my fiery flesh with ice until it went numb. Only then could I gulp down a proper breath, lost in the dark behind my clenched lids, water dribbling off my chin and into the sink. Blind, I groped around for the tap and grabbed the handle.

Yanked it too hard.

Broke it clean off.

I shot up with a gasp, Kira's whines harmonizing with the high-pitched siren screeching around my skull. Oh, *no*. Sure enough, there was the cold-water handle, right there in my palm, metallic with a matte finish, slightly crunched and warped from my fingers. No, no, no, *no*.

Okay.

At least the water was off and not spraying everywhere. Glancing warily at the door, I set the broken faucet handle on the counter as silently as I could, the ache in my lower belly sharper now. Had anyone heard what happened? First the windows, now this? Throw my stupid golden eyes into the mix and they had every reason to at least make me sleep on the porch while they decided if I was safe enough to keep indoors.

Arms crossed tight, head bowed, I stumbled into the shower stall and sealed myself in with the glass door. Not great at muffling noise, glass, but it felt less suffocating than the stone walls of a mausoleum. Never again. Never going in one of those awful places *again*.

But maybe you won't have a say in that...

I clamped a hand over my mouth to muffle the wail, then sank to the tile, stuffed in the far corner of the shower and blasted with piping-hot mist. No matter how brave and strong I'd become as an adult, the fear had its hooks in deep.

What if they kicked me out?

Sent me away?

Sure, their marks had turned to scars on my shoulders, my waist—but if whatever had happened to me at Gull River made me a threat, they'd throw me out. Toss me aside like garbage.

Just like Reed and Nikki.

I'd thought they were my family, my *only* family, my whole world, but those two had hurt me so *deep* that I still felt the blade in my back to this day. Outcast. Freak. Monster. No family wants one of those.

I wasn't a demon before; I knew that now. But what if the water had changed me into one? What if Idunn wasn't an angel, just like she said—but a demon? Demons could be beautiful. Lucifer was the most beautiful of all the angels.

No, no, no, no.

Arms thrown over my head, I sobbed into my knees, steam rising, water pounding, blood whumping between my ears. Kira whimpered and paced, giving off a warmth I'd never felt before, not even on my darkest day, in the darkest hour. We had always been terrified *together*. She bounced back faster, sure, always willing to take the first step, but we were a team.

And here she was, trying to soothe me, calm me, the scent of honey faint in the air.

Like... she was on Idunn's side in all this.

I gritted my teeth. Somehow that struck deep: Kira's first betrayal.

As the clawed fist ripped into my lower belly, I briefly wondered—not for the first or last time, probably—if it *had* been a dream.

No. Kira's memories were my memories, and flashes of us hugging, her fur so soft against my cheek, were all too real.

It wasn't a dream.

I was tainted.

Again.

Trembling, I dragged the wet curtains of hair from my face, then jumped at the blood swirling in the water by my feet. Bright red and diluted, it followed the current down the drain. As if my heart needed *more* stress tonight; breathing hard and fast, I clawed up the wall and realized—

Oh.

The blood was coming from me.

But... not from a wound.

Suddenly, the aches in my belly made a little more sense. It wasn't the tension from my mates threading with my own fear and anxiety, churning and twisting into something that made me sick and hurt. No, it was... normal.

I think?

Hazy recollections of homeschool sex ed came to mind, along with tampon commercials on muted bar TVs, pad campaigns on bus stop billboards. Girls bled when their bodies could make babies. It happened in wolf form too, but usually only once a year, during the breeding season, triggered by the alpha female when *she* went into heat. The rest of the females in the pack followed, but we couldn't mate. We rode it out and snarled at any male who sniffed too close.

At least, that was what I did.

I'd never... bled in my human form.

But it was supposed to happen monthly, right?

Twenty-six years old, fated and mated, and still clueless about *everything*.

Shoot.

I clutched my belly and sank back to the floor.

Darn.

Cried into my chest, rough and ugly, trying to get it out now where my mates couldn't see or hear.

Shit.

Was it supposed to hurt this much?

Fuck.

My heart still skipped a beat just thinking that word.

"Fuck." But given the current situation, the golden eyes and the bleeding and the windows and the tap—it felt justified.

I whispered it over and over again, through the tears and the terror, the anger and the grief, emptying my guts of it, *purging* here, alone, so that when I walked out of the bathroom and back to my mates, scrubbed clean, I could face them without tears.

And like always, keep pushing forward...

No matter what life hurled at me.

4

LUCIAN

"Cigarette?"

I flicked open the carton and offered Ewan first pick of the last three in the pack. Slumped in the wooden chair next to me, the morning breeze ruffling his sweaty black locks, my fellow alpha slid his weary gaze my way, then, with great effort, lurched forward to snag a cig. I grabbed one myself, then tossed the nearly empty pack on the table, lit the end of mine, and offered the lighter to him. He shook his head, sagging into the chair again, preferring just to fiddle with the stick, twirling it between his fingers, the look in his eyes a million miles away.

Bloody waste of a cigarette.

Taking a deep drag, I sank stiffly back in my chair, head tipped, lost in the starless black void above. No one had used this table, these chairs, since Thanksgiving when the whole pack gathered on the deck to feast on Lyssa's kill. Now, we sat here, adrift on a sea of confusion and heartache, waiting for dawn to creep over the horizon in a couple of hours. While I sported the same T-shirt and flannel trousers I'd thrown on when Soren kicked down the front door way back when, a limp and unconscious Lyssa in his arms, Ewan remained naked, sweaty and dirty from the shift, having just returned from the mountain range some ten minutes ago.

Shell-shocked, he had confirmed what Soren said: Gull River smelled like shit.

Like *always*.

Mother Nature had a way of warding off her beasties, using smell and taste to warn them that this *thing*, this divine creation of hers, would kill them. Gull River was one such killer; Ewan had noted the discovery of dead animals littered around it back when the mountains belonged only to him, and the Acker pack told their pups horror stories that steered them clear of the acrid stream.

With another puff, I glanced toward the second floor, toward the soft yellow light spilling from Lyssa's bedroom windows.

Why would she drink?

What possessed her to crouch at the heart of the monster, where the scent *had* to be foulest, and fill her belly with water that smelled like piss and sulfur?

My inner wolf unleashed a long, mournful howl, our guilt shared, our fears multiplied tenfold.

I should have gone with them. This morning—well, technically *yesterday* morning—Lyssa was in such a shit place after the run-in with the Hawthorne pack...

After Ewan ripped into her, quite unnecessarily, shouting about bloodlines and packs and the future. Absurd. *Yes*, we needed all that and more, but it was far too early to put that kind of pressure on anyone. Our mate had just bullied a handful of grown wolves out of our territory; Lyssa was a warrior, an alpha female who would stand and fight, never flee, and that ought to be celebrated. Instead, he projected *his* insecurities onto her.

His fears.

27

The same fears that ached in *my* heart like a fucking cancer—fears I kept to my bloody self because that was the proper thing to fucking *do*.

I'd nearly beaten him to a pulp, but Soren had got there first—and then she left the scene, which meant *I* left, our borders temporarily secure.

Not my usual plan of attack, to turn my back on duty and tend to someone else. In fact, my anxiety had been maxed out ever since, and while exhausted, I hadn't slept after Soren and Lyssa left for the mountains, for the day of hiking and bonding that they both needed. No, I had gone on patrol. Round and round the Redwood region I'd gone, swift and silent, scent marking more than usual, pissing on bushes and scratching tree trunks, reminding *all* of them that we knew exactly where our territory started—and if they crossed it again, the Hawthornes, the Ashwoods, *anyone*, would have a pack of alphas to deal with.

Alphas out for blood, our female included.

Then... this.

My fault for trusting Soren, a wolf with his head either in the clouds, spoiled beyond measure, or in his work. *Mine.* Should have gone with my gut and followed them, tagged along—something.

But Soren hadn't marked her yet, and Lyssa hadn't marked him. They needed a beat away from the rest of us to cement *their* connection, and while it had fucking *hurt* to send her off when she looked and sounded and felt so bloody distressed, I'd done it. For the greater good, I had held my tongue and resisted every impulse demanding I lock her in my room and make her forget everything Ewan said the night before.

Make her climax again and again until all that bloodline talk was just a thing of the past. Distract her with pleasure and food and the company of a wolf who admired her spirit.

Who had no intention of clipping her wings.

But I spent the most time with her already. Soren and Ewan maintained steady employment despite having found our fated mate, despite all of us needing to connect as a pack, which meant they were gone all day. In their absence, if *I* wasn't on patrol, Lyssa and I napped on the back deck or wolfed out in the afternoon sunshine. We swam in the lake and sniffed around the property, chased rabbits and squirrels through the trees. We tried to figure out Soren's bizarre coffee maker together and watched films in the cinema room. Not much to be had by way of conversation, but that was fine with me. Our bond wasn't based on learning each other's favorite color or how many sugars we liked in our tea.

It was deeper than that.

And I'd had the time and space to explore it with her while the others worked.

I... I'd tried to be selfless yesterday.

No more.

Not if it meant she got hurt due to Soren's negligence or Ewan's words.

No. Never again.

Should have been selfish.

Wasn't selfish enough back then and look what fucking happened.

My wolf snarled at the memories of bloodshed and fire, of screams and violence, and I closed my eyes tight, pinching the bridge of my nose as my ciggy smoldered away.

"So, what do we do now?"

I cracked one eye at the sound of Ewan tapping his unlit cigarette on the tabletop, the black-haired alpha also stuck on Lyssa's windows. No reading between the lines there: we needed a game plan going forward, because our mate had come back to us with golden eyes and some unseen energy that shook the windows when her emotion spiked. We all felt it, the shudder, the surge of primal *power* resonating through the room.

And no one had said a word.

Lyssa insisted she was fine, but that was a *lie*. She looked normal—beautiful, scrumptious, mouthwateringly divine— but she wasn't. Something had happened to her. Something beyond the poison of Gull River. Something deeper and darker.

I was terrified for her.

My wolf had loved her from the first night, the first *second* he scented apple blossoms on the breeze and discovered her. As close as we'd become over the last week or so, I felt for Lyssa as my mate. Not my *love*. Not my heart. My mate and partner, the wolf chosen for me by Lady Fate. I couldn't... love. I couldn't risk my soul like that again. Couldn't go through the turmoil, the agony, the crushing depression and loneliness when it all went to shit.

No.

Me and the beast inside adored her—but only he would ever be *in* love.

That was the safest road to take.

But that didn't mean I wouldn't sacrifice myself in her stead. I would *love* her eventually, but I couldn't be in love. The distinction mattered if I wanted to survive this life without getting torn to shreds again.

Yet the lure of her howl, her scent, her voice, her adorable giggles—

"I don't know—"

The sliding door whooshed open behind me, and out crept our girl. Dressed in too-big black yoga pants and a slouchy pink tee, she shuffled onto the deck and left the door gaping, her hair soaked, her golden eyes like floodlights slicing over stormy seas.

Swooping her hair behind her ears, Lyssa padded over to the wooden patio table, hesitantly glancing between us. She smelled fresh and clean, like vanilla bodywash and apple blossoms and a still night at the end of the dock, feet in the water...

But beyond that, beyond the images her scent stirred in my soul, there was also something *off*. My nostrils flared as I breathed deep, the air tinged with—

"I'm bleeding."

Blood. My inner wolf yowled as I shot to my feet, chair scraping over grey timber and slamming into the railing. Panic flowed between me and Ewan, the alpha also up, his cigarette abandoned and mine snubbed out on my wrist. Panic and concern and a splash of anger all threaded together, pounding through our bond sharp enough that it must have roused Soren from his fucking nap upstairs.

"*What?*" Ewan growled. "What d'you mean—"

"Where?" I demanded, scanning her figure up and down, top to bottom and back again, unable to find the source of the iron tinge in the air. Flushed, Lyssa blinked back at us, then slowly gestured to her chest, then down, down, down to...

Oh.

Oh.

Ewan joined her, both of them pointing at her crotch, Lyssa bright red and him stammering incoherently by my side.

"Do you... Uh... That is... When did...?"

Wait. My wolf whined, pawing at my chest, raking his claws across my insides, desperate to get out and scent her properly. Was our mate having her monthly—or a miscarriage? We'd all mated, but I was the first.

If she *was* with child, then it would most likely be mine.

And now she was bleeding *there*.

Choked with *feeling*, with agony from my inner wolf and the thickening scent of blood, my throat raw and burning, I took a deep breath to settle down. After all, there was no guarantee she had even become pregnant with our mating. Ewan's came shortly after, and Soren was only yesterday, so...

Despite the logic, my heart still cracked in two at the mere *thought* of losing a pup, of the pain she would be in if that were true. I glanced at Ewan—then hardened to steel. Because he was suddenly wearing the same fucking expression he had the night of the Hawthorne incursion, right before he lost it.

Eyes a copper sunset, his wolf *right* at the surface, heat swelled between us. He then parted his thin lips—

And I gut-punched him as hard as I could.

Lyssa flinched, mouth falling open, and Ewan folded over with a cough, then a snarl, lashing out to nail me in the balls. I twisted out of reach with a hint of teeth and a warning growl, and when he straightened, cheeks pink and eyes dark hickory again, it seemed the blow had reset him.

Made him think twice about whatever nonsense he had seething on the tip of his razor-wire tongue.

"I... haven't had my, uh, blood as a human," Lyssa admitted slowly, her uncertainty trickling from her to me, probably to Ewan too. It made my gut flip-flop, while my fellow alpha merely bowed his head and said nothing.

"So, no... supplies, then?" I managed, adrift at sea again, not a clue how to handle this. But it upset her, no matter the cause, and silence wouldn't do us any good. When Lyssa shook her head hurriedly, mine bobbed up and down, slowly switching gears from the golden shimmer of her eyes to the now—to this very painfully *human* problem. "Right. Okay. Why don't we head to the shop?"

Her flush sharpened. *"Now?"*

"Would you rather we waited?"

"I need... stuff." She swallowed hard, throat rippling, and her discomfort ripened in the air, zinging through our bond. "Just got, uh, toilet paper down there for now so I don't ruin my underwear."

Ewan made a face out of the corner of my eye, nose wrinkled, lips downturned, and I resisted the urge to punch him again. *Grow up.* Honestly.

"Well, off we go, then." I knew fuck all about women's cycles beyond basic biology but might as well figure it out as we went along. No sense standing around out here at five o'clock in the morning, the crescent moon reflecting off the water, the trees whispering—gossiping about us. "Chemist's open twenty-four hours in the village."

"The what?"

"The pharmacy—"

"Let me get some clothes," Ewan growled, sidestepping my colloquial phrase, the few lingering in my vocabulary after all these years, and shoving by. He stalked around the head of the table, barely glancing back as he added, "And *I'm* driving."

He then went for the open sliding glass door, grumbling about my shitty jeep, and disappeared inside. Lyssa and I watched him the entire way, our postures mirroring each other—arms crossed, shoulders slightly rounded, drained but ready for the next round. However, before I could whisper a teasing jab about Ewan's vehicular snobbery, our mate shuffled after him and climbed into the darkness of the sunken seating area inside without another word.

My inner wolf whimpered at the anxious energy buzzing from her to me, our connection flaring suddenly—then going silent.

"Fuck." Tense, I glared briefly at the jagged silhouette of

the Redwood mountain range, then trailed after the pair, wishing this night from hell would finally just *end* already.

&.

"Okay, so..." I clapped my hands and rubbed them together, woefully ill-prepared for the sheer volume of feminine sanitary products claiming nearly an entire aisle in the twenty-four-hour village pharmacy. From the wide-eyed look on my mate's face, she appeared equally uncertain, situated between Ewan and myself, seeming very small but for once not entirely out of place.

Ewan, meanwhile, glowered in the opposite direction. Even if I couldn't see the full extent of that stink-eye, I felt the rage in our bond, noting the way his jaw muscles leapt and flexed—all because some cunt down the aisle by the *sexual enhancement* stock was checking Lyssa out.

Some twat who looked like he had just crawled out of the Chalet, Redwood Grove's premiere—pretentious as fuck, just like its owner—nightclub. Sporting sunglasses and a rumpled suit, a coffee in one hand and a box of condoms in the other, the whelp had the gall to stare at our girl.

Ours.

Openly, obviously, even behind those dark shades. My inner wolf snarled suddenly, and in an instant, Ewan's wrath twined with mine. We might have all been on shaky ground right now, fated mates far more complex than any of the elders had ever let on, but one thing was certain: outside males who stared too long lost their eyes.

As I sidled closer to Lyssa, seconds away from tossing an arm around her shoulder and flashing my teeth, Ewan faced the pup completely. No more glowering profile: he stared back, meeting those sunglasses head-on. His low, rumbling growl made Lyssa

34

stiffen, but then she crouched to scrutinize a weird cup thing on the lower shelf, which allowed me to join the glaring match.

No doubt feeling the heat, the lanky little shit who smelled like whiskey, weed, and sweat shoved those condoms back on the shelf and scuttled off.

Good.

Run, run, fast as you can...

Before we rip your throat out.

Satisfied, I redirected my attention where it belonged: this wall of pads, tampons, cups—all from varying brands, all looking the exact same to my eyes but were *clearly* different given Lyssa's palpable indecisiveness.

"I... don't know what I need," she admitted, straightening with a huff. Arms crossed, her hands tightened over her biceps, scrunching the jean jacket she had thrown on after Ewan insisted she wear something *more* than yoga pants and a—quote—raggedy old T-shirt. The notion still made me roll my eyes: Lyssa's outfit was hardly the problem, not with this prick rocking up in designer labels as if we would actually happen upon anyone of importance on our predawn pharmacy run.

For tampons.

Honestly.

Prat.

"What do you usually use?" said prat asked, clearly only half listening, nose up and nostrils flared as he tracked the weed-cloud-whiskey-drenched rich kid through the shop. Lyssa shot him a frown, and he looked back a moment later to catch the brunt of my own unimpressed scowl. "Oh. Right. Never had it... Never mind."

While I once had sisters—loyal, devoted, dead sisters—I was never involved in their monthly regime. All of this was a mystery, which left me standing there like some dozy airhead, just staring, trying and failing to spot the differences between the brand names.

The only thing that differed was price, and that was marginal. Mere pennies.

Rolling her shoulders back, Lyssa strolled a few paces down the aisle, past Ewan, and then seemed to grab a box of heavy-duty pads at random. She read the label, golden eyes flying, gnawed at her lower lip, turned to *me* like I might have the answer, then shoved the box back in its place with a whine.

"I don't *know*."

"Well—" Ewan fished his phone out of the pocket of his open black trench, seeming very much in mourning with the all-black turtleneck and slacks combination beneath. "—the internet has an answer for everything. Hold on."

I rolled my eyes. We hadn't been here more than five minutes and already he had found an excuse to whip out his phone.

"Maybe we grab one of everything." I toed at the metal shop basket beside me, nudging it in Lyssa's direction. "Then you have options?"

At Lyssa's half-hearted shrug, I scooped a shitload of stuff off the nearest shelf and dumped it in the basket. By the time a bell chimed from the shop entrance about a minute later, I had the basket full and considered grabbing a second— because there was still so much *stuff*. So many varieties. Thickness, density, nighttime and daytime, and why did *those* tampons not have a plastic applicator on the box like *these* tampons—

"Way to start the party without me," Soren growled as he rounded the end of the aisle and stalked toward us. Dressed in a pair of sweats and a thin inside-out grey sweater, he felt like nothing in the bond—just the empty hollowness of a wolf running on fumes. His expression was pure frustration, dark and accusatory and brooding, but exhaustion stood tall above the rest, shadowy rings around his eyes, his shoulders rounded. Given neither Ewan nor I were all that inclined to interact with the alpha who had put our mate in danger, we had left him passed out at the foot of Lyssa's bed, snoring away.

At the very least, Ewan *had* sent a text while we idled in the driveway, informing him of the situation at Lyssa's request. She had muttered something about how unsettling it was to wake at an odd hour in a totally empty house—which didn't sit well with me.

But Soren was a big boy.

A grown wolf.

A grown wolf ready to make heads roll, apparently, glaring daggers between me and Ewan, only softening when those bright blues landed on Lyssa—then darted to the wall of pads and tampons.

"*Oh.*" He speared a hand through his dark blond locks, the sides in need of a shave again if he wanted to maintain the punkish air he adopted after his parents left. "Okay, right." Hands settling in his pockets, he glanced down at my overflowing basket, then squatted to root through it. "Uh, I don't think she needs four boxes of ultra tampons, guys."

All three of us turned on her, perhaps without realizing, and our mate went beet red.

"I don't *know,*" she hissed, overenunciating every word—something she'd picked up from Ewan, no doubt. But then the aisle trembled, boxes jittering on shelves, bagged stock swaying on hooks. Someone gasped, tremors rumbling underfoot until Lyssa blinked those watery golden eyes, and then it all stopped. Just like that, like the snap of her fucking fingers.

The anger articulating was all Ewan, but *that?*

That was Gull River.

37

Icy apprehension slithered through our pack bond, making Lyssa's blush worse as she hugged herself—like that would hide the way she shook even now that the shop had stopped.

"Are you…" Soren stood slowly, clearly fighting to maintain a happy-go-lucky energy as we all pretended nothing had happened—that her eyes weren't golden and emotional spikes *didn't* rock the literal foundations of our world. "Are you bleeding a lot?"

Lyssa shrugged again, tears barely contained and shimmering like diamonds under the fluorescent lights.

"Let's just start small and work our way up," Soren said firmly, hands on his hips as he scanned the shelves with a keen, calculating eye. "Panty liners, regular-flow tampons, regular pads, and maybe *one* pack of outliers—something for really light and really heavy days. I mean, we can always come back and restock."

Apparently, he paid far more attention to his sisters' habits than I did mine.

Yet another depressing difference between the Acker pack and my own. Not that I *needed* to know my deceased sisters' cycles, but to this day, the personal details of their lives were a wash. The Hadley pack of London—we were all about power. Wealth. Control. Tabloid darlings and journalistic assassins and aristocratic descendants. Public appearances and net gain and blood feuds and brothers against brothers…

My wolf yelped.

The scars slashed across my body burned.

And I took a step back, eyes closed, breath deep, so Soren could take the lead here. As he fished items out of the basket, I calmed the memories, the tidal wave of blood pounding from every side.

It dulled eventually, but it never disappeared for good.

Not unless I was with *her*—alone, buried deep between her thighs and drowning in her scent.

When I came back to the moment, I found Soren restocking and replacing items at a rapid-fire pace, Ewan glowering at him with that disdainful nose crinkle, seconds from baring his teeth, our bond fraught with tension...

And Lyssa's golden gaze darting between all of us, her frown deepening, her delicate hands balled to fists at her sides.

"I know you guys can see my eyes."

Soren slowed but continued feeding the basket, gingerly adding another soft pack of pads to the mix. Ewan, on the other hand, had suddenly found the floor rather interesting, ignoring Lyssa's pleading gaze, which eventually settled on me.

"Just acknowledge it," she urged, then swiped her thumb under her eyes, catching the damp before it trickled down her cheeks. I gritted my teeth, knowing this wasn't the time or place to really get into it but very aware that if we denied her *again*, she might fall apart.

We might fall apart.

"Lyssa, we... do. We see it," I told her, gesturing to the gold and waiting for the other two cunts to help. No one said anything. Soren stopped loading the basket. Ewan tapped his phone against his palm, cheeks hollow, jaw clenched. The radio played an insulting accompaniment of pop tunes, way too peppy for both the hour and the conversation. The cash register dinged. The bell at the front door chimed. Subdued foot traffic shuffled in and out, the directional flow suggesting they were headed for the ready-made meals in the fridges near the pharmacy counter.

And we just stood around, three dumb twats with a visibly distressed mate.

"I'm still me." Lyssa's voice finally cracked, her words

thick and wet. To her credit, nothing rattled this time. "I don't know what happened, but... I'm still *me*."

"Baby, we know that." Soren stood, a box of tampons in each hand, and tapped them together instead of going for her as his eyes implied he might. "We just want you to be okay."

"And we lack answers," I muttered, the discussion quiet enough that *hopefully* any nosy humans missed the key points. "We don't know what to—"

"You're not *you*."

Teeth bared, I faced Ewan slowly, danger in the air, violence in my growl. Our bond grew heated, sparks flying, this fire on the brink of getting out of hand. Yet the black-haired alpha refused to back down, stubborn as *fuck* and seconds from hurting her again.

"You're different," he rasped as Lyssa's eyes watered. "No denying it. We shouldn't tiptoe around it either. Your eyes, the bedroom windows—thinking Gull River smells *good*?" He shook his head, gripping his phone so tight the screen finally splintered. "Lyssa, you made the store shake. You're not *just* you anymore—"

Snatching a few random boxes off the shelves, she marched over to the basket and dumped her haul in. In times like these, tensions high, emotion on overdrive, her eyes would have changed—gone from cobalt to neon, her inner wolf charging to the surface.

Now—just gold. Bright, sparkling, furious liquid *gold* that gave her this divine aura. I almost expected a halo to flare around her head when she rounded on us, glaring Ewan down as she said, "Usually I steal stuff from places like this. I assume one of you will pay for it?"

While the shop didn't quake this time, our fated mate did. Words steady, she saved all the furious shivers for her hands. Cheeks sunken, she gave Ewan a moment to respond, and when he didn't, she turned her ferocity on Soren, who nodded frantically.

"Yeah, yeah, of course—"

"Okay. I'll be in the car, then."

And then she was off, stalking down the aisle and around the corner.

Once again, we just stood there and watched, woefully out of our depth and surrounded by sanitary products. Scenting our fated mate, forced to share her, had already thrown us for a loop; this was another beast entirely.

As soon as the front bell chimed and her scent dulled, Soren and I turned on Ewan, all snarls and teeth and an inferno blazing in our bond.

"What?" Ewan's coppery gaze snapped between us, canines bared, invisible hackles straight up. "She wanted us to acknowledge it... She practically begged for it. We should be fucking *honest*. Better than going through all this with rose-tinted glasses." He dodged the squishy package of pads Soren hurled at him with a snarl. "Talking is probably the healthier thing to do anyway—"

"Yes, spectacular job," I growled, rolling my eyes to the high heavens and reminding my inner wolf that no, we couldn't brawl in a human establishment, "you insensitive *cunt.*"

"And *I'm* the asshole, right?" Soren shook his head, then crouched by the basket. Blond brows furrowed, he sifted through the products and pulled out duplicates in the stormy silence that followed, our bond a mess, tempers piqued, teeth out. At the end of the aisle, an exhausted woman rounded the corner, looking like she had just finished a night shift at the Redwood Grove veterinary hospital in her pink paw print scrubs—only to stop when she spotted us, backpedal, and disappear.

Fantastic.

Scaring the villagers was hardly on my to-do list this morning.

I looked between my fellow alphas slowly; *both* had royally fucked things up in the last forty-eight hours. While Ewan had more strikes against him, Soren was the cause of our current predicament. Ewan couldn't watch his fucking mouth. That blond pup refused to accept an iota of responsibility...

Enough.

If I stayed here a second longer, ruminating, fuming, I'd snap.

Stab one of them with... something.

Without a word, I left, preferring to pour my energies into *good*—not violence. Across the small, mostly empty parking lot outside, Lyssa perched on the hood of Ewan's black Benz, arms crossed, head bowed. She snapped up as I approached, my steps loud on purpose, and then slid off the pristine luxury S-class sedan, a private jet in car form, something that had cost Ewan over two hundred grand to purchase outright, and then another couple thousand to have delivered all the way to Redwood Grove. His newest baby— now imprinted with the outline of Lyssa's ass on the hood, her body heat warming the exterior.

"I..." She toed at the concrete when I finally stopped in front of her. "I don't have the keys, so..."

Not to this beast, and not to Soren's sky-blue BMW at the other end of the lot, the SUV dust-painted and mud-splattered, a far cry from Ewan's precious darling.

Didn't matter. From what I could see, her tears had dried, leaving only bloodshot eyes and pale cheeks in their wake. Before she could mumble anything else, I snagged her arm and yanked her against me, enveloping her in a bear hug from which there was no escape.

Not that she tried. With a shaky huff, Lyssa snaked her arms around my torso, still trembling a little, and then—

Ah.

Wow.

That—

That was a firm grip.

Wincing, ribs on the verge of fracture, I just rubbed her back and took it. The soothing rhythm eventually made her ease up, and I hastily filled my lungs before the next assault.

But it never came. Always a fast learner, my Lyssa.

"You're different, little mate," I whispered into the top of her hair, shrouded in her apple blossom scent. She stiffened, then tried to wriggle away, but I held strong, hoisting her onto her tiptoes so that I could murmur the next words against her temple. "But we're not going anywhere. I'm afraid you're stuck with us... Three miserable bastards who can't get along. I'm so very sorry for that."

She peeked up at me, my quip falling on deaf ears—her eyes watery again.

After lowering her to flat feet again, I grinned and tapped the tip of her adorable little nose.

"Stare all you want," I told her roughly, my inner wolf warming to the new hue blazing at us. "That gold doesn't scare me."

This time, a thick, throaty giggle tumbled from her lips, and Lyssa pushed up again, arms around my neck for another bone-crushing embrace. I gritted my teeth and rode it out for as long as I could, knowing whatever she broke with her new strength would heal in seconds.

"Now," I wheezed, prompting her to loosen up, "should you feel the desire to, I don't know, consume our flesh, or crack open our skulls for the juicy brains, or suddenly crave our blood—"

"I'll let you know right away," my mate promised, the

humor in her words strained, perhaps a touch forced. No matter. I appreciated the attempt to make light of circumstances that would absolutely destroy a lesser wolf. *Yes*, she seemed upset with the changes, but she was still here, still standing—still fighting to live another day.

I rather admired that about her.

Lyssa had always been destined to be an alpha's mate—to lead her pack as a strong, confident matriarch, an alpha in her own right.

She would survive this.

"Good, yes, please do," I rumbled back, teasing tone unleashing a storm of gooseflesh across her neck, which I nipped at—made her giggle more earnestly. Still, as we folded back into a simple hug, holding one another, supporting each other through this fallout, I struggled to keep my own fears at bay.

Yes, she would survive whatever that fucking river had done to her, but would *we*?

And how long would it take for those golden eyes to rip her away from me—this alpha female destined for bigger, better things among the stars?

This she-wolf who smelled like apple blossoms…

And suddenly looked a little too much like a living goddess.

5

LYSSA

As soon as the Perry coven's black SUV pulled onto the end of our driveway, Rosa right up against the wheel and looking extra tiny in such a huge vehicle, I shot off the porch steps and raced across the gravel. Rocks flying, footsteps pounding, Kira whining, it was chaos inside and out, and I sprinted so hard, so fast, so head-on for the SUV that Rosa was forced to slam on the brakes, dust whooshing as it came to an abrupt stop. Engine still rumbling smoothly, I veered around the front and ripped open the passenger-side door, heart in my throat, fear prickling at the nape of my neck—fear that I'd yank the thing clean off, just like the tap.

"Whoa, honey, hold on," Rosa insisted as she scrambled to put the SUV in park. Sprawled in the seat, I slammed the door shut and rounded on her.

"Something's *happened* to me."

The witch finished ensuring we wouldn't roll down the driveway, then settled back in her seat with a gentle smile. "Lyssa, it's totally normal to—"

"No, not *that*." Heat exploded across my face; after a two-hour power nap, I caught Soren just before he left for work

45

and begged him to call Rosa over—to help with all this bleeding stuff. None of my mates seemed to know how to handle a female's period now that I had the support products, so he had been all too happy to get the witch on the phone. And here she was, dressed down in a flowy purple linen jumpsuit, black flats, and a leather jacket that smelled as expensive as the inside of Ewan's car. She came—but she wasn't here to tell me about bleeding. No, the laptop someone had left for me weeks ago would re-educate me about *that* this afternoon; the internet was an awesome place. Kind of scary, sure, but full of useful information, a virtual library that I hadn't taken as much advantage of as I should.

But I didn't need the internet to teach me how to put a pad in my panties, so, you know, one crisis averted—the other still very much ongoing.

Panicked at the knitting of her red brows, I stabbed a finger toward my eyes. "No, *this*."

Rosa looked up slowly, then stilled with a sharp breath when she inevitably—finally—noticed that my eyes were no longer the grey-blue they had been their whole lives but *gold*.

"Oh." She opened and closed those full lips a few times, blinking fast, clearly struggling. No, no, *not* good. "Oh, *gods*, what—"

I burst out crying before she could finish that thought.

Kira grumbled as once again hot wet streams spilled down my cheeks, my throat raw, my head full of thick, cottony fog. I *never* cried. I'd cried more in the last three days than I had in *years*. Crying didn't solve anything. Crying alerted predators to your presence—told them you were weak or wounded, that they could come take advantage of you in the dark.

Now, it felt like *nothing* set me off, just a gentle poke and I was gone.

Why?

"I-I'm a *freak* again," I wailed, furiously wiping at my cheeks, hating that every tear I smeared away was soon replaced by three more. "They w-won't *want* me anymore."

Still facing me, Rosa slumped in her seat with a deep breath, then straightened. When she put the car back in drive, I stopped wiping the tears and snot just long enough to notice Lucian on the front porch, his beard trimmed to scruff, his arms crossed—his expression more than a little concerned. Apprehension slithered down my back, foreign and hot like it didn't belong to me, and as soon as he stomped down the front steps, Rosa reversed out of the driveway and headed for the main road.

"Okay, okay, deep breaths, honey," she said as we peeled away from the peninsula my mates had built our home on, headed for familiar tree-lined roads that eventually led to either the village or the highway. Eyes forward, the witch reached over and patted my thigh—with two bandaged fingers.

"What h-happened?" I muttered, still catching my breath from the recent explosion. Rosa immediately withdrew, chuckling weakly as she got both hands back on the wheel.

"Oh, caught them in the door this morning like a total idiot."

Huh. I frowned, sitting up straighter and brushing the last of all that weakness from my face. Didn't she know all the healing spells? That was what she said the first night—when I hugged too hard and *hurt* her. She was a mom now, which meant she had them memorized.

So...

Why bandage her fingers like a human?

Not for the first time, a protective wave crashed over me, the hairs on my arms standing upright, Kira warbling her shared concern. Instinct told me, *again*, to grab this witch and run far, far away from Redwood Grove, but that didn't make sense. The gut feeling that had always steered me right before must have been on the fritz, because every part of me knew *this* was my territory. I'd marked each of my mates, still wearing their bites on my skin. I wouldn't leave. I... Maybe I *couldn't*.

Especially after Gull River.

Ugh, *no*.

Just catching glimpses of the mountain range through the trees, the canopy falling and burying the forest floor in an autumn-colored blanket of dead leaves, made my stomach turn.

Rosa bypassed the village, however. Whizzed right by the main wrought-iron gates and the grey stone wall surrounding it. She headed into the western woods, the foliage denser here, the road narrow and barely two lanes. Silent, her emerald gaze distant, her enormous red mane piled on top of her head like a beehive, she steered us around tight curves and winding paths, down steep hills and past the start of hiking trails, eventually stopping at a lookout point. Slowing the SUV way down, she pulled off the road onto another gravel lot, the trees cleared, and then eventually stopped at a low stone wall. It fenced in the cliffside, but seated so high up meant you could see clear over it into the gorge below, the trees slanting down the hill, a tepid waterfall slinking over the rocks.

"Okay." She cut the engine, unbuckled her seat belt, and faced me. "One... You are not a *freak*, and you never were."

I pursed my lips, only now aware that I hadn't bothered with my seat belt, and then pulled the visor down to block out the glare. While overcast, today was one of those cloudy but obnoxiously bright fall days that made your eyes tired and your skin red.

"Not a freak in the shifter sense, but—"

"*Two*," the witch pressed on, ticking these off on her

fingers, "fated mates are forever. They'll always want you—"
I scoffed. "—even when you're in a fight. *Even* when you want
to rip each other's faces off you're so spitting mad…" Rosa
arched an eyebrow, almost daring me to argue. "Seriously,
you won't always like each other. You'll push buttons on
purpose just to start a fight. You'll get annoyed over the little
things. That's life. That's how relationships work—but mates
will always *want*."

Maybe. I jabbed my thumb at the spot between my eyes
where a teeny, tiny, *sharp* little headache had suddenly
started. Even if fated mates were supposed to want each
other until the end of time, destined for the stars or
whatever, this felt… new. Strange. Were there stories about
one fated mate turning into a monster? What happened
then?

Why would anyone want a broken toy?

Rosa turned the engine back on briefly to lower the front
windows, allowing a crisp, cool breeze to filter in. "Now…"
She angled toward me again, expression serious and voice
way more intense than usual. "Tell me *everything* that
happened at Gull River."

My belly looped, flashes of fear bolting down my arms. "I
know you said to avoid it, but it was… It was different. It
smelled like honey, and it looked like diamonds."

The witch paled suddenly, even her freckles fading away,
and she nodded, gesturing for me to continue with a roll of
her hand. "Okay, from the beginning. Be as detailed as you
remember."

Details she wanted—details she got. Bat droppings, sticky
and white. The darkness of the mountain corridors. The
mineral tinge of wet rocks. The oppressive air. The sharp
whisper. The apples and honey and starlight. The freezing
water quenching my thirst. The numbness. Soren, panicked
and frightened, shouting my name.

The heavy black sweeping over me.

The orchard with its dawn-kissed sky.

Kira on the outside.

Idunn.

The thunder.

Her eyes—my eyes.

The tap. The windows. The store shelves trembling.

Lucian wheezing when I hugged him—like I'd crushed him, same as her.

By the time I finished, Kira had gone as quiet as Rosa. Mouth dry, I sat there *waiting* for this witch to say something that would make it all better—to explain it away with magic, simple and easy, like this happened all the time.

But she didn't.

She disappeared inside her own head, gaze downcast, frown deep, and with every silent second, my inner turmoil ramped up until I *felt* the blood pulsing between my ears, decades of cruel voices at the back of my mind screaming insults that I'd long forgotten—

"Are you sure the woman in the dream said her name was Idunn?"

Rosa's cautious whisper shattered it all, subdued the fear —brought me back to the moment. Licking my lips, the best I could do was a stiff nod. Yeah, never heard that name before; *Idunn* wasn't one I'd forget.

With a deep breath, Rosa finally sat up and brushed a few rogue red curls from her face, ready to meet my golden eyes again.

"I could be... wrong," she started slowly, cheeks flushed when I inched toward her, hanging on her every word, "but Idunn is a goddess." She pursed those full lips for a moment, then cleared her throat. "A dead goddess, as far as we all know."

"Great." I rubbed my sweaty palms on my leggings. "Awesome. I have the same eyes as a dead goddess—"

"It's not unheard of for spirits to visit dreams," Rosa told me, her voice soft, her smile sweet as she stilled my fidgeting with a simple touch of my wrist, her skin cool but comforting. "And, look, Idunn was a goddess of youth and fertility. She's nature based. She… She grew the apples that gave the old Norse gods immortality. In all the stories, she's kind and good and sweet, maybe even a little naïve. Don't be scared of her."

I snorted and pointed at my eyes again. Sorry, maybe goddesses were totally normal for witches, same as demons and angels, but how could I *not* be terrified of a celestial being with infinite power? That was how it worked, right? Gods and goddesses… They ranked above us mere mortals.

False idols.

Nope. Just another lie, apparently.

"Maybe she chose you from the afterlife for a reason. Maybe you inherited some of her gifts." Rosa leaned closer and squinted, peering into my eyes like they held all the answers. When she eased back with a sigh, it was clear they didn't. "I don't know. Gods are fickle. I'd never presume to speak for them, even the dead ones."

This… was really happening.

I was dreaming about a dead goddess.

I had her eyes.

And Kira was just *fine* with it.

No. No, no, no, no. Not again. Not a freak *again*.

"Can you help me?" I struggled to choke the words out louder than a whisper. If Rosa feared dead goddesses, then it seemed wrong to rope her into this. At the end of the day, it was *my* problem, but what the heck did I know about monsters and magic? A big, fat *nothing*. "Please? I keep making the walls shake."

Rosa's round cheeks hollowed for a few seconds before she nodded, and from where I was sitting, it didn't *look* like I had twisted her arm. That was… good.

"Yes, but we should really tell—"

"*No one*," I blurted, lunging across the SUV, practically in her lap as I grabbed at her arms. The witch winced, and I reared back just as fast, terrified I'd hurt her worse than before. Hands in fists, I stuffed them in my lap. *Stay. You're stronger than you were before. Remember that.* "Please, don't tell anyone about Idunn. Please. It's our secret until… I can control it, or, or, or it goes away."

The crinkle of her eyebrows mimicked the voice at the back of my head: this was here to stay. No *way* I'd wake up tomorrow with my old eyes, suddenly back to normal, no longer stronger than my mate or capable of making the windows rattle.

One could dream.

Dreams never got me anywhere before, but Redwood Grove and the three alphas who ran it had felt like a dream since they found me…

Maybe miracles were possible.

Maybe that was the one thing Reed and Nikki hadn't lied about.

"But—"

"*Please*, Rosa." If she needed me to fall to my knees, I'd do it. Go against every instinct and grovel at a witch's feet. "Please."

Her defenses fell, expression softening, her sigh full of surrender.

"For now," the witch told me, firm and solid, sounding very much like a mama with every word, "we'll keep it between us. I'll help however I can, but we'll have to wait until after Samhain."

"Saw-what?"

"Halloween," she clarified distractedly, eyes on the gorge ahead, unfocused and out of reach. Loosening my fists, I threaded my hands together and slumped in my seat. Right. Halloween. We weren't even allowed to *talk* about it as kids, spending it in prayer, warding off the devil on *his* night. Having been out in the world, my existence peppered with trips into cities and whatnot over the last decade, October 31 just seemed like another human holiday, one created to sell a buttload of candy.

Not a bad thing. I'd once sat on a bench in some suburb, watching kids in costumes run door to door, the night full of laughter and fake screams.

Maybe witches and shifters did it different, this Samhain. Ewan was currently deep into organizing a Halloween bash at the village nightclub he owned, the thirty-first falling on a Saturday this year—a cash cow, he had dubbed it, whatever that meant.

"So, why do we have to wait?"

"The night is sacred to witches and warlocks, but it can make our magic a little manic," Rosa insisted, fussing with the curly red beehive piled on top of her head. "I just don't want to taint whatever you're experiencing with my power. After, you and me will get to the bottom of it. Until then, I'll research—"

"And tell no one," I reminded her. Rosa shot me a sidelong glance, grinning.

"And will tell no one."

"Not even Ethan." He was too close to Ewan; if he thought I was in danger, he'd probably go straight to my mate with all this, and I couldn't risk them finding out yet. Couldn't risk them looking at me differently—more differently than they already did.

Rosa's throat danced through a gulp. "Even Ethan. Promise."

Keeping secrets from your mate didn't feel good; for once, I could speak from experience. I owed her so, so, *so* much. "Thank you."

Her head bobbed up and down stiffly. "Yeah, of course. In the meantime, you have to work on being calm. If something happens when you get upset, you might expose yourself."

"I…" *I've already done that. Twice.* "I'll do my best."

"And if anyone asks, you're wearing gold contacts—for the aesthetic, or whatever."

"Contacts?" *Aesthetic?*

"Lenses," she said with another distracted wave, "to explain your eyes."

"Right." Yet another thing for the good ol' internet to explain in more depth later. Before I could get another word out, my belly rumbled. And not just a demure gurgle, but a straight-up lion's roar, so loud and proud that it was a wonder the ground didn't shake. With all the dull cramping a little further south, I hadn't even noticed the usual hunger pangs, but there they were, screaming for attention. Kira huffed, unimpressed that I'd let it go on this long, and, cheeks burning at Rosa's giggle, I pressed a hand to my stomach with an apologetic shrug.

"I take it you haven't eaten yet?"

"Nope."

"Right." Rosa turned the key, the SUV humming to life, and then pressed the button to roll the windows up. "First stop, drive-through breakfast burritos, then I'm taking you home—and then it's straight to bed." As she twisted around, looking out the rear window to reverse, she patted the top of my hand once, twice, three times with those bandaged fingers—which still didn't make sense.

And still set off a protective alarm bell deep inside me.

"Because, honey, in the nicest way possible"—Rosa

wrinkled her nose at me affectionately—"you look like you really need to sleep."

"Oh, thanks." I patted my cheeks and smoothed my brows as we eased away from the edge of the empty lookout point. "Do you like it? The bags under the eyes and this pale, sickly complexion? I call it Menstrual Chic. You should take a picture—put it in your makeup book."

Rosa snorted. "Definitely first-page caliber."

Rather than heading into Redwood Grove, we took the highway south to a McDonald's just on the side of an off-ramp. The drive-through was slammed, but we eventually made our way up, and I let Rosa order for me.

Six breakfast burritos, a muffin, and a pumpkin spice drink *thing* that tasted the way Soren sometimes smelled—homey and warm, cinnamon and nutmeg and autumn spices that made my heart sing. Rosa nursed a coffee, insisting she had already eaten, while I scarfed down the mountain of fast food on the way home, and by the time she pulled into the gravel driveway, my belly had finally stopped howling.

Always taking care of me, this witch.

We hugged, me holding on longer and tighter than I should, before I hopped out and padded back to the front porch. While my lower belly still ached, the cramps dull but ever present, the rest of me was more alert. Hunger crushed, panic soothed, I could actually *think* clearly as I waved goodbye to Rosa and slipped inside.

Huh. Empty house. No mates, not even Lucian's snores to serenade me as I trudged upstairs. Off to work, on patrol, business as usual—like my world *hadn't* flipped upside down.

Again.

Not sure how to feel about that.

Gnawing on the inside of my cheek, I checked each bedroom, just to be sure the oppressive quiet was real and not a figment of my imagination. Sure enough—nobody.

Fine.

Sleeping the day away worked for me; by the time I woke up, hopefully from an Idunn-less nap, at least one of them had to be home.

And then I could show them just how normal I was despite the gold eyes and the bursts of emotional earthquakes.

My bed, however, was not as I had left it.

No, someone had made it, tucked the linens in tight, realigned the pillows—and left a gift at the head. Kira sniffed warily as I climbed onto the huge cushy mattress, and I crawled over, then settled on my knees, head tipped, staring at the velvety blue rectangle, then the sealed beige envelope beside it.

"Card first, right?"

If she could swing it, Kira would have shrugged, equally perplexed as I slid a finger under the sealed flap and ripped into it.

Oh. Not a card.

Just a single piece of thick paper—with *Quinn Enterprises* written across the top in fancy letters, surrounded by stars and other celestial graphics.

I was an ass. Please, forgive me.
E.

His handwriting was as beautiful as the man himself, but as I sank onto the mattress, scowling at the elegant cursive, the words just didn't resonate.

He had been *more* than an ass.

I tossed the card aside and went for the blue box, cracking it open to find a gold bracelet inside. Little sun and moon charms dangled off the delicate chain, stamped with diamonds—maybe? All this looked straight out of those romance movies I'd relied on so heavily at the beginning, and in those, the heroine was always deeply touched by the display.

Oh, he *thought* of me.

Oh, he bought me jewelry!

Yeah, the bracelet was nice—impractical, but still nice.

The card was… lackluster.

Did he think *this* counted as an apology for screaming at me the other night? Instead of celebrating my win against a rival pack, he had shredded me to pieces in front of the others, suggesting all that mattered was my ability to birth heirs—so the pack could maintain our territory.

And at the time, I'd fallen for it. All of it. Heartbroken and insecure, I took his words as fact.

Soren had smoothed out some of the damage the next day, but *Ewan* needed to fix the rest.

Face-to-face.

I grabbed his stupid little note again, reading it a few times, and then crumpled it up as the windows shuddered. Kira whined, an insistent reminder to *calm down*, but I couldn't—not with this beef between us. Ewan had been the bluntest of my mates in the pharmacy, so much so that it sent me running again.

Now, with some of my worries quieted, it was on to the next problem.

Apparently.

Because our connection today felt strained and distant—and if I was supposed to play it cool, not get emotional or upset or whatever to hide what could be stupid magical dead goddess powers, then we had to sort this out.

Today.

Now.

No time to let it fester into an infection.

Tossing the crinkled paper ball aside, I snatched the

jewelry box—just like in the movies, this thing—then leapt off the bed, marched out of the house, and headed straight for the village.

Straight for my mate who thought a couple of words and something shiny was enough. To a mate who always carried himself like he had all the answers.

Well, this alpha male was about to learn how it felt to be *wrong*.

6

EWAN

"Yeah, yeah, I'll make a few copies and collate the packets before the—" Jocelyn stumbled into my office doorframe, her back blocking the view—but not the heady scent of roses descending over the entire floor like a fog. "Oh, uh, hi. How are you feeling?"

Lyssa shouldered by, not as brutishly as she had the first time but still rough enough to put a fox in her place. "Doing great, thanks, Jocelyn." She then grabbed the door and closed it in my assistant's face, the very same assistant who had been with me all night during the chaos but *still* managed my professional world this morning with an iron fist like nothing had happened.

Like we weren't operating on maybe a collective hour of sleep between us.

Seated at my desk, I wheeled my chair out from behind the monitor and arched an eyebrow, seconds away from grabbing my phone and shooting a scathing message to the two dipshits who ran this pack with me. Because, I mean... Why the *fuck* was she here and not in bed? Not only had she been fucking poisoned by Gull River, no matter how *good* she pretended to be now, but she was either on her period or in the midst of a miscarriage. Given the symptoms, the former seemed more likely, but the latter made me *ache*...

Whatever the reason, my girl ought to be in bed for the rest of the day while someone waited on her hand and foot.

The sight of her standing there, fuming, unleashed a storm of emotions that I so didn't fucking need right now. Dressed in the usual yoga pants, T-shirt, black jacket combo, to outsiders my mate looked like she was headed to the gym.

The one thing out of place: a Tiffany box clutched in her fist, the one I'd put a rush order on and called in a shitload of favors yesterday to have it expedited up here at breakneck speed.

Hair wild and trundling down her back like a shaggy caramel waterfall, Lyssa hoisted the blue velvet rectangle. "What's *this*?"

Fire ripped through me, her *wrath* scorching my own feelings, the first real reminder of our bond all morning. Fantastic to feel her again—but I'd rather it not be her rage making me break out in sweats. Usually waltzing over my office threshold pushed all the bullshit aside. No matter what was going on out *there*, in here, I was in control. Confident. Assertive. Focused. *Alpha*.

For the last two hours, distraction and uncertainty were the driving forces. I had to read emails twice for the first time in fucking ages just to digest the content. Hell, I even ordered Jocelyn to rearrange my schedule, probably pissing off a few of the organizers for next week's Halloween bash, but what-the-fuck-*ever*—I wasn't in the headspace to deal with the usual shit today.

So, when Lyssa demanded to know what *this* was, I just blinked at the Tiffany box, cocked my head, and replayed the demand in my mind.

Had I... heard that right?

"Did you open it?" I drawled, sounding snarkier than intended but too wiped out to care. My mate jostled the box, probably unaware of the tens of thousands I'd dropped on it, how precious the stones in all the little pendants truly were.

"Yeah."

"Then I think it's pretty clear what it is." After wiping the sweaty sheen from my forehead, I threaded my hands together and tapped them on my desk. "Do I need to explain how jewelry works, or—"

Lyssa hurled the damn thing at me with a snarl, that velvet rectangle soaring like a fucking blue missile. I barely caught it before it slammed into my face, her aim dangerously accurate, the force behind the throw a cause for concern.

Wolves were strong, male and female, but that...

It hurt to catch.

"You think you can, what, *buy* my forgiveness?"

All the blood drained from my face, prickling down to my chest as I gawked back at her. "I... No. I just didn't have time to—"

"To respect my feelings?"

My inner wolf raked my insides like he agreed. We had been in a feud since the run-in with the Hawthorne pack at our border, which was a fucking *joke*. He felt the same way I did about our mate squaring off against four strange wolves from a vicious pack. Sure, not quite as malicious as the Quinn pack in their heyday, but still dangerous.

My mate crossed her arms and glared, waiting for me to say something, *anything*. I bristled at the thought of her expecting me to grovel, but maybe she was right.

Maybe I needed to spend a little time on my knees, because as visceral as my fears had been that night, as frustrated as I'd been at the pharmacy this morning while

61

Lucian and Soren babied her, I could have chosen my words better.

Instead, I'd taken the maelstrom inside out on her.

But women liked gold and diamonds and pretty things to dangle off their bodies.

I'd actually taken a ton of time picking the *right* piece. Her ears weren't pierced, so no earrings, and none of the necklaces in the private buyers catalogue *fit*. The sun and the moon, the delicate golden chain...

It suited her.

Lyssa was the truest wolf I'd ever met, the most connected to our primal side, our rich, rooted past. But she was also the motherfucking *sun*; her joy, her pride, the night she took down that moose for Thanksgiving and hauled it all the way to our front door... for *us*. She was the spark under our pack's ass. Her fire would unite us—forge a new legacy.

A good legacy.

A *strong* legacy.

But my reasons for selecting the piece inside this box, which I set cautiously on my desk, would probably fall on deaf ears if I tried to reason my way through this.

Still though. I had to *try*. "Lyssa, I just thought—"

"You should have talked to me," she said thickly, voice on the brink of a wobble even as the rest of her turned still and severe as stone, "and *not* like you did at the border the other night." *Fuck*. "Do you know how much that hurt? All the things you said? Is that what you really think—that I'm only good to start a bloodline?"

My blood ran cold, and I scrubbed at my face with a groan. "*No*, of course not."

It was just... a part of her.

And to ignore it, to pretend we all weren't highly aware that this she-wolf was the key to starting our bloodline, was bullshit.

Not exactly the most politically correct approach, but...

But I guess I'm willing to hurt her.

I glowered up at my forehead, at the frat-boy tone my inner monologue adopted—the tone that always reminded me just how fucking stupid *I* was being, not everyone else.

Maybe not about the core of my argument, but definitely the approach.

Lyssa shifted her weight to one leg, hip cocked, her golden stare intense—and kind of unnerving "Well?"

"I *am* sorry for that," I started, selecting my words as carefully as possible. "What I said... It was all fear, and—" *Fuck it.* "—a little truth." I raised a hand when Lyssa sputtered. "You *are* our fated." This time when she stared, unblinking and intense, I met the gold head-on and refused to back down. "We'll never want another like we want you. There is no better mother and matriarch for this pack and territory than *you*. Lady Fate designed you that way—"

"I'm a person first," she gritted out, then shook her head with a huff. "Or, you know, shifter, wolf, whatever. But I'm not a label or a thing—I have feelings and wants and my own desires."

With a deep breath, I slowly stood and planted my hands on my desk, balancing precariously on my fingertips. Fights like this were unheard of in the Quinn pack: civil and conversational. Reasonable. Rational. My pack had always been about blame, about who was responsible for the fuckup and who was about to get walloped. We tossed responsibility around like a fucking hot potato, fought for *ourselves*, sometimes literally, and hoped that at the end of the day, someone else looked guiltier in our alpha's eyes.

My dad was a mean drunk, and, even totally shitfaced, packed one hell of a right hook.

So, yeah, deflection had been a way of life for the Quinn kids, and it fucking followed me all the way up here.

Because, looking back, I did the same thing with Soren and Lucian.

Always them, never me.

And it had to stop.

I couldn't bring this disease into our pack—to my mate and whatever pups we had in the future.

Brows knit, I hung my head, shame burning all over. "You're my mate, Lyssa, not a walking womb." I straightened and stared deep into the gold, my wolf and I finally in a ceasefire, the vicious heartburn easing a little. "I'm so sorry I made you feel that way. What I said—how I said it—was uncalled for and beyond rude."

"And wrong," Lyssa growled. She then sucked in a sharp breath, eyes darting around my office. I joined the hunt, bracing for something to shake or rattle or—

One of my pens trembled in the coffee cup Jocelyn bought me the first Christmas we spent together. Just a silly old University of Toronto mug from the campus store.

I'd never drank from it.

And it always had a home on my desk, even as my tastes and style refined over the years.

One pen of the bunch shuddered, nothing more, but the air thickened around us, her scent sharper, stronger, more intrusive than ever before.

"And... wrong, yes," I said slowly, still eyeing the pen.

"Okay." Her arms finally dropped, body language open for the first time since she had marched in here. "Ewan—" *Fuck.* Wildfire consumed me every goddamn time she said my *name*, and it was really starting to piss me off. "We're both alphas. Me, you, the others—we're the mating, uh, pair times two."

"Quad," I muttered, which made her eyes narrow.

"Whatever." She fidgeted with her hair, tucking it behind her ears, exposing that sharp jawline as it rippled through a clench. "Alphas are equal in the pack. Don't you ever speak to me like that again. I won't take that from *any* of you. If I want to defend my territory, I will."

All that lusty fire turned to rage at the thought. Gritting my teeth, I looked away—to the bar cart where we first mated and where she sobbed after, desperate for companionship, needing just *one* of us to stick around. How far she'd come in just a few short weeks.

No matter how out of line I'd been the other night, I couldn't have her running into stupid situations—alone—where she might get hurt. Unfortunately, if I harped too hard on it now, she'd resent me. The sentiment made the angry flames snap and spit, made my inner wolf pace and snarl, but that didn't change the fact I needed backup for this conversation.

Soren and Lucian had better agree: our mate could *not* charge into the wilderness alone against an unknown number of foes. No way. Not a chance in hell.

I squared my shoulders and changed tactics.

"What happened to your eyes?"

"I don't know," she said a little *too* fast. A gulp and a shrug followed, her anxiety prickling at the nape of my neck like TV static. "Side effect of the river?"

"Why did you drink?"

"Because it smelled good, and I was thirsty." Lyssa stiffened when my eyebrows rocketed up my forehead. "It's that simple."

Gull River did *not* smell good. I had scented it out on my first trip to the unclaimed mountain range years ago, and while it was a blemish on my newfound territory, I accepted it because it was *mine*.

That and there was nothing I could do to change it. Ethan and I had talked at length about Gull River, mulling over the source of its poison, about why some animals drank and died while others turned tail and bolted. Lounging in our usual VIP booth at the Chalet, my shot girls feeding us bourbon all night and security keeping the ritzy rabble at bay, we had discussed curses and toxins, magical and natural alike, but at the end of the day, it was just talk.

No clear answer.

No insider knowledge from the only warlock I had ever trusted.

Who never sneered down his nose at me because I was a shifter, some beast the magical folk considered lesser.

Gull River had been fouled and sullied and fucking *gross* from the day I first found it until this very morning when I trekked out there to confirm.

It didn't smell like fucking *honey.*

And if that was what Lyssa scented inside the range, then she ought to be banned from there too.

I nearly said it, but instead—

"Lyssa, twice now in as many days, I thought my mate was at risk of *dying.*" Her anger finally dulled from a dagger to a butter knife in my chest. "You understand why that might make me protective, right? Maybe an overprotective asshole, but I *will* protect what's mine... and I won't always do it nicely. You need to hear that."

Cheeks sunken, Lyssa glanced back at the door, then down to her shoes, voice hard as she said, "Protective of me —or the territory?"

Both. Couldn't say that though. Not now. Not today or anytime in the near future. I held my tongue, not trusting my stupid mouth to keep the truth where it belonged. Lyssa finally looked up expectantly, waiting for me to soothe her worries, her anxiety prickling at the back of my neck ramping up to little acupuncture needles. Teeth gritted, I swatted at the invisible sensation, glad to be feeling her again but *annoyed* that we had only mated once and the cross-contamination of *feeling* hit so hard already.

Our staring match dragged on, her begging, me withholding, until finally my mate headed for the door.

Fuck.

Fuck.

"Protective of you," I insisted roughly, making her pause well within reach of the doorknob, seconds from storming out and leaving us hanging. Before her, I would have let it go —let the opposition think whatever they wanted so long as it was clear that I'd won. Now, it needed to be quashed or I would feel it, literally, all day. "We don't really have a choice anymore, right?"

Lyssa wheeled around, golden eyes narrowed again yet somehow screaming *What the fuck did you just say?* loud and goddamn clear. One step forward, two steps back: that was the Quinn way in relationships. My parents had been fated, sure, but crime and booze and money soured the bond shortly after I was born. The pups that followed? Fucked. Born into chaos, their destinies set in stone.

"I'm just... trying to be honest with you," I told her, tongue tangled around the words—around the honesty. "I could lie. I lie to everyone." Bright and squeaky as my holier-than-thou persona, I was still a Quinn at heart. "I built all this..." I gestured at the wall of windows behind me, out to the parkette littered with pine trees, Halloween décor already hanging from the boughs. "I built it on hard work, sweat and tears and blood, sure, but also on a few lies and false promises along the way."

Hell, that was practically the Quinn creed.

But I wasn't the only shark to spin the truth for gains. My professional world was pretty on the outside and rotten on the inside; I usually tried not to let the rot stain my suits.

"I'm doing my absolute best to be totally honest with *you*,"

I pressed on, only now realizing why I had been such a mess since I met her. I'd never freaked out on a woman before. Never exposed myself. Never peeled back the layers. My fated mate deserved that, not only because Lady Fate deigned it, but because Lyssa was a blank slate. A good she-wolf. The same old shit just wouldn't and—given how she'd called me out this morning—*couldn't* fly with her. "And you may not always like it. Sometimes the truth is ugly, but no one else gets this. *That* is a choice I *can* make. Fate put us together for a reason, but *I* choose when and with who to share my heart. Honesty? That's from the heart. It fucking sucks. It makes me feel..." *Wrap it up, asshole.* "Anyway. I choose to be honest with you. I think we're all learning we can't always control how we act around our fated mates. It's irrational and frustrating, but this... The cold, honest truth? That's all me."

I held my breath despite needing to gulp it down by the lungful, that rambling speech taking a lot out of me. My inner wolf stilled when her cheeks hollowed again, but we both breathed easier when Lyssa bowed her head, hands on her hips, in a thoughtful quiet. No fire licked across my bones. No anxiety stabbed at the back of my neck. Nothing from her but a contemplative calm that threw me for a fucking loop, because arguments *never* went like this.

It wasn't two parties laying out the facts from their perspective, acknowledging them, and then conceding on certain points. No, it was a duel to the death—and then someone got fucked over *hard*.

Her golden gaze lifted slowly. Fuck's sake—so intense and penetrative. Sometimes pups shed their bright blues as they aged, growing out of their birth color into something more settled. My eyes shifted from dark, dark brown to copper when I changed from man to wolf, but this was different. This was... magic.

Accursed or not—that was the question of the day, wasn't it?

And none of us had a clue what to do about it.

But that hue was impossible to ignore. Couldn't pretend it wasn't there, not when it gave Lyssa an unnervingly ethereal beauty now, like she could see down to the soul and beyond.

People who had met her before today would know something was off. Normally Ethan would have been my go-to about anything outside the physical world, but this felt different—and private. This was pack business for now, and I went with my gut.

If anyone asked, our mate was trying out cosmetic contacts.

Because...

They were...

In?

I shook off the gold, hyperaware of it but refusing to let it dictate our interactions, then extended my arms. "Hug it out?"

She might have sighed like *I* was the one who stormed in here and hurled a Tiffany's box in a snit, but Lyssa agreed with a stiff, quick nod. Darting around my desk, I was on her in a flash, scooping her into a hug that felt lukewarm at best. Her arms slumped around my torso, locked at the wrists and not exactly squeezing, but at least she didn't bail. I ducked down to bury my face first in her hair, then her neck, dick twitching with interest, blood surging.

Her scent was so much *stronger* today than yesterday, the roses headier, the musk more apparent—a louder, bolder siren song to my inner wolf. Trembles shuddered through me when I caught him at the last second trying to force the shift, desperate to sniff her for himself.

"I *am* sorry, Lyssa," I murmured, voice deeper and

rougher, growly and beastly and fucking *stay in there, you asshole*.

"You can be honest with me," she whispered back, sounding annoyingly in control and not like her wolf was trying to stage a coup. "Doesn't make you free of consequences—honesty isn't an excuse to be a... a... *jerk*."

"You're absolutely right. Fair enough."

"But if you can just talk to me like this," my mate pressed, "and not through a stupid note or with gifts, then I'm good."

"Heard," I growled back, finally caging the beast even as her scent drowned me, imprinting on my suit, in my hair, across my skin. Warmth blossomed in my chest, the sensation coming straight from her, and Lyssa squeezed tighter. I returned the pressure, nuzzling in deep, throwing caution to the wind and succumbing to the rosy deep.

We stood there for ages, holding each other, almost like we needed the other's strength to process the day.

I mean, Lyssa should have died.

Gull River should have killed her.

But she was here, in my arms.

That was quite the fucking victory—and it was time to treat it as such.

Question it another time.

When we finally eased apart, I swooped her hair behind her ears, noting the dark rings around her golden gaze, the impact of her body's turmoil obvious. *Please don't be a miscarriage. Please just be her period.*

Miscarriages were extremely rare for shifters, but not impossible.

With the river—

No.

No, it was probably just her period, and clearly her three mates sucked at their end of the baby-making bargain.

"You look tired, blue ey—"

She sucked in a sharp breath when I stopped, both of us aware that she *wasn't* blue eyes anymore, that my pet name didn't apply.

Fuck it.

"Blue eyes," I finished properly, softening my tone, my touch, *everything*—because she would always be my blue-eyed mate. Always. "Want to nap on the couch?"

Lyssa rolled her shoulders back, shaking off that little hiccup—one of many—like a fucking champ. "No, I want my bed."

Possessiveness flashed through me at the thought of her considering that room, that bed, in *our* house, hers. The beast in me wanted to lash out, pin her to the wall again, fuck her until she screamed.

I kissed her cheek instead, followed by a gentle peck to her lips.

We hadn't mated again since the first time; interactions around the house were all so tepid and uncertain, the four of us maintaining a frustrating level of social distancing like we were still figuring out this coexistence nightmare. Despite the longing looks, the blushes, the suggestive lip bites, Lyssa seemed more focused on her mates getting along—doing shit together without fighting—when, really, this minx probably wanted to jump our bones.

All our bones.

Because she had been *just* as eager to scratch that itch.

And yet—nothing.

It was driving me *fucking* insane.

"Go home, then," I rumbled, tipping my head toward the door. Lyssa nibbled at her lower lip for a moment, then arched an eyebrow.

"You going to be there for dinner?"

I frowned, knowing it would disappoint her and ruin this

71

cozy bubble we found ourselves in, but still saying it anyway. "No—not tonight."

I never *did* dinner anyway; there was always so much to do here.

The workday didn't stop at five for the *real* workaholics.

After patting my chest, kissing my cheek, and staring deep into my eyes until my inner wolf whimpered, Lyssa headed for the door.

I went for my desk and grabbed the jewelry box.

"Hey." She glanced back, then whirled around to catch the velvet rectangle when I lobbed it her way. As Lyssa hugged it to her chest, I nodded pointedly at the blue, adopting a stern, no-nonsense alpha stance as I growled, "You'd better be wearing that when I *do* get home."

Rather than bristle at the domineering tone, Lyssa smirked, then sauntered out the door with a torturous sway in her hips.

Alone again, the exhaustion hit hard. Heaviness whittled into my limbs, and rather than going for my chair, I trudged over and flopped onto my couch.

Stretched out, just to alleviate the dull ache in my lower back.

Closed my eyes because, you know, the sun was suddenly a little too bright.

Let the heaviness take over—

And then, minutes later, boom—dead to the world, snoring away.

7

SOREN

"But these are Halloween classics." Freddy, Mike, Jason, Ghost Face—gang's all here, literally in the palm of my hand. I motioned to the DVD boxset with a dramatic flourish. This baby had been a part of the Acker pack legacy since I was a kid. Dad shared my love of cheesy horror movies, and we had watched this set so many times over the years, slowly initiating my sisters one by one into the ring, that it was a miracle any of the discs still played. Corners frayed, ink faded, the girthy box set moved with me to this house—and given Halloween was only a week away, it was time for the psychotic stars of the season to make a new pack debut.

And, I mean, where better than our basement cinema room?

When if not on a freakin' stormy Friday night late in October? *Seriously.*

"I don't want to be scared though," Lyssa protested. Swaddled in blankets and sweaters and obnoxious wool leggings, my mate had tucked herself into the far corner of the mammoth wrap-around sectional, comfy, hormonal, and ravenously eyeing the movie marathon spread I'd organized earlier on the coffee table.

She had no idea what my sisters and I would have done to watch these classics in a room like *this* when we were kids. For years, we fought for the best seat in front of the tiny TV in the living room, and even when Dad upgraded our tech, it was still a brawl over who bagged the spot where all the acoustics hit just right.

While Ewan might have had a firm hand in designing the pretentious upscale accents of this cottagey mansion, I had pushed for the *perfect* cinema suite. Windowless. Black walls and ceiling. Old-school movie theater carpeting so ugly it insulted Ewan's sensibilities. Screen that stretched an entire wall with the most expensive sound system we could squish into the budget. The enormous couch hugged three walls, big enough for twenty—and meant for a huge pack to enjoy.

I'd designed this place with my future pups and their friends in mind.

Lyssa had used it the most so far. Rosa came in at a close second, frequently here for girly days, chick flicks galore. Lucian wasn't exactly a TV guy, but film and television was a quick way to update our mate on the modern world, which meant he put up with it. For her, he sucked it up.

We all made concessions for Lyssa, even more now after Gull River, her eyes still a soul-piercing gold, her period—not a miscarriage, thank Lady Fate, after the pregnancy stick read negative for any baby hormones in her system—wreaking havoc on her mood this week, her sleep fraught with dreams that made her cry out and sweat and moan and gasp.

Me and Ewan carried on working, yeah, but we did what we could—*all* of us—to cater to her *especially* hard this week. Whatever she wanted, she got. Specific meal? I had that covered. Treats from the village? Ewan came home with it in droves. Jaunts down south just to *move*? Lucian escorted her on top of his usual excessive patrol schedule.

"They really aren't that scary," I argued weakly, tapping the box set and motioning to the screen. "We—"

"She's made her choice," Lucian said gruffly. Scratching at his dark brown beard, trimmed and neater than I'd ever seen it, he glanced between us with a *sigh* like he was *over* this discussion—and very clearly in Lyssa's corner.

"We watched these when I was a kid. Like, they're *funny*, not scary."

"They're horror movies." Lucian pinned me with a menacing look. "Enough."

My eyes narrowed right back, inner wolf pacing around, uncomfortable with the tension. Seated in the middle of the sectional, legs spread wide like he had a thirteen-inch dick that needed the breathing room, Lucian was usually a go-with-the-flow wolf. Historically, *Ewan* was my main opponent, but I guess when it came to Lyssa, the British dickweed was ready to go to bat, even using his *words* tonight rather than communicating with caveman grunts and eyebrow raises.

"But if it's scary..." Lyssa drew the blankets up to her chin, eyes rounded as she studied the box set. I shook my head, willing my excitement to rub off on her.

"It's really not."

"Not if you've seen it a million times," Lucian interjected again, and we quickly resumed our glaring match, waiting for the other to back down. We'd been at this for ten minutes, ever since the food arrived, and, *no*, I refused to fold —not again. *No one* wanted to do any of my usual October traditions. So far, the guys had shit all over my suggestions, and then Lyssa would side with the majority. Once again, *I* was on the outskirts, even after we'd mated. Definitely a crappy feeling, and not one I expected to go through after marking and being marked by my fated mate.

Seriously, wasn't it supposed to get easier, not harder?

With Ewan bogged down in next week's Halloween-bash nightclub preparations, the Chalet forecast to rake in tens of thousands as rich kids flocked north for *the* premiere party of the spooky season, a Friday-night movie marathon seemed perfect. A little time to bond as a group, the most obnoxious alpha absent, and with the storm, the moody October ambiance—Halloween movies were a given. I'd come up with it this morning, offering to order pizza, wings, cheese sticks, lava cakes, popcorn…

Lucian sucked at food stuff. The guy couldn't cook to save his life, nor did he have a clue how to organize a chill hang in a basement.

This was my gig.

My *thing*. The first themed night anyone had agreed to so far.

No one wanted to carve jack-o'-lanterns, and the guys laughed off my suggestion of taking Lyssa on the wagon ride out to the pumpkin patch down south so she could pick her own. Caramelizing apples? Nope. Decorating the house for the zero trick-or-treaters headed our way next Saturday? Hell no. Group costume suggestions? Get *out*.

Lucian had given me hope this morning that just *one* Acker fall tradition could finally happen—and now this?

This was *bullshit*.

Yeah, the new pack wasn't the Acker pack. We had to make our own traditions, forge our own path—whatever. But my old pack had fun traditions. The kind to endure through generations. Pack-bonding activities that strengthened our connections. And, frankly, it was really starting to piss me off that no one wanted to try *any* of them. I had worked hard all day to be out of the office at a reasonable hour. Ordered the food. Organized it on the table in the center of the sectional. All my bases covered. Beer chilled. Pop fizzy and cooled.

I pulled my weight for this pack, yet time and time again, the two grumpiest assholes on the planet outvoted me.

And my mate just rolled with it.

I kept waiting for Lyssa to realize all this was important to me—but nope.

"Babe, trust me, they're really good—"

"Stop pressuring her." Lucian looked about two seconds away from punching me, but the feeling was mutual. I groaned, pinched the bridge of my nose, then redirected my frustration onto him, our alpha bond sizzling with it.

"*You* stop being a *wuss*." I patted the box set again, determined to plead my case—determined to *win*, just this once. "Halloween movies are a cultural staple. We all did this kind of stuff in October growing up—"

"Strong disagree," he rumbled, his mouth twitching like he was fighting back a grin—like suddenly this amused him.

My inner wolf rustled up a growl, but almost because he felt like he *had* to. All packs had that one wolf who soothed tension by being a clown; of course I got stuck with him.

"Can you seriously, for once, just—"

"Soren, you're throwing a fit over a bloody *movie*." Never heard the guy talk this much. Our fated mate had put us all through the ropes lately, made us reexamine who we were as wolves and alphas, but with Lucian, her presence made him vocal. *Very* vocal. Unfortunately, he had always seemed happy in his little hermit bubble, and arguing about this— just a *bloody* movie, apparently—had his hackles up and his eyes like golden honey. He jerked his chin toward the blank projection screen, all teeth as he added, "Stop being a *child* and just put the *fucking* Lion King on already."

Ugh. As soon as Lyssa spotted the cover art online for the world's most recognizable kids movie, she jumped and squealed and pointed; it was the only film she remembered from her childhood, and instead of all these gorgeous, hilarious, gruesome classics, she wanted... that.

Cartoon lions.

"But..." I hoisted the box set one last time, my inner wolf whining like he could smell defeat. Lyssa finally tore her gaze from the stack of pizza boxes, brows knit, our connection shivering with want—want for something *else*. Lucian, meanwhile, slumped into the couch and glared, waiting for me to grow up.

Fine.

Fine.

Scowling, I tossed my beloved DVD collection onto the couch, then rustled around with the laptop connected to all the tech. Roughly a minute later, the movie started up, and the recessed lighting dimmed.

And I bailed.

"Soren?"

My mate called to me just outside the door of the cinema room, the basement hallway dark, her voice wanting, her concern like an ice pack plunked squarely on my chest. Sighing, I leaned back through the doorway.

"Be right back."

This was supposed to be a group hang, and with me as the organizer, it seemed shitty to leave.

But I needed a second to *breathe* so I didn't snap.

Neither of them deserved that.

Lyssa just wanted to watch a movie from her childhood, which we still knew nothing about, but the memory seemed to make her happy. And Lucian... That bastard was just sticking up for our mate. Obviously he wasn't chomping at the bit to watch a stupid cartoon, so, yeah, couldn't exactly snarl at *him*.

But couldn't they see I was just trying to build fun pack traditions?

That this mattered to me—and it should matter to them?

I stomped all the way upstairs to grab a beer from the kitchen fridge, ignoring the ones I'd left chilling in the wine cellar. While my inner wolf had always been a goofy dufus despite being destined to rule as an alpha, he delivered when it *mattered*—we had that in common. After my colossal screw-up with Gull River, I just wanted to distract everyone.

Make it better.

Make it *fun* and seasonal and cozy.

Make this place feel more like a home, not just a house we all slept in, unsure how to interact, uncertain what to do with each other. I mean, it sure as hell wasn't sex. Despite the desire thickening in the air anytime Lyssa walked into a room, all three of us stayed polite—like finally we were ready to *not* step on each other's toes.

The vibe was weird.

Something had clearly happened to her in the mountain.

The Hawthorne wolves had howled along our eastern borders twice this week. Work, duty, connection, protection, *feelings*—it was a lot.

Why wouldn't they let me *fix* it already?

I could.

I threw a great party.

Cracking open the bottle, I tossed the lid on the kitchen island and trudged back to the cinema room, where I found Lyssa and Lucian scarfing down pizza, half the meat lover's supreme already gone. With the excitement of what could have been an epic movie night extinguished, I hunkered down in the far corner, appetite dead right alongside my original plans, and nursed my beer as the movie's opening montage played out. Lyssa couldn't look away, shoving food in her mouth and barely blinking, still buried in cozy blankets, happy as a clam and focused on the screen.

And Lucian—

I flinched when I glanced his way and found the alpha staring *directly* into my eyes. A few cushions over, we had enough of a gap between us that if one took a swing, the other could dive out of the way—maybe. But his glare had softened. As he chewed a massive mouthful, tomato sauce in his beard, grease smeared across his white tee like he had wiped both hands there instead of taking from the mountain of napkins, it wasn't anger flowing between us.

But disappointment.

Disappointment in me, my behavior, my sulk at the far end of the couch.

But he didn't get it—how it felt to be constantly put down by Ewan, overruled by them both, and boxed out of the decision-making.

If he did, he would have gone along with my plan—been on my goddamn *side* for once.

Head cocked, I flipped him off. The alpha rolled his eyes and grabbed two slices of pizza, sandwiching them together as he relaxed into the couch to watch the movie. He grinned when Lyssa pointed out baby Simba, so absolutely smitten with her that even *this* was tolerable.

I sipped my beer in silence, a little disappointed in my behavior too...

But determined to build seasonal pack traditions for us if I had to drag all of them kicking and screaming into the fun.

The next holiday season in December would be better.

Not scary. Family oriented. Tons of stuff to do around the village. Loads of Acker traditions to float.

I needed to strategize. Suggest stuff casually—and sell Lyssa on it first.

But if Ewan and Lucian pushed back, if they refused to so much as drive around the suburbs just to look at the lights and decorations, I'd fucking riot.

8

LYSSA

"Can I see some ID, please?"

I blinked up at the enormous man in black, distinctly human—I'd started to notice the difference in posture, complexion, and temperature the more time I spent around my mates—and attractive in a TV-show villain sort of way. Blue-eyed and bald, he wore a fitted suit and a wool cap, steely and stern as he asked clubgoers for identification. Having shuffled through the line that wrapped around the red-bricked building for the last thirty minutes, I'd watched this unfold time and time again.

Stupid to think he wouldn't ask. Well over the legal drinking age, I should have breezed by. Instead, I stood before him, a head shorter and gawking, then groped at my empty purse. No ID. No phone. No nothing that people on TV had when they went to places like the Chalet. Still, while the nightclub scene might have been totally foreign, bars were old news—and I'd been sneaking into them since I was fourteen. Usually a smile and a flutter of your eyelashes did the trick if anyone questioned you.

"Uh…" Not this guy. I didn't even bother to try; Kira

probably wouldn't let me fake flirt with another male now that I was marked and mated with our fated. The thought made my stomach all topsy-turvy anyway, and I licked my lips as I gestured to the red doorway down the brick corridor behind him. "I'm here for Ewan Quinn. He… We…"

Ugh, what did we even call ourselves to humans? *Hello, the wolf who owns this place is my fated mate. Step aside, human.* Yeah, not going to fly.

Probably.

Just as I drew a breath, about to *try* and pull rank somehow, a gruff interjection cut me off.

"You Lyssa?"

I flinched when the second bouncer joined the conversation, the pups he had been questioning when I initially stepped forward slinking away, tails tucked, IDs rejected. Just as tall as his colleague, he was leaner, his skin a rich onyx and his eyes a warm chocolate brown.

The warmth frosted over a little in the silence that followed, and I hastily nodded, struggling to speak—to sound calm, cool, and collected like the *teenagers* on the shows I'd streamed to prepare for tonight.

"She's good, man." The second bouncer swatted at the first. "Boss said she might drop by a few weeks ago—has a VIP room reserved for her if she ever showed."

My face lit up like a firework as the pair scrutinized me, like they were trying to decide *why* I deserved such special treatment. Kira's unimpressed huff slipped out *my* nostrils, and I swallowed hard when they frowned, waiting, waiting, *waiting*—

Then disbanded and let me pass, already on to the next people in line.

A cold, shaky feeling washed over me as I scurried by. Not very alpha-like, quaking before club security, but one day I'd find my confidence.

Rosa kept telling me that, anyway.

Put us out in the wild, deep in the forest in the middle of winter, and those two would be *dinner*. Here, they radiated predator—and I *had* to stop feeling like prey.

The hairs on the back of my neck stood up.

Kira stilled.

I stopped just a few paces from the entrance, all that security stuff falling to the wayside.

Eyes roved my back, up and down, side to side...

Someone was watching me.

Kira snarled as I twisted around, searching, scanning my surroundings for a source. It couldn't just be the bulbous cameras mounted on the walls; a mechanical eye wouldn't make my entire body erupt in goosebumps or douse my blood with adrenaline.

For a Tuesday night, the Redwood Grove village was really *alive*. Nestled in the trendy high street area, flashy restaurants and packed bars surrounded the Chalet on all sides, people milling from one locale to the next, the nightlife bustling when everywhere outside these walls would have been dead hours ago. Just past eleven, the place felt like a major city, not a cozy hamlet at the foot of the mountains.

Must be something in the water—

I shuffled aside as a group of males barreled down the corridor, okayed by security and headed for the door like a pack of wolves—moving as a unit, glancing at *me* as one, totally in sync.

Gnawing at the insides of my cheeks, I stood taller and ignored them. They weren't the first males to leer inside the village walls, and they wouldn't be the last. *They* didn't set my body on fire though.

Wait.

My belly looped and my heart sank.

Oh. Right.

Those eyes boring into me from nowhere probably belonged to the same dead goddess who had turned mine gold.

Stupid.

Of course she was watching me—from the inside of my skull, no doubt. I dreamed about her every night.

Well, I dreamed of the orchard. The endless rows of apple trees. The sky pink, her world beautiful and empty and lonely. *She* hadn't made direct contact in a few days, her whisper occasionally on the breeze, encouraging me to try an apple. Sometimes I caught her out of the corner of my eye, flitting between trees like a ghost, but anytime Kira and I charged over to investigate, she was gone.

"Snap out of it," I muttered, fluffing my soft waves as a couple locked in each other's arms sauntered by, their hips swaying in unison. Shoulders back, I followed them into my first nightclub—

Overwhelmed. Instantly.

Oh.

Oh.

Kira stiffened again, both of us plunged into a deer-in-headlights daze at the assault. Lights dimmed, music blaring, scents clashing and mingling—sweat and beer and liquor and perfume galore. The couple ahead of me veered left, and I just followed along blindly to the free coat check booth tucked into a corner just off the main door. Slowly adjusting to the intensity of it all, the music and the smells and the *bodies* everywhere, I peeled off my black coat and swapped it for a ticket stub with the smiling woman behind the counter. Stepping aside for the next in line, I shoved the slip of paper inside my purse and pressed back against a stone wall, just breathing—processing.

Thank goodness I'd come today and not Saturday. While Rosa had my costume covered, Halloween scared the pants off me—and not for the usual spooky, horror-y reasons. Here, just four nights from now, the others and I would attend Ewan's big October 31 bash.

And I didn't want to make a fool of myself.

Like I was doing right now.

Just a fawn on the ice, legs everywhere, panicked and bleating for her mama to rescue her.

So, to avoid *this* happening on a night that Ewan had been preparing for the second his Thanksgiving market wrapped weeks ago, I had decided on a trial run. Lucian and Soren were both out on patrol tonight, hopefully squashing the beef from our movie night last Friday. Alone at the house with nothing to do, head full of TV moments just like this, I took a risk.

Did the bare minimum makeup-wise.

Washed and brushed my hair.

Put on a form-fitted red dress, sleeves to my wrists, the neck scooped but not showy. Added a pair of black stockings and one of the fancier pairs of flats I owned. Ewan's bracelet dangled from my wrist.

I'd thought...

The articles online said this would be a good club outfit, but as I tugged the creeping hemline down my thighs, glowering at the male by coat check who brazenly checked me out and then seductively licked his lips, I realized it wasn't enough.

Once again, *I* wasn't enough. The women here—they were *sexy*. Short-short dresses. Cleavage out. Sequins and sparkles. Black and sleek. Smoky eyes. Red lips. Sky-high heels. Bare legs that were waxed and shiny and perfect.

I felt overdressed and out of place.

But at least my monthly blood had wrapped up yesterday. Hard to pull off such a tight dress all bloated and achy and grumpy.

You can do this.

Purse strap cutting across my figure like a security blanket, I made a firm little nod before striding deeper into the club. I mean, I'd done the hair, makeup, and outfit all by myself. Got out here and waited in line like everyone else. Made my way inside, now almost adjusted to the sensory overload.

I was twenty-six and mated.

I could walk around a nightclub, for goodness' sake.

Still, when the place offered a literal road map, I flocked to it like a moth to a flame. Designed to look like a park trail map, an enormous landscape hung on the wall of a log-wood corridor, the final frontier before I hit the main club. Arms crossed, I quickly studied the layout of the Chalet. First level: dance floor in the center, bars and booths on all sides. Second level: private VIP rooms that seemed to overlook the dance floor below if I had read the sigils right. Third level: booths, pool tables, bars. Rooftop patio: closed until spring.

Right.

Let's do this.

Much like our house, the interior kept up with the club's namesake, stone, wood, and other raw natural elements everywhere. Only the wood was dark, the floors black, and the stone had a rough coarseness to it that could probably draw blood if you hit it right. Outside the log corridor, *bam*, the dance floor was just *there*, a few steps down from the perimeter seating and bars, mostly full of dancing, writhing bodies. A heady sensation washed over me, this scene so *human*—not wolf at all. Kira retreated, unimpressed with the music's volume, the colliding scents, the ogling males.

I padded forward, past the railing that wrapped around the dance floor, then down the two steps onto the glittery black tile. Out of the corner of my eye, a male strode toward me, only a couple of inches taller and brimming with confidence.

Our eyes met. His hazels widened, then ducked, almost like he *knew* not to mess with an alpha she-wolf.

He pivoted fast, weaving back through the crowd alone.

Good.

The wrought-iron balcony above would have provided the best vantage point, but something told me I'd learn best *here*, in the thick of things. Not only did I want to look the part for Saturday, but I needed to *act* the part.

I had no clue how to dance.

No idea what to do with my feet, my hands, my hips.

But nudging through the crowd wasn't exactly the learning experience I had hoped for; everyone moved differently. Some jumped. Some writhed. Some bodychecked —mostly males to other males. I managed to find a partially open space in a corner, arms still crossed, and swayed to the deepest beat coming from the speakers.

Was this it?

Was I... Was I doing it?

Rosewood suddenly tickled my nostrils, rising above the rest, dominant and insistent, demanding my attention. The hairs on the nape of my neck stood on end again, but for a *way* different reason. Kira stirred the moment we scented our mate, her low whine urging *connection*, and I hastily tucked my loose waves behind my ears, searching for him in the crowd—

And finding him well above it.

Descending a spiral staircase nearby, Ewan emerged from the shadows like a fallen angel, all dark beauty and sharp angles and raw *power* as his hand ghosted the iron railing, his steps slow and deliberate, his hickory gaze locked hard on me. Effortlessly stylish in a pair of black slacks and a simple crisp white button-up, he blew all the males here out of the water, females glancing his way, gravitating toward him like he had this unearthly pull.

A pull I understood.

A pull that immobilized me, trapped me in the corner of the dance floor, the rest of the club elevated around me, railings at my back and a wall of humans at my front.

I'd needed to elbow my way through at first, dancers crashing into me with their wayward arms.

Ewan glided on *air* here, totally in his element, the crowd parting for him. Strong, confident, *utterly* alpha, it was like no one else existed as he cut through the dance floor, not stopping until he was practically on top of me. Kira shivered inside, eager to scent her mate, taste him, *bite* him like he and the others had done to me, give them a feel for *my* teeth.

I just stood there, her excitement slicking my palms and making my belly squirm, gazing up at him and feeling kind of small all of a sudden.

Cornered.

Caged.

Pinned by his dark, dangerous beauty and a smile sharp enough to cut glass.

"Hello, blue eyes."

My sex clenched with interest, hot pleasure twisting in my core. Even though my eyes were far from blue these days, I *loved* that he still called me that—loved the way he growled it, possessive and assertive, like only *he* could say it and anyone else who tried would feel his wrath.

Hands easing gracefully into his pockets, he tipped his head, dark gaze sweeping over my body and making Kira even more antsy.

"What are you doing here?"

Right. The super-embarrassing reason I'd done all this.

"I wanted to get a feel for the place," I told him. All around us, humans shouted over the music to be heard. Ewan set the tone, speaking at a normal volume, and I followed his lead, capable of reading him just by watching that sinful mouth—but also hearing him fine despite the roaring beats. "Kind of nervous for Saturday."

My mate huffed a chuckle. "Why?"

"My bar experience is... not this." I waved a weak hand around, the jingle of his bracelet on my wrist snaring his attention. Cheeks warm, I tucked my hair behind my ears again, keenly aware that he was tracking the movement of the gold strap, the diamonds catching the light with every rustle. "I don't know how to dance, or how to—"

"Let's fix that," he rumbled, low and dangerous, his copper wolf eyes sliding back to mine, his body angled closer. I swallowed hard, flustered, the *itch* suddenly back.

"We don't have to if you're busy." He was always busy. Always working, even at home. As persistent as the itch was, flaring like gasoline on the fire the longer he looked at me like *that*, I hadn't come to the Chalet for him. Sure, Soren had spilled that he'd be here every night this week, monitoring the club and preparing for the Halloween party, but the goal hadn't been to catch his eye.

Get him down here.

Make him smile like that, oozing temptation and sin. Lucifer was said to be so handsome—

"I think I can take a break," Ewan rasped. "Come here."

He caught my hand and jerked me to him, whirling us around at the last second so I faced the sea of grinding strangers. Masterful, totally in control where I had struggled to walk in the front door, Ewan snaked his arm around my waist and yanked me back, molding me to his chest, his hips, his thighs.

"*This* is how couples dance at the Chalet," he whispered in my ear, lips caressing my skin with every word. Back to chest, we mirrored plenty of pairs around the dance floor, I now realized, but they couldn't feel like *this*—like their entire body was an inferno from a single touch. His large hand smoothed down my waist, my belly, all the way to my thigh. The other pressed me back to his hips, which started a slow, easy sway that I couldn't help but follow. Mouth dry, I drifted back and forth, keenly aware of his body thrust against mine, the way his much bigger frame cradled me, his knees bent to make up for the height difference.

Kira retreated, just as she had when we all first mated, leaving me to what was *mine*. No distractions from the inside —nothing but my own body reacting to his, my skin tingly, my head empty. No thoughts. No whispers. No stupid apple orchards. Just—*feeling*. Him. Me. His hands on my hip, my thigh, his wicked mouth brushing my ear.

"That's it," he murmured with a hint of teeth, the sharp nip making my nipples stiffen. "Just like that... Easy, right?"

Flushed and flustered, the heat under my skin blazed south without delay. Somehow, Ewan's arms left me feeling... safe too. After his blow-up in the forest, I hadn't thought that would be possible. Lucian made me secure with nothing but a look, just a flick of his green gaze in my direction and *bam*, everything was right in the world. Soren wavered, sometimes a steadfast support, others surly and distant and pouting—usually when he didn't get his way.

Ewan?

Ewan had become my wild card.

But here and now, in his arms, I could fight a whole pack by myself.

That was how he made me feel.

And I might not trust the feeling, but it was... good. Nice.

Like we'd found ourselves again.

Breath whooshing across my cheek, his mouth leaving a trail of barely there kisses at my jaw, Ewan snagged my arm and brought it up, a snarl rumbling between us at the way the diamonds glittered. The charms jingled, suns and moons alternating, slipping over my red sleeve and up my forearm.

"Looks good on you," he whispered roughly, his words all grit and gravel, his mouth hot and my core pleasantly twisty. Ewan brought my arm closer, my hand limp in his grasp, then dragged his parted lips up over the bracelet and straight to my palm. Desire zinged from where his lips pressed *straight* to my low belly, and I muffled a moan, focused on my breathing, on keeping calm.

What if I made the room shake with *other* emotions?

What if it wasn't just anger?

What if, when one of my mates made me explode, a building collapsed?

My tempered breathing only seemed to excite him, and he threaded my hand back into his hair, stretching me, arching my body over his as that dangerous smile found my neck. Kissed it. Nibbled and licked and sucked while my lashes fluttered and struggled to stay open.

I'd missed this—the itch.

Ever since my mates came home, we were all so careful around each other. Eager as I was to let them mount me again, anytime, anyplace, forming a pack bond was *crucial*. Without that effortless connection, we still weren't strong.

And if those Hawthorne wolves taught me anything, it was that we needed *strength*. Cooperation. Support and wordless communication. Trust and transparency.

We did better lately, my mates on their best behavior around me most of the time, the fights fewer and the snarls subtler.

But we still lacked a few key ingredients.

So, with Gull River and my golden eyes and my stupid monthly bleeding, plus three stubborn mates who almost *refused* to work together, my focus had been elsewhere. Desire fell to the wayside.

Oh, but it felt so *good* to let it back in.

Like my body was *alive* again after stumbling around in the dark for way, way too long.

When the song bled into something faster, I tried to pull away. All around us, the humans moved differently, jumping more, smiling and laughing and singing along to lyrics I'd never heard before.

Ewan just swayed faster, blanketing me with his scent, and tucked me deeper into his embrace.

"Look at them," he rumbled against my temple, one arm crossed possessively over my torso, his free hand snaking up my chest to my throat. Our hips rocked in perfect unison, his interest hardening against my backside, his words taking on a wolf's growly edge. "They're all here for something… Upstairs, they can drink in the quiet. Talk and flirt, negotiate their courtship. They can even *fuck* in the private rooms if the males pay us enough to look the other way." My breath hitched at the thought, pulse pounding beneath his hand. "But down here? It's all about the hunt. You know the *hunt*, don't you, blue eyes?"

"B-better than you." Trapped in his thrall, I stumbled over the feisty retort, the alpha in me a little too happy to roll on her back for him. Ewan chuckled, sounding—*feeling*—very much like a predator who had run down his prey.

"Those girls in the big groups—just here to have fun." He steered me around the dance floor by my chin, each word nibbled under my ear. "The pairs? Looking for men to buy them drinks. Compliment them. Worship them. The males circling—on the hunt. Prowling. Searching for weakness…"

He gripped harder, the pressure on my windpipe sparking the alpha in me again. I turned my face into him, our noses brushing, our skin touching, breaths mingling.

"If one of those little human shits *touches* you," Ewan

snarled, "tonight or Saturday or any time after, any-*fucking*-time between—I'll break his hands."

A smitten whimper slipped past my lips, making his dick harder, more insistent as his hips ground against me.

"If one of these staring females touches *you*," I fired back, capturing *his* chin and forcing *him* to meet my eyeline, "I'll break her nose."

My mate flashed his canines. "Naughty girl." He slipped my hold as his fingers gritted into my thigh. "Behave yourself."

"If you can do it," I glared at a blonde whispering to her companion and pointing at Ewan, the want in her eyes *obvious*, "so can I."

Totally oblivious to the female's attention, my mate clucked his tongue at me, the sound followed by a chastising nip at my throat—then a harder bite over my dress where I still bore his mark. His hips bucked harder, more determined, more dominating, the beat of the music be damned, and as I finally surrendered to the black, eyes closed and lips parted, I wondered if it was against the law to mate *right* here on the dance floor. I mean, he could just pull up my dress, rip down my stockings, and really—

"Hey, guys—sorry."

Ewan stilled with a growl, and my eyes snapped open when Jocelyn's voice popped our bubble.

No, no, no, no, no.

Sure enough, a quick glance over my shoulder, and there was Ewan's stylish assistant in a burgundy romper and black stilettos. The look transformed a fox shifter shorter than me into a giantess, her short at the back and long at the front white-blonde bob sharp, defined, and curtaining her foxy features as she leaned over the railing with a grim smile.

"Mr. Quinn, I'm afraid they need you upstairs."

Ewan's snarl made her flinch and me sigh.

"Can't it wait?"

Jocelyn arched a white eyebrow, and my mate disengaged completely. He tucked me back in the corner where he had found me, eyes stormy and mouth no longer sinful, the twist of his lips stiffly apologetic.

"I'll be right back, blue eyes," he insisted, stealing a hard kiss before disappearing into the crowd again. His arrival had been like the seas parting. Now, his disappearance had a lot less fanfare, my dark angel disappearing into the shadows again without a backward glance. People ducked out of his way, sure, but it was because he stalked through his club like a bullet, ready to plow through anyone who didn't *move*.

Safety net gone, I folded my arms, shoulders hunched, and suddenly felt way too alone and exposed out here—

"Come on, wolfy." Jocelyn leaned over the railing to pinch my sleeve and steer me toward the nearest set of stairs. "They don't need *me* up there." The fox grinned when our eyes met, her warm browns chasing away how raw Ewan's sudden absence left me. "Lemme buy you a drink."

Relief thawed the ice water in my veins, and I hurried up the steps after her toward one of the bars in a quiet corner. Perched on leather stools, I let Jocelyn take charge with our drink orders. Sure, I'd tried beer and cider before, but my palate, like my fashion sense, just wasn't sophisticated enough for Ewan's world.

In the end, she ordered herself a martini and me a margarita with half the usual amount of tequila, promising me the next could be stronger if I liked it. Pleased to have company, I took a beat to scan the Chalet from a different viewpoint, all these pretty humans looking like they well and truly *belonged*.

"Everyone here is so…" *Flawless.*

Lean legs crossed, Jocelyn snorted as she slid my drink over. "Wasted?" She then scooped up her martini, the glass and the olives and *everything* just like on TV, and took a quick sip. "Yeah, kind of embarrassing no one can hold their liquor, but that's the Chalet crowd for you. Just rich kids who want to get tanked and haggle over drink prices. Like, the *worst*."

"I-I was going to say"—I poked at the rosemary sprig sticking out of my glass, voice dropping—*"intimidating."*

Another snort. Jocelyn's features then softened when she realized I was serious, and she patted my arm, her nails a sharp french manicure—only they were black on the bottom, not pink, with a crisp white line on top.

"Girl, they're just humans."

"I know, but—"

"And you're a *wolf*," she added with an arch of her brow. "An alpha wolf. You're so above them."

"But..." I gestured to my outfit. "I don't look it, and everyone who sees me and Ewan will know it—"

"Fuck them." She downed half her glass and set it on the napkin with a scoff. "Seriously. *Fuck*. Them. They don't know *anything*. You could wear a plastic bag and still be better than them, so let it go, wolfy. Be who you are, and fuck what the rest think."

Before I could thank her, not entirely boosted by her little speech but still appreciating the effort, Jocelyn hoisted her glass for a cheers. We clinked drinks, and I tried my first tequila-based cocktail.

Not bad.

A little... sour-sweet for my liking, but the rosemary smelled familiar, and the lemon had a pleasant zingy bite that made me come back for more.

"Jocelyn?"

"Yeah?"

"Can you... tell me what to expect for Halloween?" I nudged my glass around the countertop, drawing shapes in the condensation. "After everything with the river, and..." I pointed to my eyes, knowing she saw them but was too polite to stare. "And *these*... After everything, I just don't want to disappoint anyone. I'm good at the wolf stuff. I'm... less good at all this."

The fox's burgundy lips dipped into a luscious frown, the kind that caught the bartender's eye and kept him loitering.

"Halloween is *fun*, Lyssa," she insisted, oblivious to the male—all the while eyeing a pair of females chatting at a nearby high-top table. "And I don't think you could disappoint those assholes if you tried. From what I've heard, *they* need to step up, not you."

Once again, the sentiment was great—but the landing didn't stick.

Jocelyn sighed as I guzzled the rest of my drink, then snapped at the bartender and pointed to our empty glasses, flashing two fingers and angling herself toward me, her back to him.

"Okay, sure. I'll give you the breakdown, behind the scenes and front of house. You'll go into Saturday knowing how the sausage is made."

I frowned. "Uh, what?"

"Never mind, never mind." She propped her elbow on the bar, chin on her fist, and patted my arm again—not like she was *better* than me, but in a way that felt oddly reassuring. "You think of any questions, just cut me off and ask."

"Got it."

As Jocelyn kicked things into high gear, firing information at me left, right, and center, I glanced around quickly for any sign of Ewan.

Nothing.

Not even a whiff of his rich rosewood scent in the air.

Ignoring Kira's disappointed sigh, I slowly sank into the rhythm of Jocelyn's husky voice, committing all the details to

97

memory as best I could, determined to go into Saturday night *totally* prepared...

And confident as an alpha with three mates should be.

§♦

Of course it was raining.

And not just a spring showers type thing, but a *we angered the clouds and now they want to punish us* downpour. Sheltered beneath the brick corridor that led to the club's main door, I squinted into the grey wall, then braced when the wind changed direction and blew it straight at me. Misted with just a taste of what was pounding the village, I wiped my cheeks on my jacket sleeve, then flinched when thunder cracked overhead. To my left, a group of huddled females roughly my age screeched, the drunkest in their pack seated and slouched against the wall, mumbling about street meat under her breath.

Lightning flashed a few steady beats of my heart later, the storm right over us and slowly headed north. Midnight had come and gone without Ewan, and once Jocelyn shared that it was always a late night at the Chalet since the nightclub didn't close until three, I decided enough was enough.

My mate had taught me how to dance.

The females here had shown me how to dress.

Jocelyn had given me a tour of all three levels, front and back of house.

As of this moment, I had a fairly good idea of the layout and expectations of a place like this, which settled the anxious static in my belly. Kira had retreated deep inside for most of it, bored to tears without her mate for company, Jocelyn's rundown of the upcoming Halloween event thorough but a bit dry despite the liquor involved.

Even now, tequila warmed my chest, four drinks deep,

two of them with the full portion of alcohol, but I was still in control. Not wobbling in heels. Not crying in the bathroom. Not vomiting in a stall—and definitely not sitting on my butt outside, ignoring my friends and mouthing off to the increasingly annoyed bouncers.

Jeez.

Humans were messier than I thought.

Another thunderous *boom*. Another chorus of shrieking females. The lightning came faster this time, turning the empty cobblestone street ahead white, the storm hovering. I felt for Lucian and Soren on patrol tonight; whenever weather like this hit, the pack and I hunkered down somewhere dry—or as dry as possible, anyway. All of us in a pile, warming and comforting each other, pups near Mama while the thunder kept them awake and shivering.

My mates had to keep moving tonight, keep marching the perimeter. Soren might trot back if things didn't ease up, but Lucian would walk the whole territory no matter the conditions.

I... I wanted to have something ready for them when they got home.

Something hot and comforting, delicious and soothing.

But cooking wasn't exactly my forte.

Throw it in the microwave? Fine. Eat it raw? Perfect.

Simmer and season and baby on the stove? *Nope*. But I'd try.

Hot chocolate was always a nice treat on a night like this.

Kira stretched inside, toes spread wide, her stiffness carrying to me. She sniffed, each *whoosh* tickling between my ears, then grumbled; even she didn't want to go now, Jocelyn's bland tour sounding better than a trudge through the storm.

Lips pursed, I watched a male jog by in a drenched suit,

his briefcase a useless umbrella. Ugh. This... was not going to be fun. Head down, I stepped out of the shelter.

Instantly soaked.

Right down to the bone.

Great. No point in rushing, then. I was used to the rain and had never caught a cold. Still, as I plodded down the cobblestone street, the lure of all the soft, warm light spilling out from bar windows was beyond enticing.

Only I had no money.

No ID.

No nothing to barter with for another drink somewhere else—and I couldn't keep dropping Ewan's name like that was currency, right?

Arms crossed, I pushed onward, headed for the main gates but not in a hurry. The village grew dark and empty the further I walked from the high street neighborhood, store windows black, only the odd light or two on in the low-rise condo buildings. Every so often, an automatic porchlight flashed as I passed a chalet, probably triggered by motion. Fewer and fewer humans crossed my path, the sights and smells drowned out by the rain.

The sounds muted by thunder.

A light flickered on behind me, sparking in the corner of my eye. Kira growled low, confused and alert. Frowning, I glanced over my shoulder. The row of nestled bungalows faced a small park, and that particular light had already brightened when I passed, then turned off on its own.

Motion sensor again.

Triggered—again—even though I was five houses down.

Strange.

The hairs on the back of my neck rose.

My vision sharpened, Kira nudging to the surface, both of us scanning the one-story chalets, the vacant stretch of nature across the street full of pine trees and winding stone paths, garden beds brimming with late-season blooms and a few fake tombstones for Halloween.

Nothing.

Thunderstorms always played tricks on you. Made the shadows dance—made scary sounds out of nothing more than raindrops.

But one street over came a sound the storm *couldn't* fake: feet splashing through a puddle. Behind me.

I spun around, eyes widening as lightning lit up the narrow roadway.

The *empty* narrow roadway, the corner grocery closed, the spa beside it silent.

"Idunn?"

Run along home, little wolf.

For the last week and a half, I'd heard the dead goddess in my dreams. Tonight, she whispered through the rain, voice sweet and high and clear, shimmering all around me, slinking down my body in heavy icy droplets.

Another splash, feet charging across a puddle, loud and a little too obvious at my back. Kira snarled as I whirled around, senses on high alert, on the lookout for danger and finding none.

Go home, Lyssa.

"That's what I'm trying to do," I gritted out, barely moving my lips, unwilling to let whoever was watching catch me talking to myself. At the next splash, striking like the storm's heartbeat, I jogged down the street, my own feet pounding through puddles, the sewer drains beneath the sidewalks gurgling as I passed.

Two distinct sets followed me.

Or...

Or the storm was playing tricks and the tequila had hit harder than I thought.

No. I swore those were—

One behind me.

One everywhere else, sometimes to the left, to the right, motion-activated lights flicking on when I was nowhere nearby, illuminating a whole lot of nothing. Between her snarls, Kira whined and nosed at my insides, desperate to come out, to swap places and *hunt*.

I kept her right where she was, refusing to let whatever was happening scare me.

Ewan owned this village—mostly.

And I was his mate.

And I wasn't about to be run out of it by thunder, lightning, and rain.

And more splashes of puddle water. Eventually, I darted through alleys and between houses, zipped and turned and backtracked. I'd lost predators before—not because I feared their claws and teeth, but because I just couldn't be bothered to deal with them.

Tonight, I didn't want to water the streets of Ewan's village with blood.

Home, little wolf.

"Shut *up*," I hissed, skirting around a dumpster and slowing at the mouth of an alley, officially lost. All this darting around, turning on a dime—no idea where I'd ended up, but the neighborhood was still soft and subdued, sleepy and still.

Except for the feet in puddles.

I took a deep breath and blinked the rainwater out of my eyes, vision sharp—and narrowed on the shadowy alley across the street. A street for cars this time, pavement not cobblestone, the gap situated between two dark cafés with hanging flowerpots and pumpkins at their doors.

Oh.

Oh *no*.

This was what they'd wanted. It or they or him or *whatever*—the *thing* I kept hearing?

It had herded me.

Make noise to the left, I went right.

Splash around behind me, I pushed forward.

"Stupid," I whispered, rolling my eyes as I poked my head out and looked up and down the road. Empty.

But the shadows across the street suddenly moved.

A black cloud eased away from the café door, dropping low and creeping along the side of the building, then darted into the alley.

Okay.

This wasn't the storm.

Kira's snarls stopped. Her growls dulled. We became one, hearts beating together, thoughts aligned, staring down the grizzly without fear. Enough was enough.

I was a wolf.

An alpha.

Wild to my core.

You don't scare me.

A strange darkness smothered that alley. I paused at its opening and squinted into the black, unnerved that for once, the night *wasn't* my friend. Iron scented the air, and as soon as I crossed the threshold, my breath fogged.

Footsteps ahead.

I broke into a sprint, charging into the inky cloud, hissing when my knee clanged off something metal a few paces in. Aching, I pushed harder, relying on my sense of smell, tracking the metallic tang, the frost sharpening, swelling, *hurting* the deeper I ran.

Still nothing.

Light returned like a beam of sunshine slicing through the grey fog after a storm. I slowed. Ahead, this alley emptied into the village square, silent tonight but well-lit with enormous iron lampposts.

Someone drew a breath just beyond the exit, right around the corner. Teeth gritted, I charged.

And—

"Oh!"

Crashed right into Ewan's steely chest. My drenched mate swept me up, chuckling, his smile positively wicked as he thrust me back into the alley and pinned me against the brick.

Shock echoed through me.

"Hello, blue eyes," he rumbled, snagging my wrists and trapping them against the wall, holding me captive in his powerful grasp. His midnight-black hair, usually so stylish and full, curtained his dark beauty, softening some of the sharper angles of his face, and he peered down at me with copper wolf eyes.

Victory pulsed between my thighs—a sensation that didn't belong to me—and my heart hammered as Kira cautiously withdrew, my world suddenly upside-down.

"W-what are you doing here?" Had he been following me? Was this... a game? Pups played predator and prey all the time; was it as simple as that?

Had it been my mate all along—and the storm up to its usual tricks?

"I needed to say good night before you went home," Ewan whispered, ducking low so that his sinful lips caressed mine with every word. Each flutter of skin to skin quieted my racing thoughts, his rosewood scent, complemented with a musky sandalwood cologne, muted by the rain but still ridiculously alluring. He snapped his sharp teeth at the tip of my nose, a rumble vibrating in his chest, and my body bucked off the wall without my consent, arching into him, into the memory of his intimate lesson on the dance floor.

Without warning, he licked a raindrop from the crest of my upper lip, his touch fiery and distracting. "I'm sorry work is so... busy."

What?

Oh. Right.

Distracted by the chill in the alley, the darkness to my left, and, most of all, *him*, I gulped, skin on fire, heart a drumbeat, and shook my head. "I-I get it." His obsession with living in his office was the *last* thing on my mind right now. Lost in his wolf eyes, I struggled to think, to form simple *words*, never mind a coherent sentence. "Were you... Did you f-follow me?"

Ewan's grin was all pearly whites and bad-boy allure. "You're not the only hunter in this pack, darling."

He kissed me hard, *finally* closing the distance between us with his hungry, laughing mouth. It was a kiss to claim, to possess, dominant and rough. His tongue thrust between my lips in seconds, teasing mine, coaxing it to forget everything that had just happened.

Begging for me to accept that it was just the storm playing tricks.

Still trapped against the brick, my hands curled to fists, and I moaned, surrendering to his brutal good-night kiss a little too easily. Most days it felt good to conquer, to pull my weight with all these males who towered over me. I was the better *wolf*, through and through, but my mates were really good at making me feel like a woman.

Just a woman—desired and coveted and *wanted*.

Wildfire jumped from his skin to mine, burning away the autumn frost in the air. A good-night kiss should have been quick and fleeting, a promise for more to come tomorrow, but Ewan barely gave me room to breathe. He couldn't get enough, his yearning pluming in my belly, tainting the pleasurable clenches, turning them electric like the hum of a farmer's fence. Before I could even try to escape his hold, my mate shifted his grip, pinning both my wrists above my head suddenly and clamping down with one hand.

My eyes snapped open. I glowered into the merciless sunset blazing back, his free hand skimming my drenched figure, our kiss rain-slick and a little desperate.

He found the hem of my dress with a snarl. Yanked it up to my hips. Attacked my stockings so that they *ripped*, louder than the clap of thunder above. Lightning swiftly lit up the alley, chasing away the last of the creeping shadows. I glanced left, just for a moment; nothing there but brick and concrete, a metal dumpster with the lid open and a door to one of the cafés with no handle.

Stupid storm.

Playing tricks.

Dealing *lies*.

When darkness fell again, I submitted to the moment, to Ewan's powerful hand between my thighs, beneath my underwear, stroking me, massaging me—

Fucking me.

I clenched my eyes tight, still struggling to *think* the word, but that was what his fingers were doing: pumping in and out of my slickness, our kiss slowed, breaths crashing. He groaned with every plunge, working me inside and out, toying with the tender bud at the peak of my curls, the one that made my belly squirm and my thighs shake.

Whimpering, I tried to wiggle free. Needed to—*touch*. Stroke him. Maybe even taste him. Ewan and Lucian had tasted me, knelt between my thighs and licked me into paradise.

I... could do that.

Did it feel the same?

From the way they reacted to my cautious touches before, it had to.

Only my mate had his own plans tonight. On the brink of an explosion, the kind that bled like lava through my whole body, dragging with it a white-hot pleasure I had never experienced before Redwood, before *them*, Ewan withdrew.

Didn't let go of my hands, mind you. No, he kept them trapped against the brick, stretched above my head, claimed and captured, his grip like steel anytime I twisted and squirmed. He wrenched down his slacks. Freed his shaft. Fisted it, glaring at the rigid length, not realizing that with every rough pump, he was teaching me what he liked—what I could do to him if he would just let my hands go. I licked my lips, eager to do to them what they did to me.

Eager to make them *burn*.

Almost against their will—a surprise every time.

But then he speared me with that impressive shaft, slamming me hard into the wall, impaling me to the hilt. A twinge of delicious pain swept through the mounting pleasure, and my moan tangled with his snarl, our bodies *home* in each other. He stretched me. Filled me. *Fucked* me, right there, right in the open. In the rain. Beneath the booming thunder and the brilliant flashes of lightning, we *finally* mated again.

Ewan, pounding me furiously.

Me—taking it. Him. All of him. Hands bound above my head, I had no choice but to submit, even when I wrapped my legs around his torso. Pulled him closer. Stabbed him with my heels. Nothing I did slowed him or made him pause.

My mate had me, claimed me, until the glorious, almost *violent* end. Bliss ripped through me during a symphony of thunder, multiple *cracks* rattling the village, the lightning show that followed as I squealed and writhed the sort you'd expect on Judgment Day—the world ending, angels descending, demons clawing out of the pit.

Stark white seized my vision, taking over no matter how

fast I blinked, the pleasure of our coupling intense and all-consuming, gobbling me up and spitting me out a mumbling, rambling mess.

I bit him this time.

His shirt was in the way, the undershirt beneath that muffling my teeth, but he still hissed and snarled and bucked harder, not stopping his brutal claiming until—

Ewan stiffened all but his trembling hips, then exhaled my name against my neck like a prayer.

A painful prayer.

Like it *hurt* him. I ducked my head to the side, the alley coming back into focus slowly, pops of white light still sparking behind my lids whenever I closed them. Panting, I nuzzled at his temple, his soaked and slick hair, whimpering, whining for his attention.

Ewan released my hands and kissed me again, cupping my face, cradling it gently, his lips tender and mine sore. When the thunder rumbled this time, it did so somewhere else, the storm moving on, leaving only the rain to slowly put out the fire.

"You know," I murmured between kisses, "I think I'm going to need to change my definition of a good-night kiss now…"

Grinning, Ewan nipped at my neck with a playful growl, then lowered my feet to the ground. Right into a puddle. Rainwater flooded my flats as we untangled and adjusted clothing, hair, everything. My stockings were toast, and I ripped them the rest of the way off, then tossed them in the general direction of the dumpster. My panties, meanwhile, were too cold and wet to put back on, but their survival after Ewan's assault earned them a spot in my purse instead of the ground.

Lower lip snagged between my teeth, I watched Ewan tuck his shirt, his black brows furrowed, his movements rough and stilted as he wrenched his zipper up and moved on to the belt.

"You're not coming home with me, are you?"

My whisper carried over the pitter-patter of rain, and Ewan slowed, buckling his belt without glancing up. Eyes down, chin tucked—that was answer enough. Frustration plunged down my spine like an icy finger, accented with disappointment and regret.

None of it mine.

All his.

Mates... felt things. They felt each other. None of my three had explicitly taught me that, but Rosa had said it was a thing when I asked, and the more we mated, the more time we spent together, the stronger the sensations became. Kira snorted, mildly unimpressed that he felt like that—frustrated and disappointed in himself, upset that, *no*, he wasn't going to walk me home in the rain...

Why go back to the club if that was how he felt?

Why?

She didn't understand, but I was starting to.

Sort of.

"It's... okay." I caught his chin and forced him up, throwing some of my new brute strength behind it to get this stubborn alpha to look at me. "I know Saturday is a big deal. I'll just see you at breakfast."

It wasn't okay. A party *wasn't* a big deal in my books—but it mattered to him. More than the others, Ewan's job was his life and his passion. It might wear him out, but he didn't seem miserable doing it.

He put his all into this side of himself.

So...

I wanted to be a supportive mate. The others teased him about it, and not always in good fun, which meant he *needed* someone in this pack to believe in him.

I'd want the same, honestly.

But I would rather have him at home.

This alpha with his hickory gaze and jet-black hair—he risked a disconnect from the pack if he never showed up.

And, sure, wolves roamed solo all the time. Sometimes wolves left *my* pack and never returned, full-grown adults ready to start their own families far away from ours. But the mating pair? They wandered. Papa left for days, weeks sometimes, and then showed up out of the blue like he had been with us all along.

A few weeks ago, I told Lucian wolves wandered—that all I needed was confidence that my mates would come home.

Maybe that would be enough for a wild wolf, but as the days passed, I was starting to realize that wasn't enough for me. I wasn't *just* a wolf. Shifters needed more than the basics. Food, shelter, family—it was a start, but now I craved *more*. Connection. Conversation. Laughter. Learning. Movie nights and sushi lunches and napping all together on the deck. Hikes into the forest and strolls through the village.

Togetherness. I needed more.

And they were trying.

I couldn't leave them now, not after mating and marking —and definitely not after whatever happened at Gull River. But if we didn't push beyond the basics soon, especially with Ewan, things would nosedive fast.

It's only been a month.

I swatted at the nothing beside my ear, unsure if that comment came from Idunn in the rain or my own thoughts rolling around my skull—but it was fair.

And annoying.

A month in the wild might as well have been a *year*.

My mate fixed me with a long look, eyes heavy and muddled, beautiful mouth arced in a frown so sorrowful that I just wanted to kiss it away.

He did that instead, kissed me deep and slow, cradling the back of my head with one hand and stroking my cheek with the other. Wildfire sparked. Kira howled. Thunder grumbled way up north.

"You stay in bed in the morning," Ewan whispered against my lips. With a soft breath, my eyes fluttered open to warmth and promise, his gaze straddling the line between man and wolf, the hickory rimmed by coppery fire, almost *glowing*. When I arched a curious eyebrow, he smirked and eased back, then tapped me under the chin with his knuckle. "I'll bring you breakfast there, blue eyes. Give you a taste of my hollandaise, a little smoked salmon and eggs benedict, eh? Just me and you—we'll eat together."

I had no idea what hollandaise and eggs benedict were, but my mouth watered at the thought of him climbing into *my* bed with food—though the moan that followed was kind of embarrassing.

"Yes, *please*," I said shyly, cheeks heating when my rumpled mate chuckled.

"It's a deal." He stole another toe-curling kiss, then murmured right in my ear, breath hot and tickly, "And a promise, blue eyes."

Fingers entwined, we strolled out of the alley together, snuggled close and heads ducked against the chilly downpour. Ewan led me through the village square, then reoriented me, steering us back to the main roads and pointing me in the direction of the front gates. Thankfully, he didn't insist on walking me home—as if Gull River had stolen my fight or ability or smarts. Lucian would have. Soren might have offered. But Ewan didn't. If he escorted me home and then left, back to the village for another few hours of work, that would have been confirmed these males assumed I couldn't take care of myself out here anymore.

We kissed goodbye one last time, then went our separate

ways, him back to his world and me to mine. Just as I crossed through the gates, Redwood Grove village at my back, I heard it again...

Feet clomping through puddles.

Boots, actually, given the sound and the echo, the huge *splash* that came with it. Kira perked up from her post-mating snooze, and I turned slowly, proof that whoever and whatever might be watching hadn't startled me.

After all, they couldn't hear my racing heart.

Right?

Nothing. Again. Just an empty two-lane road leading in and out of the village lined with blocky green shrubs, little lights that looked like golf tees dotting the curbs.

I cocked my head. *Listened.* Just the rain and the wind and the thunder drifting across the mountains. Tires rolling over wet pavement further inside the village. Light glowing from the depths around the entertainment hub.

Nothing here. I turned away, headed out—

Splash, splash.

No. Not nothing. *Something* was toying with me.

And it wasn't the storm.

Ewan wouldn't...

My next breath fogged, the temperature in freefall.

With a low growl, I darted into the foliage along the stone wall that circled the village. Stripped down behind the bushes, ditching my clothes somewhere they wouldn't be seen from the main road.

Let Kira free.

Then ran all the way home, swift as the wind, Idunn's voice in my ears—urging me to go *faster*.

And—*please, please, please, little wolf, heed my warning*—to lock the door behind me.

9

LUCIAN

"We don't have to go if you're not feeling it."

I wasn't feeling it, but when had I ever been in the mood for some capitalist human holiday inspired by the same magical folk who made my hackles rise and bloodlust soar?

Never.

Not when I was a pup.

Not when the Hadley pack warlock betrayed me.

Not now, Halloween in general so bloody commercialized, all shiny and pretentious and destined to be packed full of pissed, sloppy humans tonight at Ewan's club.

Lyssa had been a bundle of nervous energy since dawn, rousing me and the others from our, oh, hour or two of collective sleep. Soren and I had patrolled until the wee hours of the morning, while Ewan had practically lived at the Chalet all week in preparation for tonight. Had we been humans, we would have been *the* most miserable prats—more miserable than usual, anyway—operating on literally no sleep. Instead, our shifter bodies allowed us to function on only a few hours, hauling ourselves out of our separate beds as Lyssa crashed around in the kitchen.

Bless her. She so wanted to whip up a feast as effortlessly as Soren did most mornings, but the stove really was her nemesis.

After a meal at the ass crack of dawn, Ewan headed into the village—no shock there—and Soren joined Lyssa and me for a morning forest run as wolves, then a brisk swim in the lake, then a game of Go Fish at the coffee table in front of the enormous sitting room hearth.

After lunch, the blond alpha left for Redwood Grove proper.

He... had promised to help Ewan prepare for the party.

Strange, the thought of those two coordinating *anything*, but business management in a public place surrounded by humans meant they couldn't snarl and pound on each other if a disagreement arose. Apparently he had sensed some distance between Ewan and the rest of us lately, and ever the happy little pup, Soren had found a way to lessen that.

Which made him a better wolf than me.

Like I'd ever *willingly* go to a nightclub, *especially* the Chalet, unless my mate was in danger.

Before today, that was the only reason I'd drag my surly ass into the village, past the doormen, and into a club meant for humans ten years my junior.

Unfortunately, all my firm stances and noble intentions went out the window for Halloween, Lyssa's energy off the charts. Our usual afternoon nap never came despite eating a massive breakfast and lunch *and* afternoon tea. Be it excitement or nerves, I couldn't get a proper read on her. Even my wolf struggled when he tussled with hers, both of them frisky and bouncy and all over the place, vocal and a little rough in their play.

I hoped it was excitement.

Sort of.

Excitement was harder to dampen, but as the sun dipped

below the horizon, this was my last chance to alter the course of what was bound to be a truly hellish night.

"No, no," my mate called from the bathroom, the objection followed by a burst of water, then the *clunk* of the metal tap closing. "I really want to go."

Muffling my growl, I rolled my eyes and flopped back on her unmade bed, arms outstretched, feet on the floor —*dreading* what was to come. Sensing Lyssa's minxy wolf half wasn't going to have an encore anytime soon, my inner wolf had already retreated as far away as he could, equally horrified at the thought of spending the night at a club. So loud. So smelly. So... drunk and human and *fucking* Halloween. Soren had been hyping the holiday up all week, and that paired with her pleasant visit to the Chalet Tuesday night really cemented our mate's opinion on things.

Rosa had her costume sorted.

Ewan had reserved a VIP room for the pack, which was bound to be stocked with only the finest champagne and liquor and snacks money could buy.

Soren had promised to teach her dorky dance moves.

Yeah. I really only had a few bargaining chips left.

"Are you sure you wouldn't rather stay in?" I floated, upping the English charm, voice as velvety as I could swing before it got ridiculous. "Cuddle right here..." I popped my head up just as Lyssa poked hers into the doorway, and my feral grin turned her cheeks crimson. I patted the bed, smoothing a spot by my side *just* for her. "Spend some *quality* time together, little mate... Just the two of us, all alone—"

"I know what you're doing," she insisted, pointing at me with a playful frown, her eyes narrowed and cheeks still flushed—nipples pebbled through her T-shirt, braless and ripe for the plundering. Even if tonight wasn't dreadful as *fuck*, in my opinion Lyssa needed some downtime after days of restless sleep, her nights plagued with fits loud enough for the rest of us to hear and feel all the way in our own beds.

Two nights ago—she screamed.

Nearly six in the morning, the sun cresting the horizon line, and the most terrifying shriek I'd ever heard ripped through the house.

Dragged me out of bed. I'd crashed into Soren on the way to her bedroom, a groggy-eyed Ewan bringing up the rear, and it took all three of us to shake her from the nightmare.

When she came to, she insisted it was fine.

Just a dream.

Just a *lie*.

She passed out as soon as her head hit the pillow again, silent and unnervingly still.

All three of us loitered outside her bedroom door until we heard the toilet flush a few hours later, our mate officially up, then scattered before she caught us.

At the time, I would have given anything to curl up beside her in this massive king—hold her, fight the nightmares for her, banish all of it with my touch and kiss and murmurs.

And from the feeling in our bond that morning, thick and morose and heavy, the others felt much the same.

Yet we still slept in different rooms, in our own beds, longing and heartache shivering through the collective bond every night, touching me even if I was miles away on patrol.

Given all that, Lyssa really ought to stay in.

Talk about it. Unload onto one of us, so maybe, just *maybe*, she could have a good night's sleep again.

Mind you, perhaps she just needed a distraction—and a huge obnoxious costume party in the village offered precisely that.

Bloody *hell*.

"Haven't the faintest idea what you're talking about," I purred before sitting up and slowly peeling my shirt off, flexing all the muscles most males didn't even know existed. I then tossed it aside innocently and fanned my neck, making sure to roll my shoulder a bit too. "Rather warm in here, no?"

"Stop tempting me."

Speaking of bloody tempting, there stood my fated mate in the bathroom doorway, hands on her hips, wearing nothing but a too-big tee and a pair of black frilly knickers. Good *grief*. How did she expect me to allow her to leave the property, let alone this fucking room, dressed like that?

"Oh, little mate," I growled, prowling upright, looming way over her and that delicious pout. "I've only just begun—"

"Well, put a pin in it, wolf!" Rosa suddenly barreled into the bedroom, jerking both me and my mate out of our hazy, flirtatious tug-of-war. As soon as I saw her, the witch's scent detonated like a bomb, heavy on the honey and amber, warm and cozy and innocent. How I hadn't noticed it before, never mind the obvious footsteps slapping over the hardwood, was kind of pathetic.

Sporting a pair of stretchy pants and a turtleneck jumper, in all black today for her beloved Samhain, Rosa had a face full of silver makeup, looking like a sea nymph ready for a night on the town, and her usual mane of red curls stacked around her head in massive rollers. She tossed her armful of laundry bags on hangers at Lyssa's bed, a little too at home here for my taste, and then beamed up at me. "Your mate and I have a lot to do and not much time to do it in. Keep it in your pants, mister."

Biting back a scowl, I offered a deferential nod and bowed out of the fight, odds stacked way against me now. While I loathed most of her kind, Rosa was... fine.

Pleasant.

A nurturer who had taken Lyssa under her wing the past month—which I *supposed* put her in my good books. My wolf rarely bristled in her presence, unlike her stick insect husband. Ethan Perry smelled fake, his smiles too wide and his eyes too calculating, and it fucking *infuriated* me that he had someone as rational and logical as Ewan Quinn under his thrall. Even Soren had taken a liking to him, connected by proxy now that we were a united pack, and that just...

Ugh.

Definitely not my favorite person, that warlock, but from the way Lyssa bounced out of the bathroom and into Rosa's arms for a hug that nearly tackled her to the ground, this witch was one of *her* favorites.

I'd respect that—until the witch and her husband inevitably gave me reason not to.

"*Rosaaaaaa*," my mate squealed, the pair spinning around at the end of the bed. "I just finished cleaning my face!"

"Then we are officially ready for Samhain costumes," the witch fired back, Lyssa's energy lifting her, both suddenly giddy and giggly and falling all over themselves.

"I love your makeup."

"I'm basically doing the same for you, but in gold."

"*Oh!*"

"It'll go great with your eyes."

"I can't wait to see our outfits!"

Fuck me. My wolf padded closer to the surface, smitten with our mate's eagerness, in love with her smile—touched by their friendship. *I*, on the other hand, teetered on the brink of a ruptured eardrum given the pitch and volume of this conversation. Before I could ask what, exactly, Rosa intended to do with my mate, their joint costume scheme a coveted secret, Lyssa skipped over, grabbed my hand, and hauled me toward the door.

"Time to go," she insisted, sounding as confident and certain as I'd always wanted for her. The thought made me smile; Lyssa was born to be an alpha, a leader, a matriarch. As males, we *could* impose our will. We outnumbered her.

Outweighed her. But... Lyssa had an *energy* in her soul that no one could tame. This she-wolf was on par with the rest of us, an equal in every sense, and I knew that with some time and support, she would find her strength in our world.

Unfortunately, I hadn't expected it to be wielded against me as she tried to literally shove me out of her bedroom.

"Right. Why?"

"It's a *surprise*," she stressed for the millionth time today, darting behind me and shouldering into my back, really bearing down to get my stubborn ass out. "I want you to be —" She grunted at the effort. "—really surprised when you—" Another grunt. "—see me tonight."

I peered over my shoulder with a sigh. "But—"

"And I hear you have a costume to work on anyway," Rosa added from across the room, arranging the clothing bags into separate piles on the bed, smirking at me when our eyes met. Mine dipped to her wrist, exposed when her sleeve had scrunched up at some point—revealing a smattering of purplish-green bruises. The moment she caught me staring, she hastily tugged the fabric back down and focused on her organizing, all the teasing humor gone.

Odd.

Shifters couldn't bruise permanently, any marks left healed in seconds, but those without supernatural healing abilities could. Witches and warlocks, however, relied on balms and potions to mend their wounds *almost* as instantaneously as we did.

Was that fresh?

Had she run into trouble on the way over here?

"Yeah," Lyssa growled, really giving it her all and barely moving me an inch, "I-I want to be surprised by *your* costume too."

I rolled my eyes. Like I had an *actual* costume for this ridiculous night, some stupid outfit that I put time and effort into. Ewan and I had already agreed over breakfast the other morning: black suits all the way, and should anyone ask, we could say we were the night personified. Simple. Easy. Straightforward. The bastard then asked if I needed to borrow something, which had earned him a scowl. A lifetime ago, I wore and abruptly discarded suits finer than anything in his overpriced wardrobe.

Three had survived the transition to the wolf I was today: black, charcoal, and light grey.

"Out, out, out," Lyssa ordered, and I finally gave in, shuffling through the doorway as if she were pushing me along with every step, her newfound strength from before seemingly absent. As soon as I faced her again, about to tell my mate not to get her hopes up in terms of costume creativity, she pounced. Literally. Lyssa jumped up at me, hooked an arm around my neck, and hauled herself up for a kiss. Hard and a little manic, her mouth made me forget, just for a moment, about the night ahead. Scooping her off her feet, I crushed her against me, bending her backward to deepen the kiss, tasting and claiming and marking her with my scent. Her giggles eventually shattered the moment, and I begrudgingly set her down, inner wolf just as riled as my fucking cock.

"It'll be worth it," she said breathlessly, flushed and adorable as she backpedaled into her bedroom.

Fuck. *Fine*. I'd... pretend to have fun tonight.

Because as long as she was happy, so was I.

Smitten, I tapped the tip of her nose, unable to stop my lips from matching her grin. "Little mate, you're *always* worth it—no matter what you wear."

"Oh, good line," Rosa called, not looking up as she sorted her bags but smiling to herself all the same. Lyssa, meanwhile, buried her blushes behind her hands and finally tiptoed out of reach. Behind her, the witch straightened, and an icy finger slicked down my spine when she leveled her wand at me. "Goodbye, Lucian. No peeking—because your mate is gonna knock you on your ass later."

She winked, then flicked her wand at the door.

Which slammed in my face with a *whoosh* and a *bang*.

Grumbling, I dragged myself away only after listening to my mate giggle and bounce around on the other side of the door for a few moments. All right, all right. Let it be a surprise. This was the first time Lyssa had been able to dress up for any of us, and clearly she wanted to make the most of it.

Fine.

The least I could do was put on my suit.

Which was a little big, actually. Not by much, but it used to hug my frame better.

Clearly, life as the forest hermit didn't exactly lend itself to maintaining the bodybuilder physique I'd been known for back home.

Dressed, hair brushed, beard combed, and cologne spritzed, I eventually departed without a farewell. The Perrys' black SUV sat parked out front, which meant Rosa would drive my mate to the village in a few hours when the Halloween party launched.

And that left me plenty of time to grill Ewan's security team, scope out the club for myself, and scent-mark the perimeter.

Halloween always spelled trouble in this part of the world. From children to full-grown adults, humans leaned heavily into the shenanigans the night promised. Supernatural folk tended to go a little wild as well, shirking the secret *living together but apart from humanity* thing we did for the sake of our survival.

All for this fucking night.

If my mate was going to be surrounded by all sorts,

humans flocking north for the party of the season alongside witches and warlocks driving down from nearby Hampton to get pissed at the club and then head to the Redwood forests for dark Samhain sabbats—then we couldn't take any chances.

Before this party started, I personally would bulletproof the shit out of that building.

And if anyone tried to stop me, I'd put them through a fucking wall.

10

EWAN

"Happy Halloween, wolf."

Struck by the scent of yew and mint, I grinned and braced for the inevitable clap on my shoulder, Ethan's greetings always the same. Leaning on the thin black railing that lined the second-floor balcony, I'd been lost in the moment for a little while, mind racing, thoughts pinging, mental checklists flying.

It was finally here.

Redwood Grove's exclusive Halloween Bash at the Chalet.

In the last twenty-four hours, my nightclub had become unrecognizable. Starting with the jack-o'-lantern and skull chandelier hanging over the dance floor, timed to erupt with confetti at midnight alongside an explosive DJ set, we had dressed the building like a haunted house—but classy.

Spiderwebs in corners, grotesque face illusions in mirrors, Halloween puns on the bathroom doors. Carved pumpkins with flickering candles at the bars. Themed drinks and appetizers. A militant private chef managing our kitchen. Costumes were mandatory. Tickets cost a small fortune to keep the riffraff college assholes from Hampton out. Guest DJs from all over North America had flown in and rented chalets from me for this one night, allowed to play any set they wanted so long as they had mixes with Halloween classics.

Kind of a mindfuck to hear *Monster Mash* whumped from the speakers alongside heavy dance beats, but whatever.

The clap landed like a whisper, Ethan known more for his shrewd intellect and business savvy than brute strength. Temporarily shrouded in his scent and magical hum, I straightened and went for his hand, for long, bony fingers that always felt like a bear trap whenever we shook.

"Blessed Samhain, warlock," I offered in return, knowing tonight was sacred to his community. He could have been anywhere else—but he chose the Chalet. He had picked *me*, lending a subtle magical hand to really up tonight's atmosphere.

Those little touches that we added—they'd sell next year's tickets. The unearthly *feeling* shivering down a human's spine when they stepped over the threshold would stick with them. This was only my second year organizing such a big Halloween blowout, but given we'd been sold out for months and only forty minutes in the club was packed with ticketholders and a line stretched all the way around the block for those *hoping* they might be let in at some point, willing to pay the outrageous cover charge...

Fuck yeah, this was going to be a yearly thing. My team dropped a fortune on it, but from ticket sales alone, we had been in the black for weeks. The pricey cocktails and specialty snacks would only further the divide between loss and gain.

While Ethan and I had both stuck to classic tailored black suits, he went a step beyond that, dressed as a... fancy skeleton? Gangly, tall, all limbs and sunken cheeks, Ethan

Perry passed as Skeletor on a regular day; tonight, Rosa must have gone to town on that face paint, because the shading was *impeccable*.

He looked legit.

And the top hat?

This guy.

Always willing to go the extra mile for my events.

"Looks amazing in here," the warlock mused, both of us back to leaning on the railing, humans giving us a few feet of space—almost like they *knew* tonight of all nights not to invade our personal bubble. Shifters might not recognize Halloween or Samhain as anything special, but even I couldn't deny the electricity in the air, magic sizzling, thick and heady.

"Thanks, man." I motioned to the chandelier. "Make your kind feel right at home?"

All our supernatural ticketholders organized their admittance through Ethan, a massive group of them bussing over from witch-run Hampton at our northwestern border. Unlike the mass of humans squished on the dance floor and crowding the first- and third-floor bars, Ethan's ilk opted for private rooms.

And good for them.

Cost *way* more, but it got you privacy, space, and security. A tinted window overlooking the club below. Bottles on bottles on *bottles*, all night long, for a set fee.

On weekends, our private rooms averaged a sixty-percent occupancy. Weekdays—forty.

Tonight we were at one hundred, the rooms stretched along the east and west walls of the second-floor balcony, hallways on the perimeter connecting the north and south viewing decks for those who couldn't afford the privacy.

One room, however, was roped off for my pack.

No idea if any of them, giddy little Lyssa included, would

make use of it, but I'd wanted the option available. No club attendant either, just in case things took a turn for the scandalous.

"Everyone's really happy," Ethan insisted, his huge smile kind of unnerving tonight with the face paint, his teeth hauntingly white. His faint brown gaze flitted around the dance floor, both of us waiting for our girls to arrive. "This is going to make *waves* over there." We bumped fists without looking, our friendship instinctive at this point. "Next year, these humans will have to fight to get tickets."

While I smirked, my inner wolf huffed, dreading the thought of doing this all over again after such a brutal week finalizing everything. This bash was a *performance*, ten steps above what standard clubs did on theme nights. The chef, the bartenders trained in fire shows, the DJs, the private rooms—it was an art. Throwing a party, the kind people willingly paid a shitload for and still talked about months after, was a fucking *skill*.

Thus far, no hiccups.

My crew knew their stuff.

In precisely forty minutes, the lights would dim so that only the chandelier illuminated the first floor. Fog would roll out. The music would take a turn for the creepy and sexy, and our graveyard-themed hour would commence.

As always, Ethan and I immediately dug into the nitty-gritty business talk no one in my social circle put up with. Stats. Numbers. Profit margins. Some gossip about the dick chef who charged way more than he was worth *but* whose name was a fucking Pied Piper for foodies. It flowed fast and easy between us, so much simpler than conversations with Lucian and Soren—until I scented it.

Her.

Roses in the air, floating high above the standard nightclub scent storm. Over the colognes and perfumes, the

BO and the bad breath, the liquor and the chicken-and-waffles circulating the crowds—my mate.

I straightened, nostrils flared, vision sharpening as my inner wolf let go of the alpha male shit we used for the club —and tapped into the alpha *beast* who craved his fated girl more than *anything*. Possessive. Dominant. Wild. My lips twitched, threatening to peel back and reveal canines as I searched the crowd. Beside me, Ethan chuckled and nudged at my arm.

"Scent your mate, did you?"

My low growl and stiff nod was answer enough, and he let me search the first floor in peace, scanning, scanning, scanning—

Found you.

Slack-jawed delight ripped through me, probably *pounding* through the alpha bond and alerting the others that she was here—and she looked fucking gorgeous.

"Lyssa looks like a goddess tonight," Ethan remarked as he slowly straightened beside me, his tone respectful, our minds—no surprise—forever aligned.

And he was right.

My golden-eyed mate was a vision, loitering at the helm of the dance floor, above the crowd near the steps, alongside Ethan's wife.

Their couple's costume *so* obvious now I should have seen it coming.

Lyssa in gold, Rosa in silver—the sun and the moon.

They always said not to look directly into the sun or you'd go blind, but if I did right now, locked on Lyssa, the rest of the club fading away, I'd go happy that *she* was the last thing I saw before the abyss claimed me.

Ethan wasn't far off the mark either: she definitely had a Greek goddess *thing* going on with the toga-length dress cutting off mid-thigh, gold and shimmery beneath the moody chandelier lighting. Golden gladiator sandals looped up her bare calves—had she shaved for tonight? Because those legs *glistened*. Gold rings glinted on her fingers, and she wore a straight-up Statue of Liberty crown, seven golden spikes reaching for the stars, her hair wild and wavy. Soft, too, controlled and styled. Complementary makeup for her tanned skin and ethereal costume, obviously done by the witch at her side. Gold and brown and a beigey-nude lip.

Exquisite.

Lyssa nearly hacked me off at the knees in that getup.

So *fucking* beautiful.

I gripped the railing hard, white-knuckling through my wolf's desperate howl—calling to his mate, beckoning her *here* so we could taste her.

In that, my girl *was* the sun. No question about it. Radiant, her smile lit up the nightclub. She outshone everyone here, males and females alike, and they ought to bow down to her—recognize that Lyssa was the center of the *fucking* universe.

I blinked out of the lovestruck stupor, suddenly *very* aware of Ethan's teasing stare burning into the side of my face.

"Breathtaking," I muttered. Not wanting to leave his wife out, I begrudgingly looked Rosa over as well, in need of a compliment so he didn't think I was a completely whipped wolf.

"What's with her eyes?"

"Contacts," I said without thinking, the lie we as a pack had agreed on coming a little too easily for a friend like Ethan. Even though he and Rosa had been heavily involved the night Lyssa drank from Gull River, we needed to get a grip on her changes first and foremost. She seemed fine—but she wasn't.

And none of us knew how to manage that.

And I'd been so busy *here…*

My inner wolf snarled at the thought. Yeah, yeah, fucked-up priorities and whatnot. *I get it, stop giving me fucking heartburn.*

"Contacts?"

"She saw it on Instagram," I told him distractedly, massaging the burning ache in my chest and taking in Rosa's unflattering silver sheath dress with a frown. "Thought it was cool. I ordered them from some specialty shop in LA."

"Ah." Ethan chuckled, his head bobbing, his skeletal smile unsettling. "Makes sense. She's got a lot of social media to catch up on… Prepare for *that* nightmare while you can."

"Hmm." I cocked my head, still scrutinizing Rosa in that oversized pillowcase. Sure, her hair spilled over her shoulders like a red waterfall, similar to Lyssa's in that it seemed soft and fluffy as a cloud. But that *dress*, those sleeves creeping up her hand and looping around her middle finger. That muted crown. Solid makeup, but clearly she had organized Lyssa's outfit; she could have *rocked* something similar. "How's Rosa feeling about the baby weight stuff lately? I mean, she looks fantastic—perfect pair, our girls."

"Yeah, it's hit-and-miss," Ethan remarked with a sniff, fidgeting with his black bow tie, eyes locked on his wife. "Some days she's fine, sometimes it's a lot of sobbing and stress eating. I just try to help where I can." He then glanced my way, his frown exaggerated by the face paint. "Why?"

"No, it's just…" Shit. Had I just dug myself a hole? "Not to be rude, but she has a great figure."

I mean, hourglass was *in*, and Rosa was all curves, womanly and full. Ethan snorted, blackened brows rising.

"I'm not a shifter, bud. Feel free to tell me my wife is gorgeous—I know she is."

My inner wolf rumbled, mildly annoyed at the potshot, but the warlock wasn't wrong. If a male told me Lyssa had a great figure, I'd have to *really* fight the urge to gouge his eyes out just for looking.

"The costume just makes her, uh…" Hands in my pockets, I left it at that. Even a blind man could see that circus tent made her appear ten times bigger than she actually was, her nipped waist lost, her bountiful curves muzzled.

"Well—" Ethan dug out a pair of black gloves from inside his jacket with a shrug. "—she just knows better than to dress like a whore."

Uh. What… the fuck? I turned away from the girls as he shoved his gloves on and tilted his top hat. "What did you—"

"Have you seen the way some of these humans dress?" Ethan's lip curled as he motioned to the throngs of women in skimpy Halloween costumes. "Despicable." The sneer threw me almost as much as his use of the word *whore*. "Anyway…" Another lukewarm clap on my shoulder, followed by a great white's grin. "Gotta go sweep my moon goddess off her feet. Amazing event, man. We'll do drinks to celebrate next Friday."

Still a little shell-shocked, I managed a nod and a thin smile, then watched his back as the warlock wove through all those so-called whores, politely laughing and bowing if he accidentally jostled any of them, then descended the nearest spiral staircase to the first floor.

That was… fucking weird.

I'd never heard him talk like that before.

As I tracked him below, headed toward our females and towering over many in the crowd, I probed my inner wolf for an opinion. Generally, the beast had an aloof, standoffish approach to just about everyone except Lyssa and, annoyingly enough, Soren and Lucian—but only in their wolf forms. Tonight, however, he was too busy clawing up my lungs, desperate for me to refocus on our mate, to notice what had just happened.

Not great, in the grand scheme of things. Growling, I massaged at the hot twinge in my chest, then returned to her.

To my golden girl—utterly alone as soon as Ethan whisked his wife away, steering her onto the dance floor from behind and whispering in her ear while Rosa giggled and plodded along.

My soft, affectionate grin turned feral: this was a familiar picture, my mate alone by the dance floor, in need of a rakish professor to teach her the seductive art of the grind.

Unfortunately, she wasn't alone for long. Just as I was about to push off the railing and stalk down there myself, she was swept into the arms of another.

A fucking *Viking*.

Blond, massive, shirtless, and muscular, he scooped her up and twirled her around, my mate's expression exploding from startled hesitance to giddy exhilaration in a heartbeat. Warmth pulsed in my chest, her feelings twined with his, touching me, tickling me, coaxing me to… join them.

Fucking Soren. Of *course* he had an actual costume for tonight—and from the look of it, he went hard. Dark linen trousers and a rope belt with a plastic axe hanging from it. No clue what the shoes consisted of, the view obscured from here, but that bare sculpted torso had just about every female on the first floor drooling, even if it was artfully dirt and faux-blood splattered—like he had just returned from battle. He'd shaved his hair at the sides since I last saw him, runes carved into the cut, the long top tousled. Blackened eyes with streaks down his cheeks like war paint.

Yeah, he definitely looked the part.

And Lyssa, her back now to me, couldn't stop *touching* him, her hands all over his abs, his pecs, his biceps. From his expression, the light in his amber wolf eyes, he loved every second of it. Again, a whoosh of molten heat bloomed in my chest, their reunion happy and giddy and overtly affectionate.

My inner wolf held his breath, waiting for *my* jealousy to erupt and reverberate back to them through the bond.

Nothing.

In fact, as Soren ushered her toward the dance floor, all that mattered to me was that Lyssa was having a good time.

That she was happy.

And her smile—brighter than the sun.

Good.

I schooled my features when I realized I was gawking at them like a teenage girl who had just *finally* watched her dream fictional couple share their first on-screen kiss.

Fuck's sake.

Below, Soren marched her to the middle of the dance floor, his huge frame and—for once—imposing presence clearing some space. However, while Lyssa backed into him, as though expecting the type of dancing *I* had taught her, Soren Acker busted out the nerdiest shit I had ever seen.

The sprinkler.

The shopping cart.

Dorky Dad moves galore.

Yeesh.

He really looked the part, seductive and brooding and dangerous, and then *that*?

You blew it, buddy.

Or… not?

Because there was our mate, *howling* with laughter, clapping her hands and mimicking his moves, much to the delight of the crowd around them. Hell, a few of the humans even joined in, the blond alpha effortless in the way he connected to strangers with a smile and a bit of self-degradation.

Dick.

Women *loved* a man with a sense of humor, but, really, that just wasn't my bag.

On the brink of sauntering down there and stealing my mate away, Jocelyn intervened. Costume-wise, my assistant went a half step above me and had thrown on a headband with fox ears on top, all fuzzy and velvety, to pair with her burnt-umber pantsuit.

"Issue in the delivery bay," she told me above the pounding bass, her hand on my shoulder, her mouth next to my ear. I ducked down to accommodate, very aware of how intimate the conversation looked, but Jocelyn was like a little sister at this point. I had *real* sisters—two were in prison, forever loyal to the Quinn code of psychotic conduct, and the third had died of a wolfsbane overdose like Dad. I'd always choose this fox over any of them. "Something with the payment."

"Fuck's sake."

"I know, I know, I *told* them..." She rolled her eyes, positively bristling. It wouldn't be the first time the vixen could have handled a problem on her own, yet they always demanded *me*. One day these pushy chauvinist assholes would feel the sharp bite of her little fox teeth. Scowling, I brushed by her, off to deal with the first disaster of the night that warranted my attention.

As per usual, it was shit Jocelyn could have handled on her own, something I drilled into those thick human skulls before returning to the party. I did a quick check-in with the fussy Montreal chef in passing, then exited from the kitchen doors right into the scheduled graveyard segment of the night. Fog hovered about two feet off the ground, lights dimmed, patrons *loving* it. Slower, more sensual music pulsed from the speakers, the DJ dressed as the devil spinning like this was the party of the year, really selling it, really earning that outrageous price tag—and really setting the mood for seduction.

Following the scent of wild roses, I tracked her back to the dance floor, where I found Lyssa alone, loitering by the railing overlooking the pit of writhing bodies.

No Soren.

No Lucian—but no surprise there.

While Soren had showed up this afternoon to *help* with setup, happily following Jocelyn's orders and doing a lot of the heavy grunt work without question—and most importantly, without stepping on my toes—Lucian had been a handful. Normally he stuck on the sidelines, watching, mapping perimeters and exits, but he had arrived this evening shortly before the bash started demanding security information.

Right in my face, asking about the men I had working the door, the bouncers inside, who the hell were all these *strangers*—fucking nightmare.

I dumped him onto the head of club security, telling them both that Lucian had authority to call the shots and override exterior protocols. Infuriating as it was to have him barking at me an hour before opening, he did it for Lyssa.

So.

Whatever. Let him sniff and patrol—because, really, what the fuck else did he do with his time?

And what had happened in his past that made him so goddamn anal about safety?

At one point, literally ten minutes before we let ticketholders in, he blocked me in a men's room stall and growled that the air in the delivery bay smelled like iron.

Like that mattered.

I told him I'd have someone look into it, breezing by to wash up and get out where I belonged.

Hadn't seen him since then, and I appreciated every

blissful second of his absence; the huge wolf really knew how to body-block when my stress levels were at an all-time fucking high.

For now, however, a lull blanketed my schedule.

Technically, I had nothing to do but nitpick and micromanage—as Jocelyn put it—which meant, in theory, I too could do whatever the fuck I wanted.

And right now, I wanted *her*.

Strolling through the fog, I snuck up behind my golden goddess. She stiffened, then relaxed, sinking against the railing, her anticipation suddenly humming in my chest like a beehive.

She'd scented me.

Expected me.

One day I'd catch her off guard properly again.

For now, I relished her submission, her body soft and curvy and fucking *mine* as I strolled up behind and smothered her with my own.

"Hello, sunshine," I rasped in her ear, mindful of the spiky crown about an inch from gouging my eye. Lyssa moaned and arched into me, ass to my front, wiggling ever so slightly, her cheeky smile telling me she knew *exactly* what she was doing down there.

"Hello," she purred as she tipped her head back against my shoulder. I grimaced and reared out of the nearest spike's reach. "Where have you been?"

"Putting out fires." Swooping low to safety, I dragged my lips across her shoulder, over bare skin and gold silk, then up her neck, tongue flicking out to tease her pulse point. If Soren hadn't made it clear, *I* staked my claim on the most exquisite female present, not subtle in the way I snatched her and declared *mine*. One arm snaked around her waist, I let the other wander, stroking her curves, her exposed thigh, even hiking up her dress *just* enough to make her squirm. "But I'm all yours for a little while…"

Lyssa chuckled, dragging her nails over my arm, *gritting* into the suit material. "Really?"

"Yes," I murmured against her jaw. I then nibbled just below her ear, reminding her that while she had claws, I had *teeth*, and I had no qualms in marking her right here and now in front of everyone. No one questioned a bit of blood on Halloween. "Whatever will you *do* with me?"

My mate whirled around—or, at least, she *tried* to, only to stake me in the face with her crown. I hissed and fully disengaged before she took out an eye, and Lyssa clapped her hands to her mouth, apologetic but giggly, then smoothed out the pinprick of pain where a sharp little spike had stabbed my cheek.

"Where's Soren?" I snagged her hand, smitten with her tender care but hungry for something darker, then kissed the underside of her wrist. Face-to-face now, my mate sidled closer, her figure flush against mine—against the erection that had been building since I first spotted her looking like the fucking sun.

"Getting us drinks," Lyssa told me with a nod toward one of the larger bars we had installed just for tonight.

"What a gentleman." Threading our fingers together, I stepped back, then jerked her forward into my orbit again. "Well…" *You snooze, you lose.* Wasn't that Soren's sentiment when he stole my *perfect* bedroom right out from under me? Now I was stuck with his boring, unimaginative space the furthest from Lyssa, wardrobe storage severely lacking. "How about a tour of a private room in the meantime?"

Lyssa tiptoed after me as I backed toward one of the spiral iron staircases. "But Soren—"

"He's a wolf," I growled, ignoring her concerned point toward the bar. "He'll find you."

With that flawless logic, she trailed after me upstairs, through the mass of humans, the stifling costumed crowds, then down the west corridor of private rooms. All the way to the end, past the bathrooms and beside the emergency exit stairwell, I whipped out my personal access card and swiped it over the reader. Tonight, Lucian and Soren had a copy as well—as should this she-wolf.

You know. Later. For now, I just wanted to *enjoy* her, not teach her the nuances of a key fob.

Locks unbolted, clicking and clacking and catching Lyssa's attention, her head tipping side to side like she was in wolf form and listening to a strange noise in the bush.

Fucking adorable.

Eager to prove that despite the danger in my smile, I too could be a gentleman, I nudged the door open and bowed low as it swung inward, gesturing for my mate to pass. Shoulders back, head high like the queen she was, Lyssa sauntered by with an added sway in her hips—then squealed and scampered in when I pinched her ass and snarled, prowling after her like a starved man in sight of his first meal.

Kicking the door shut behind, I gave her just a beat to acclimate to our new surroundings. Keeping with the low-light nightclub vibe, the private rooms were all black—walls, floor, ceiling, black, black, black. Black furniture, two crescent moon couches in the center, leather and luxe, separated by a round coffee table with a tray of pricey champagne already chilled. To my immediate right at the door stretched a buffet table, tonight's Halloween-themed canapés tented under coolers or warmers depending on the type. The club's music thrummed from the corner speakers, muted enough for actual conversation, and Lyssa charged over to the wall-to-wall tinted window, practically shoving her face against the glass to take it all in.

My gaze narrowed, the hunter rising, adrenaline prickling in my fingertips the longer I scoped her figure. Lyssa inhaled sharply, and when she peeked back, her flushed cheeks told me she *felt* the desire—felt the predator eyeing his prey, mouth watering, hackles soaring, instinct about to take charge.

She wet her lips on the casual stroll toward the half-moon couch, golden eyes flitting my direction every so often as she drifted around it, running a finger over the leather. I let her dangle, hands clasped behind my back, let her *guess*—then lunged when that glittery orange-and-black bow on top of a champagne bottle caught her attention like something shiny ensnaring a magpie. Ever the fighter, such a quick little wolf, Lyssa pivoted *just* in time, shoving at my chest when I was nearly on top of her.

"Nooooo," she whined, half-hearted in her attempt to escape my rough hands all over her body. "My makeup—"

"Blue eyes," I growled, palming her ass and yanking her against me. "I'll *pay* Rosa whatever she wants to fix it."

And fix it she would, because the way I kissed her, rough and deep, squeezing her ass like I *owned* it while the other hand cupped the nape of her neck, this golden shimmer and nude lip wouldn't survive the assault.

Lyssa responded like a she-wolf who had no interest in being tamed, all teeth and claws, fierce and fiery. Snarling, I cuffed her neck harder and wrenched her back, fully aware that despite the theatrics, she had already hooked a leg around my thigh, her dress hitched, her hips undulating— grinding on me in search of relief.

"You think you can walk into *my* club looking like that and not expect to get fucked?" I demanded, relishing the way her eyes rounded and her hips stopped, the threat landing hard enough that she gasped. I tipped her head back further, fingers twined in her bronze waves, the other hand cupping her, bucking her over my thigh. "Blue eyes, you're lucky I didn't mount you right where I found you."

Oh, *fuck*. The thought of that—hiking up her dress, yanking aside her panties, and *fucking* her right there over the railing…

Like my dick could get any harder.

Whimpering, Lyssa wrenched me to her by my tie, fisting it with both hands and using it like a leash. Typical. I had her cornered—yet she had all the power. We crashed together furiously, each desperate to consume the other, fire sizzling from her skin to mine and mine to hers. Heat swelled around us, the air thick and suffocating. Hands *every*where. When Lyssa finally pried her mouth away, I had her hoisted up, those bare legs snapped around me, her dress up to her waist and her eyes beyond wild.

Golden *fire*.

"Actually," she whispered breathlessly, her grin savage as she dragged a rough thumb across my bottom lip, "there's something I want to try…"

My eyebrows shot up, every last drop of blood officially in my cock. "Oh?"

She nodded, eager enough to make me second-guess the hellfire in her eyes, then wriggled free. Grabbing my hand, Lyssa escorted me to one of the half-moon couches, then pushed me into it, hands on my shoulders. I surrendered to the intrigue and crashed down, curious, hungry, envisioning her sprawled over my lap with her dress up and panties down.

Lyssa nudged my knees apart, putting them in an aggressive manspread, then slowly—*fuck* me, so slow and slinky—sank to the floor. Kneeling before me, she smoothed her hands up my inner thighs to my belt.

"You're all so *good* with your mouths," Lyssa mused as she brushed those wayward fingers over my cock, featherlight

139

and teasing enough that my hips jerked. Smirking, she didn't stop until she reached my belt. "I did a little research…"

"Did you?" I growled tightly. This exquisite sun goddess nodded as she undid my belt. Goddamn it, I *knew* that laptop would be a worthwhile purchase.

"I want to be *just* as good," my fated purred, my belt open, my zipper next, her smile sinful and her eyes powerful. "Sit back, mate. I want to taste you."

Dead.

Officially dead.

Arms outstretched across the couch, I threw my head back and groaned. Fuck it. No more work tonight.

And if anyone barged through that door right now to interrupt her, I'd snap their necks and deal with the body in the morning.

11

LYSSA

Tonight I learned there was power in kneeling.

I'd never want to totally control my mates, just as I would hate them if they did that to me. No, this wasn't that. It wasn't power and control over *all* aspects of our connection —just this moment. On my knees, cradled between Ewan's strong thighs, I had him. Every inch of him. His attention. His eyes like a sunset on fire, his primal heart right on the surface as I nudged his briefs down. The slightest touch of his shaft made him twitch and hiss, his hands flexing in and out of fists along the back of the couch. His dick sprang free as soon as I tucked the silky fabric under his balls, hard and yearning, reaching for me with a beaded wet pearl at the tip.

Desire made his expression tight.

His teeth clenched.

His eyes almost... pained.

Wow. I licked my lips, fascinated by how *open* he was suddenly, my mate who was always and forever in control. No wonder he and the others liked licking between my legs —because this was exhilarating. While Kira left me to it, her *need* threaded with the excitement pounding in my chest, lightning in my veins and damp between my thighs.

Even though I had mated with all my alphas, I'd never been this up close and personal with any of their manhoods. Sure, I'd *felt* them—intimately. Ewan's was as thick and long as I remembered whenever it speared me, pinned me to the wall and pounded me into paradise. A smooth head. Hefty. Two stand-out veins twining around the shaft. Smooth and relatively hairless, the black coils at the base as neat as the hair on top of his head.

I'd read about blowjobs on my gifted laptop. Always when my mates were out of the house, I turned off all the lights and huddled against the headboard, knees up, laptop on top, and hastily skimmed articles about the mechanics, the how-to, what to expect and how not to gag if he stabbed the back of your throat.

Reading about them always made me feel silly and embarrassed; most of the articles were written for teen girls, *maybe* early twenties.

I was twenty-six this year, twenty-seven in January. At this point in my life, I shouldn't need to *research* blowjobs, but all that background reading came in handy now.

Some women in forums seemed to dislike giving them.

I just wanted to return the favor. Lucian and Ewan had knelt between *my* thighs; fair was fair. Mates were equal in all things—including this.

The internet had told me to mind the head because it was sensitive; Ewan groaned and closed his eyes when I traced its ridge, his hips bucking. My research had also insisted I not grip the thing like I was mad at it, so I tempered my grasp, highly aware of my newfound strength, then licked him from base to tip.

One long, fluid sweep and this alpha male was *mine*.

"*Fuck*, Lyssa," Ewan growled, a hand slapped to his

forehead, his face crinkled. I hesitated, worried I had somehow messed this up already, but when he didn't push me away, didn't snap his teeth or snarl or stand up and run, I did it again.

And again, grinning when the fiery sunset crashed to my face and locked on my eyes.

Goodness, the power here was thrilling.

Power had been the name of the game since waking up after Gull River. My limbs felt stronger, my endurance better, my strength heightened. Still, I tailored that last one around my mates so we didn't slip into a power imbalance. It had taken us *weeks* to find *some* sort of stability in the house, and with my males, it was precarious, ready to fall apart on a gentle breeze.

Plus, I didn't want to scare them away.

Refused to give them yet another reason—on top of the golden eyes and the trembling windows—to reject me.

So, I held back. This evening, shoving Lucian out of my bedroom, I had barely pushed. He seemed to enjoy me struggling, and I liked the way his warm affection resonated in my belly. Win-win. Still, it was a learning process, one that I didn't consider mastered yet. Sure, I had adjusted to my eyes—but not my strength, not the raw, ancient power buzzing in my fingertips.

Not the way plants bowed in my direction like *I* was the sun.

And definitely not the nightmares.

Ever since my first visit to the Chalet a few days ago, my dreams had been full of darkness, cold and suffocating. Shadows hunted me through the orchards now; before, the endless rows of apple trees were just that—endless. Annoying. No escape. Now, something sinister stalked me, its icy breath on the nape of my neck. No relaxation. No sitting around wondering if Idunn would show.

Because she was there, in the thick of it: up a tree.

Hiding.

Terrified, just like me. Anytime I saw her through the foliage, the goddess just held a slim finger to her lips, begging me to keep quiet.

Kira protected both of us. For the most part, she circled me, but if the shadows stretched their cold fingers up Idunn's tree, there she was, snarling and scratching at the bark, bullying them back.

Four horrible nights of that.

Of being hunted.

Never caught—but the world of magic and goddesses was new to me, and I had no idea what would happen if the shadows *did* coil their hands around my neck.

I always woke in a cold sweat.

One night, my mates had roused me. Apparently, I'd been screaming.

In the orchard, I couldn't breathe.

Tomorrow, Rosa and I were headed south to really work on this curse. I planned to share every detail then with the one person who couldn't kick me out of the house and turn their back on me for being *different*.

Tonight, I let the rest go and surrendered to the power, to Ewan's raw expressions, to the perfect distraction this nightclub and its private room offered.

After a few more exploratory licks, his skin salty and velvety, I took him completely in my mouth—

And gagged.

Whoops. Too deep.

Eyes watering, I coughed and adjusted—combined my fist and mouth, moving both together to create a rhythm that had Ewan's breath erratic and sharp, his fingers twisting into the leather. Totally in my thrall anytime my eyes flicked up to tangle with his, the alpha occasionally toyed with the ends of my hair, feathered and styled to perfection by Rosa's glamor charm. With all the bobbing, it took some tact not to stab him in the chest with my crown, but we managed. A part of me said to take it off, but this costume was divine—that crown wasn't going anywhere, not with the way my mates complimented me while wearing it.

I nearly took *all* of him after a while, getting used to breathing through my nose, relaxing my jaw, maneuvering my tongue—when the locks clicked and clacked open like they had when Ewan swiped his card. Gasping, I reeled back when the door flew open, and Ewan lurched forward to cover himself. I hastily wiped the saliva from around my lips, wide eyes landing on Soren.

Soren with a beer bottle in one hand and a cup with smoky orange liquid in the other, a skull-tipped straw poking out the top. My blond mate cocked his head to the side, then stepped inside.

"Uh-huh," he said, his voice rough but playful. "Just what I thought."

He then kicked the door shut as I settled back on my heels, Ewan covering his dick with his untucked shirt.

"What's *this*?"

Soren's eyebrow wiggle set my face on fire, and I pressed my hands to my cheeks, mortified to have been caught in the act—but not as guilty as I should be. All of this was sinful by Reed and Nikki standards, but in my heart, having three mates didn't feel *wrong*.

My eyes? Wrong. My strength? Wrong. My connection to a dead goddess? Very wrong.

But not them.

By now, I really believed a divine being had linked us all together—even if I struggled and they bickered and we all fought to connect some days. It was a mess, but it was *my* mess.

And there was no shame in kneeling before my mate to pleasure him while the other watched, right?

Especially when the other looked so *rugged* in that costume. Bare-chested with an axe hanging from his rope belt, Soren was clearly an ancient warrior—and that was about as specific as I could get. The war paint streaking his cheeks and smoky-ing up his eyes had to mean something. Females drooled over those abs, those defined pecs and steely biceps, his forearms oddly powerful.

And he could have been so seductive on the dance floor.

I for one was ready to submit to his prowess.

But my mate had been silly. Goofy. Embarrassing for another female, maybe, but his dance moves made me shriek with laughter. It drew the humans into our bubble, the connections made friendly and shallow but really, really fun.

Now, he was still here for fun, but the way he prowled toward the couches in the center of the room—it was a sinful pleasure. Carnal and devious. Only a sliver of his blue eyes remained, snapping to full amber with a blink and a savage grin. Nibbling my lower lip, I glanced up at Ewan, also sporting his wolf eyes, and when Soren finally slowed, drinks in hand and head still tipped, the alphas faced off with each other.

All teeth.

Snarls rumbling in their chests.

Ugh.

"*You* left our mate unattended," Ewan growled, still covering himself, glowering at Soren like the wolf had beat me to a pulp and left me for dead. Like, come on—it wasn't that serious. "Unacceptable."

"She's a big girl," Soren fired back, sounding just as savage, just as dangerous, his hands tightening around our drinks. "She doesn't need a babysitter." Then, with a deep breath, the rage stoking embers in my lower back eased. He wandered over to the door and set our drinks on the food table, then rounded on us with a smirk, arms crossed, an eyebrow arched. "So, what are we up to?"

I flushed again when his amber gaze settled on me, demanding and pressing and oh, *no*, how was I supposed to resist that look? Did he want full details, or...?

"Soren," Ewan motioned to the door, "fuck off already, or I'll—"

You'll do nothing. Instinct propelled me; I shoved him back into his lazy couch-slouch. Surprise nibbled up my spine just as it flashed in his eyes, and I yanked his shirt up—then got back to it.

Taking him deep on the first stroke, I gripped the base of his dick and found my previous rhythm in a heartbeat. This time, Ewan muffled his groans, his hisses tempered and strained. Soren chuckled somewhere over my shoulder, his surprise threading with Ewan's, brightening up our connection as only Soren could.

Seriously, they were *not* about to start a fight here over nothing. This was really the only way to calm him down, body language and words and expressions otherwise useless. I was mated to *all* of them. They had marked me. I had marked them. We were connected on a deeper level than the usual relationship, and that was that.

It felt wrong to bully one of my mates out just so I could be intimate with the other.

We were all deserving of affection.

Fated mates—in our case, anyway—was a team sport.

Right?

Or was I out of line?

Was this a step too far?

My mated answered for me.

Ewan bucked ever so slightly into my mouth, his hips

jerking, and Soren hovered *right* behind me, the heat of his presence suddenly stifling.

"T-take a picture," Ewan snapped after a moment of Soren's loitering. Heat sparked at the nape of my neck, sharpening at the *click* that sounded behind me immediately after. My black-haired mate snarled and lunged forward, getting tangled with my crown and shoving his length down the back of my throat.

"Chill." Soren chuckled. "It was facing me."

Squirming free, I sucked down a deep breath and glanced at Soren over my shoulder. If they could *not* push each other's buttons when I was working around a choking hazard, that would be great. My blond mate slipped his phone back in his pants pocket, then held up his hands innocently. I shot him a narrowed look, all discipline in the eyes but humor in the quirk of my lips, then got back to it, rising higher on my knees, legs spread for balance, and taking Ewan deep enough again to make his groan sound more like a whimper.

A gentle *whoosh* tickled the backs of my thighs, Soren dropping into a crouch behind me. Without a word, he tugged my dress up and over my backside, exposing the drenched white cotton beneath, then traced the stretchy hemline. Refusing to get distracted, I leaned deeper into Ewan's lap, focused on using both hands now, my lips and tongue devoted to the silky tip, to the way his thighs trembled and his moans snagged in his throat every time I swirled my tongue.

Soren snapped my panties, pulling back and letting go at just the right distance so that it *stung*. My warning growl went unheeded, muffled by Ewan's dick, because seconds later, my mischievous mate tore my underwear right along its seams. Haphazardly, with no regard for my limited supply back home—*rip*. Mouth full, I whined and wriggled my hips as he peeled the shredded fabric off, then tossed the heap on the couch next to Ewan. Just as I was about to press pause here, maybe remind my mates it was *their* money I spent every time they tore a pair of my panties, Soren *licked* me.

Front to back, he had ducked down without me noticing and dragged his tongue through my slick, swollen folds, all the way up to cleft of my backside, avoiding the puckered hole there by wandering over my left cheek—nipping hard enough to leave a mark.

My rhythm faltered. I sat up, hands still working Ewan's saliva-slick shaft, then whimpered when I found my mate on his back behind me, spreading me wider to accommodate for him as he scooted between my knees.

I soon lost sight of that smirking mouth; his hands shot up, cupped my cheeks, and hauled me down. My yelp milked a chuckle from *both* of them, the jerks, but any surprise melted away as soon as Soren's tongue showed me he too was *also* very good down there. Like his fellow alphas, he knew me. Knew how to lick just right, the pressure perfect, his fingertips bruising into my hips, spreading me wider. He tasted me inside and out, then up to the crest, to that little button that, *oh*, they all knew how to play.

It wasn't fair—Ewan seemed especially sensitive around the head, but their attention on *my* most sensitive spot made my knees weak and my thighs tremble and my mind blurry.

Imbalance. This was where they had me.

Determined not to be outdone by the skillful mouth lapping between my thighs, I resumed sucking Ewan as best I could—but rhythm escaped me this time. I struggled to focus, to maintain any sort of control as pleasure whumped in my lower belly like it had a heartbeat of its own, sparking, soaring, like electricity on *fire* the longer Soren tasted me.

As if sensing I needed a hand, Ewan rocked his hips into my mouth with long, languid sighs. When my gaze flicked up, I tripped right into the inferno, and all it took was a gentle tap of his one finger to each of my hands for me to withdraw. My mate rearranged them on his thighs, almost for the sake of my balance while Soren shoved me closer and closer to the edge. Ewan then took firm hold of my crown— and *pumped* into my mouth. He went as deep as I could take without coughing, then retreated. Again and again, he thrust into my mouth as he had done my sex.

He...

He...

Fucked my mouth.

Oh. Oh, *no*—that nearly punted me into the black, into that slightly scary moment when I lost all control of my body and lit up with pleasure so bright I swore every time *this* was the end.

"Oh, *shit*, blue eyes—"

Ewan's fingers twisted in my hair, and his shaft pulsed, followed by an explosion of salty warmth that flooded my mouth. Scrambling, I did my best to swallow it all down and not spill a single drop on the couch—on my beautiful costume or his expensive suit. A shiver of delight rippled down my spine, skirting the mounting heat in my core, separate and independent and *his*. Soren groaned between my thighs like he felt it too, Ewan's bright moment spreading through all of us, passing from one to the next like a contagious yawn.

As his shaft softened somewhat, I finally eased back— because I *did* it. I did a blowjob. *Yes*. Pride blossomed in my chest, affection sparking in Ewan's eyes as they straddled the shade between man and wolf, the fiery sunshine setting into dark hickory.

Coolness tickled my thighs, my sex—Soren was gone. He vanished so fast that it made my head spin, but then there he was, kneeling behind me, one hand clutching my hip as the other steered his dick into me. My blond mate claimed me with one rough thrust, me moaning and him grunting as soon as his hip bones slammed into my backside. Goosebumps shivered down my arms; he had taken me on the edge of my own explosion, the pleasure heady and a little painful, *hovering*, my sex aching for release. Whimpering, I braced on Ewan's sturdy thighs, hopelessly full, stretched and stuffed and *oh*. My head bowed, then shot up at his pointed throat clear, both of us highly aware of my sharp crown and his sensitive member.

With a low growl, Soren found his grip: the hand on my hip held tighter, while the other smoothed over my shoulder. A familiar position for us, just like the first time he hunted, caught, and *fucked* me on the mountainside. We'd tried just about every other position the rest of the day, our game ongoing until...

Until Gull River.

But never mind.

This—folded over on my knees, his hands dominating me, his strength pushing me down and bending me to his will—made the heat in my belly spiral.

The first firm buck of his hips made me squeal.

A third hand soon found my body, Ewan's fingers creeping up my throat until he cupped my chin and forced my head up. My midnight mate eased forward, the fiery sunshine back, his wolf eyes boring deep into mine as Soren pounded me from behind. I jostled and jerked, nudging into the couch, into Ewan's spread thighs, back against Soren's strong figure...

But Ewan held me still.

Captured me with that hand cuffed on my chin, with his eyes promising no escape.

It was all too much.

I tried to close mine, scared of the intensity in him, in the fire churning in my low belly, but his fingers gritted into my jaw.

A warning.

A plea.

Please, look at me.

And I did. I forced myself to stay with him, to be in the moment and not in the dark. As soon as Soren abandoned my hip and reached around for the sensitive bud between my thighs—I was done. Gone. The pleasure finally erupted, shooting like sparks from a bonfire, melting my limbs, turning me molten and limp between my mates.

And Ewan held me the entire time.

Made me look in his eyes as I broke apart and blew away on the breeze.

The sensation between my thighs turned sharp and deadly, Soren still teasing and touching and tormenting, even as I whined and squirmed. I swatted back at him, unable to take it, and then they both chuckled again—like they were in on it together.

At least *something* united them.

Apparently all it took was my sexual suffering and they were a team.

When his torturous fingers finally relented, Soren found a punishing pace, slamming into me from behind, both hands on my hips, his teeth gritted and his expression dangerous over my shoulder.

So he had found it too—the power in kneeling.

My mate had his way with me, Ewan's thighs supporting me, his hand under my chin, until his pace faltered and his hips finally stilled. As if my own pleasure wasn't smothering enough, the heat suffocating, the sort you died happy in, Soren's bliss touched me too. Tickled the backs of my knees and skittered up my thighs, zinging right at the bud he had tormented.

Strange that the undeniable urge to bite and scratch at them when I exploded like a dying star wasn't there anymore; maybe marking a mate was a onetime urge, an itch that *needed* to be scratched the first time. From here on out, it was like we could just... enjoy ourselves.

And tonight, I had most definitely enjoyed myself. My mates released me at the same time, Ewan easing up on my chin, Soren sliding out of me. My supports gave way, and I just wanted to sink to the ground—pass out, snooze the party away with Ewan and Soren on either side of me—

"You think it's that easy, baby?" But Soren scooped me onto my knees, my back to his bare chest, his skin a raging wildfire that made me sweat. He nipped at my shoulder, my neck, then licked the shell of my ear. Soren was my sweetest mate—until we mated. Then he turned wild, like a switch flipped inside him the moment we kissed, and I arched into the monster with a moan, exhausted but perking up again at his dark chuckle. "You've got *three* mates..."

Ewan tipped his head to the side, watching us through heavy, hooded lids, casually fisting his shaft, slowly bringing it back to life so that it stood tall and proud.

"It's never going to be just one of us," Soren rasped, his voice dropping to a silky purr. "We *all* want a piece of you— and we're going to take what we need."

Before I could get a word out, he *lifted* me off my knees and plopped me down on Ewan's lap. They both widened my thighs, positioning me over him, arranging me however they saw fit. Limbs weak and shaky from pleasure, I let it happen, breath hitching when the silky head I had showered with so much attention earlier nudged my slick entrance. As soon as Soren released me, Ewan took over, our eyes locked again as he slid me down his shaft, down, down, down, right to the bottom. I whined the whole way; I'd already... *exploded*.

But Ewan's touch, his gaze, his intensity, made the

pleasure throb in my belly again, the *need* for release swelling. I steadied myself on his shoulders, trembling, our foreheads finding each other, our breath hot and gusting over each other's cheeks, lips, everything. Across the room was the clink of glassware, and out of the corner of my eye I caught Soren slugging back half his beer, then lifting the lids off the platters, perusing whatever made that *heavenly* meaty scent in the air.

I perked up at that, at the food over there, at Ewan's possessive hands kneading my backside.

He set the pace. I rocked half-heartedly; that first explosion had drained me.

Only... Soren was right.

I *had* three mates.

Three males who needed my attention—and I was the one who insisted they all be in the room at the same time. Sure, we were missing Lucian, his scent strongest outside of the club tonight, but as Ewan rocked into me, lifting my spent body and slamming it back down, I was almost grateful.

I couldn't...

My eyes squeezed shut as I gritted my fingers into the leather backrest. *Oh.* I couldn't do this again. Couldn't... Couldn't have one of them drag me to such blissful heights and toss me into the abyss.

And from the determined gleam in Ewan's eyes, his mouth as sinful as Soren's, that was exactly what my mate planned to do.

Refusing to be a passive participant, I did my best to keep up, whimpering, moaning, growling, totally at my mate's mercy. Every time I tried to outpace him, he smacked my backside or nipped at my throat—let me know that *he* had the power here.

Power I happily surrendered, a little sick of keeping it all to myself.

As we turned frenzied, grinding and rocking, Ewan pumping his hips off the couch just to take me as deeply as he could, I finally threw my head back—and came face-to-face with Soren. A few feet away, my mate loitered behind Ewan, shirtless, pants up, war paint smeared. He nursed that beer, a hand in his pocket, casual and distant to outsiders.

Intense and hyperfocused on me. Just as Ewan had forced me to maintain eye contact, a challenge among wolves but a secret intimacy in our pack, Soren ensnared me. Molten amber blazed bright as a shooting star, and I fell into it willingly, needing the burn.

He liked to watch me explode. My mate had demanded it every time he caught me on the mountain, refusing to let me close my eyes or look away, even if he was behind me. I knew the drill by now—knew better than to fight his command.

Tonight was no different. As the hot, sharp pleasure in my belly reached its peak, Soren stiffened, his knuckles white around the beer bottle. Ewan inhaled sharply, then cursed under his breath as my body succumbed to the ecstasy. Pleasure scorched white-hot, tearing through me without mercy, without compromise, drowning me from the inside out. Soren gritted his teeth, every muscle taut, and Ewan choked my name, fingers bruising my backside.

With a snarl, my black-haired mate stilled, his shaft pulsing inside me, his grip like a steel trap. Pleasure licked between my thighs once more, separate from my own and less intense, and Soren finally closed *his* eyes, Ewan's explosion touching all of us again.

Too hot.

Too intense.

Too much *pleasure*.

I whined and buried my face against his neck, riding it out, loving his snarls as Ewan did the same. Still, even with exhaustion worming into my bones and contentment washing over me like a gentle tide, something was missing.

Lucian.

Sure, the thought of being dragged to such sublime highs one more time, from a mate who knew just how to touch and lick and caress, a mountain of a man so scarred yet so tender, made the heaviness worse. But he should be here.

Soren and Ewan could have erupted in another fight, just another one of many. Of my three mates, these two really liked to beat on each other.

They hadn't.

The night could have taken a steep dive into hostility and tension and alpha males baring their teeth just to get a piece of me—to get *all* of me while his rival had nothing.

But we managed to keep the peace. Each of them had me in one way or another, and in the hazy aftermath, neither had started hurling insults again.

This was good.

This was *progress*. A big moment for our pack—and Lucian should have been here to celebrate. His heart deserved to feel just as whole and happy as mine did right now. When I'd asked Soren about his whereabouts earlier, my blond mate had no idea beyond the fact that he was outside pestering security—his words, not mine—and that he probably wouldn't show his face until the crowd died down.

While that fit what I knew of Lucian, I didn't have to like it.

I wanted him here, with me, on this couch, his lips on my skin and his hands everywhere...

But as Soren handed me the pumpkin cocktail he had originally left to fetch downstairs, the straw tipped with a skeleton skull, some little floating ice cube thing still giving off fog—was it a magic trick?—I lacked the energy to make my case.

Next time.

Lucian would be in the thick of it *next* time—I'd make sure of that.

After sitting up and slurping down the tart liquid, the liquor muted by the zesty mix, I fed an equally sweaty Ewan a sip. My spent mate's face puckered as he shook his head.

"Fuck, that's so sweet."

Not for me.

But I kept that to myself, gulping down another icy mouthful with a grin and a shrug.

"So…" Soren set his empty beer bottle on the back of the couch as he perched next to Ewan's head, *right* in his personal space, determined to be involved, and then smirked when his fellow alpha glowered up at him and I smothered a giggle. "Anyone in the mood for round two?"

LYSSA

"I'll be right back." *Wait.* I hesitated in the doorway, fixing my two sweaty, disheveled mates with narrowed looks. Fog kissed the corners of that huge tinted window across the room, and the buffet table to my right screamed my name. Knowing wolves as well as I did, I pointed a warning finger from Ewan to Soren and back again. "Don't eat all the food while I'm gone."

Sprawled on one of the half-moon couches, Soren chuckled—then sat straighter when my no-nonsense expression darkened. Tough as it was to be serious after our first group mating, I held my warning composure like an elder wolf checking a mouthy yearling.

"All yours, baby," Soren insisted. When I looked to Ewan, an eyebrow up, my black-haired mate grinned and raised his hands in surrender. Honestly, the sex had been fun and amazing and great and all that. I still burned bright and hot, the aftermath clinging to me, cloying between my thighs and threatening to stain my dress. But those sausage things under one of the tray covers? I planned to eat all of them. Then the fancy cheese. Then the garlicky spread for those fancy crackers, *then* the cookies shaped like little bats.

Yum.

Great sex *and* delicious food *and* my mates getting along?

Dream. Come. True.

Having staked my claim, I slipped out of the all-black private room, then flinched when the locks clicked and clacked into place as soon as the door shut. How... was I supposed to get back in? A special knock?

Even in this narrow corridor away from the main event, the Chalet struck like a charging bull. The heady smells of sweat and cologne and body odor and liquor. The pounding music. The fog hovering a few inches off the ground, artificial and tickling my nose enough to make me *and* Kira sneeze. Too loud. Too busy. Too—human.

I'd had my club fun for the night. If I had my way, we'd all spend the rest of it in there, separate from the chaos but still able to check on things through the window overlooking the first floor. Heck, if it were up to me, I wouldn't leave that room until sunrise. Sure, Ewan would inevitably come and go; that was expected. So long as he came back, Soren stayed, and Lucian eventually found us, it would be the *perfect* night.

The perfect distraction.

Something wet and thick oozed down my inner thigh, and I squished my legs together as I waddled down the hallway to the women's bathroom. Man, what I wouldn't give to be a witch right now instead of a shifter. On one of our lunch dates, little Aster had spit up all over her onesie, and Rosa whooshed it away with a flick of her wand and a softly murmured spell. *Bam.* Gone. Baby clean. No one had even noticed.

Shouldering through the dark wood door with its glossy rose-gold lettering, I stumbled into a space just as packed as the nightclub itself. Wall to wall females crowded the bathroom, the smells and sounds no less intense here—but the air... different. Electric, humming, like there were fifty Rosas in one place. Swallowing thickly, I glanced toward the sinks, catching the purple eyes of a woman washing her hands, her reflection watching *me*.

More witches?

Rosa had said her kind traveled here from nearby Hampton for the Samhain weekend, dropping a fortune on Redwood Grove's hotels, chalets, restaurants—and Ewan's nightclub. Suddenly self-conscious after a glimpse at my own reflection, my hair a mess and my cheeks a telling pink, I tugged my dress down, feeling almost like that purple-eyed witch could see right through it.

"Babe, you got a tampon?"

A human—something about her smell, her energy, her *look*—suddenly bobbed in front of me, dressed like a bride.

A... dead bride?

Half her face was rotted, but given the smell, it was just makeup.

I blinked back at her. Tampon? *Me*?

I didn't even have a purse tonight.

I came to the Chalet with nothing but myself and a crown.

Throat thick, mouth dry, I shook my head and croaked out, "No, sorry."

"Here, girl." A voice echoed from one of the stalls to my right, and seconds later a packaged tampon skidded across the tile in our direction. "I got you."

"Oh my god, *yes*, you *lifesaver*!"

Half-dead Bride scooped it up and skipped into a stall the second another female slipped out. More electric, bright-eyed women gathered by the sinks, fixing their hair, their makeup, all of them *very* stylish on a night dedicated to costumes. A toilet flushed. A door opened. I zipped inside the stall before someone else claimed it, feeling oddly at peace in here.

Surrounded by female strangers.

The air was different with all those witches, sure, but there was this strange feminine comradery here in the second-floor bathroom. Everyone stunk of booze, of the tart orange drink that I'd guzzled before leaving our private room. But it was nice. Drunk compliments flowed. Laughter. Hand dryers whirring and toilets flushing and heels clacking.

Until last month, I thought the only world I belonged in was the one out there—in the forest, in the wild, with the wolves. There was no room for a freak, an abomination, a daughter of sin and evil, among humans. I was too strong, too fast, too savage.

But as I sat to pee and clean up down below, I fit.

Just a little.

Not completely. Not yet.

Still *so* much to learn—about history and tradition, about blending into both humanity and shifter culture. About how to walk effortlessly in high heels. Seriously. Still on the toilet, toes exposed and tapping in my golden sandals, I bent over a little to gawk at the massive stilettos on the woman in the next stall. How did those things not just totally murder her feet?

But despite the hurdles ahead, I belonged here.

Kira whimpered.

Well. So long as Rosa and I could get Idunn's… *gift* under control.

Who knew—maybe I didn't have any of her powers. Maybe it was a fluke, the windows trembling and the pen on Ewan's desk rattling and… me breaking the faucet in my bathroom.

My mates still didn't know about that, and I just stuck to

the other tap, forced to do everything with scalding hot water, the cold officially inaccessible.

I gulped at the thought.

Right here, right now, I belonged.

But that could change.

I had worked hard to keep all this new crazy inside, lying to my mates, pretending it *wasn't* happening—refusing to give them a new, very valid reason to turn me out into the cold.

The longer I sat there, trying to focus on the good but forever dragged toward the terrible, the bathroom quieted. Females filtered in and out, but the crowd eventually thinned to a lone pair of whispering women.

Then… just me.

Alone.

Like always.

Nope. Not tonight, stupid inner voice. Sniffing, I stood and flushed the toilet, then sauntered out to wash my hands, makeup ruined, golden gaze a bit bloodshot. After smearing my hands dry on my dress, I wiped under my eyes, banishing the old sorrow before it *dared* leak out. If I kept up the playful attitude—which would be easy once I was back with my mates—no one would notice.

If I didn't think it, *they* wouldn't feel it.

And then we could just have a fun night like any regular pack.

Hair smoothed, sadness squashed, I stared hard into the mirror—and gold stared back. My first instinct was to insult my new eyes.

Instead, I rolled my shoulders and stood taller, willing the tension away.

That gold looks great with your costume. Very on theme for the sun.

Kira huffed, unimpressed with my attempt at a positive attitude.

I glared harder at my reflection, this time directing it to my forehead as I pointed at the mirror. "Don't you start with me."

She fired back with a teasing yowl, just a little something to let me know she wasn't serious, then stomped around inside, bored and eager to get back to Ewan and Soren.

On the same page, girlie.

Feeling marginally better but still chasing the post-mating high, I left the bathroom—

And was immediately hooked around the waist and ripped back into a body so hard it had to be stone. All the air *whooshed* out of my lungs, like taking a punch to the gut, and Kira snapped and snarled inside my cotton-filled skull, her fury slicing through the shock.

No scent except the buckets of bergamot-accented cologne.

Roughly my height. Thin. Not a physical threat, but—

A hand snapped around my throat at lightning speed, the touch ice-cold and brutal.

"You smell like honey and sex," the strange male rasped in my ear, breathing me in deep, the air around us cooling.

Tinged with iron.

Down the hall, next to the emergency exit door, the shadows shifted and *moved*, just like they had a few nights ago.

"If I bite you," he carried on, crushing my windpipe as Kira fought me, desperate to shoot out and rip this guy apart, "is that what your blood will taste like?"

My vision sharpened, locked on the shadow morphing into the shape of a man.

A man in black.

Skin deathly pale.

A walking corpse in a fitted suit.

Handsome. Grey eyes. Cruel smile.

Coming right at me.

I blinked once, twice—and then the fog lifted.

Goodbye, shock—hello, *murder*. I elbowed back hard enough that something *cracked*, probably a rib, and my captor grunted. Whirling around, I hiked my knee into his groin— and found myself face-to-face with a mouth full of sharp, dazzling white teeth.

Two elongated fangs.

Not fake.

Not a costume.

Vampire.

This night was full of trickery, costumes and sparkles and illusion, but those weren't fake. Those were very, very real. Snarling, I shouldered forward, throwing all my new strength around, and knocked him a few paces back. Also ghostly white and in an identical dark grey suit as his shadowy companion, this buzzed blond staggered and struggled to regain his footing, surprise flashing in his gaze, his irises shaded like a wilted daffodil.

"Don't you dare *touch* me," I sneered. No one but my mates had a right to my body—and even they needed my permission. Kira and I aligned, hearts pounding as one, I attacked. Nails. Teeth. Brute strength. I bullied and pushed and kicked, snarling and growling and snapping.

I was strong.

But so was he.

And fast.

So fast he blurred right before my eyes, in front of me one second, behind the next—then *two* of them on me. I could take one if he just stood still for a beat, but two?

I wasn't strong enough for two.

All my fight, tenacity, confidence—trapped in their steel

grips, both of them behind me, one gripping my wrists, the other clapping a hand over my snarling mouth.

So I bit him.

As the pair shoved me down the corridor toward our private room *and* the emergency exit door, I clamped down on that frozen flesh with everything I had.

"*Fuck.*" The hand's owner tried to wriggle free, but clearly he had never had a wolf bite before. We chomped hard and never let up, even as thick, gloopy, cold blood filled our mouths—made our stomachs turn and Kira gag and *ugh* vampires tasted like death. But I held on. Clamped down until my teeth nudged bone. Snarled like an alpha. Didn't even flinch when one of them pounded his fist into my side, right over my kidney. "Fucking wolf *bitch—*"

"Just get her downstairs," the original lurker hissed as they plowed me through the heavy metal door. "Don't break anything."

"Fucking cunt won't let go."

"Well, you'll *heal*, won't you?"

"Fuck off."

"*You* fuck off."

Both of you... fuck off.

We stumbled into a dimly lit stairwell, one giant heap of arms and legs and bodies all moving in different directions. Mouth so full of vampire blood it leaked out the sides, I planted my feet and fought the whole way down, these two throwing everything they had into moving me—their curses suggested as much, anyway.

I'd been in fights before.

Faced scarier foes.

Always alone, sure, but always a *survivor*.

After Nikki and Reed and the two years of horror following my first shift, nothing out there could compete.

Not that I had tangled with a vampire before, never mind

two, but if they wanted to shove me out of this building—do it. Outside was *my* territory, and they had no idea what they were in for once I let Kira stretch her legs and bare her teeth in the alleyway behind the nightclub.

What I wasn't ready for, however, was their speed. Again. Once we all struggled down a single flight of stairs, like slogging through quicksand courtesy of sheer wolf grit, the pair paused on the landing, the stairwell suddenly *too* quiet except for my heaving breaths and snarls, and then the world just... blurred. Nothing in focus, we moved so fast my belly flipped, and I finally choked on all the vampire blood.

Gagging, hacking, I folded over when the stairwell finally came back into focus, surroundings crystal clear again, heart in my throat and Kira just as loopy. Blood so dark it was almost purple splattered the concrete and my sandals. Kira found her balance first, snarling, hackles up and lips peeled when the men behind me snickered.

"At least we know something shuts her up."

The one death-gripping my wrists, circulation cut and my fingers white, whipped me around and marched me toward the metal door at the end of the corridor.

"You tell me when the world stops spinning, puppy," he sneered in my ear, even his breath cold. Swallowing hard, I blocked out my hatred for *them* and focused on my breathing, on finding my feet again so that as soon as we hit fresh air, I could cut them off at the knees.

Literally, hopefully, only I had no clue how much pressure you needed to snap vampire bone.

But, hey, always up for learning something new.

As the pair ushered me roughly down the corridor, muffled music pounding away, Kira and I braced for the next attack. The first had happened so fast it was tough to take stock of my opponents, but from the lingering cold damp smeared around my mouth, I knew they bled.

And I knew they *hurt*.

On the brink of the final exit, the duo muttered to themselves in a language I didn't understand, fluid and low with a lot of hard *R*s. I took a deep breath. Kira stilled. They shoved me through the door—and right into a furious Lucian.

My mate took *me* by surprise, never mind the vampires. Dressed in a fitted black suit like Ewan, my mountain man pounced with a roar that lit up the night sky. Savage. Wild. Raw *fury* slammed into me, knocked the wind out of me, jumping from his heart to mine and setting it on fire. He lunged for the vampire on my right, and a gush of cold mist hit me from the side. The other vampire dragged me away, cursing, my skin painted with the blood of his friend.

Silly man.

Didn't he remember I could take them one-on-one?

Drawing on Lucian's wild, fusing it with mine, Kira *right* on the verge of a shift, I twisted my arm, loosening his hold, and spun into him. My fist met his nose *hard*, bone snapping, blood gushing, more curses filling the air. He regained control fast, snatching my wrist, but I ducked under his arm, not caring if I dislocated a shoulder in the meantime, and leapt on his back.

Raked my nails across his face.

Bit into his neck and tore off a hunk of icy skin. Down the alley, Lucian wore a mask of deep purple, vampire blood smeared up his snarling face, his neat beard dripping with the stuff.

"Should I shift?" I called over the fray, legs snapped tight around my bucking opponent.

"*No*," Lucian bellowed back. "Not here."

As if the human population of Redwood Grove *mattered* to either of us; I was ready to let Kira taste vampire flesh, and he sounded more beast than man, his voice impossibly deep

—demonic, almost, as he slammed the throatless vampire's head into the pavement over and over again.

Unfortunately, these guys seemed to heal as fast as we did: my nose crinkled when I noticed the gaping wound across the vampire's neck stitching back together, ugly and crude. Lucian needed to bash his skull *now* or he'd have a warrior back at full strength in no time.

The momentary distraction was my undoing. Two strong hands shot up, grabbed my shoulders, and *ripped* me forward. I toppled down with a rough screech, Kira's snarl leaking through, and crashed into the ground. At the last second, I'd tried to cushion the fall, but the impact snapped my wrist, bones breaking with a sickening *crunch*. Agony seared up my arm. I hissed, knowing it was only temporary, and tried to squirm away.

Lucian broke the other vampire's jaw, drowning in a sea of rage, and my vision tinted red for a few seconds until I blinked *his* emotions away.

Not good in a fight.

I looked to him, frantic, hurting, needing this huge wolf to get a grip on his emotions—

The emergency door flung open, clanging off the brick and rebounding into a snarling Ewan and Soren. My mates charged into the fight, wolf eyes out and teeth bared, their anger, fear, and *wild* twisting with mine and Lucian's, the air thickening, the four of us briefly so in tune I swore I heard their heartbeats, felt their blood pumping through *my* veins same as my own.

My fingers tingled.

Heat exploded in my chest, scary and sharp and so *bright* my eyes watered.

A nearby trash can shook violently enough to jostle the lid off.

Dead weeds turned green, soaring out of the cracks along the building's foundation.

"*Shit.*" The vampire on top of me took off, blurring down the alley, his friend at his heels, just two shadows racing for the main streets. Without a word, a shirtless Soren sprinted after them, followed swiftly by Lucian, who ripped off his jacket and tie as he ran, hurling them aside and skidding around the corner.

Groaning, I pushed up on my elbow and rolled my previously broken wrist. While still a little crackly, it rotated in two circles with minimal pain—good enough. What had me more concerned were the weeds that had crept along the Chalet's foundations; yellow and dead to green and vibrant, one had even sprouted a flower head and a few white petals.

"You all right, blue eyes?" Ewan crashed to my side and bundled me up, his wolf eyes assessing me for damage. I nodded. Technically, I was fine. *Technically,* my body healed fast and I lived to fight another day.

Inside, however, the fear turned to reaching ivy, spiraling around my bones, threading through my rib cage, *strangling* my heart.

Not only had two vampires tried to kidnap me tonight, but I made dead plants grow.

I shook that garbage can so hard the lid popped off.

I—

"I'm fine," I muttered when Ewan's search for injuries got rougher and more panicked. Groaning, I brushed the hair out of my face and—oh. *Come on.* One of them had ripped my crown off at some point. Jerks. Annoyed, I sat up properly and dusted the dirt off my legs, then grimaced when I noticed the ocean of purplish blood splattered everywhere. "Why did they do that?"

"I don't know." Now that he had confirmed nothing was broken or permanently damaged, my mate eased off to send a rapid-fire text, thumb flying across his phone's screen before he locked it and stuffed the thing in his jacket.

Then he was all mine.

Ewan hauled me into his lap, arms steelier and stronger and much, much safer than those blocks of marble with fangs. While I wanted to be strong, prove to my mates that once again I could stand on my own two feet against pack enemies, this was nice too. Just for a moment, the world went quiet. Me and him, alone in a dark alley, the ground damp with rain that must have fallen sometime in the last hour. On the other side of the building, the Halloween crowd chatted and laughed, the dull roar punctured by the occasional girlish shriek. Arms folded into my chest, I snuggled closer, burrowed under his chin and nestled into his throat, breathing in his scent. Eyes closed, I bathed in his support—

In his wrath.

Unlike before, Ewan seemed to be trying to keep his emotions under control—which worked great for me. Not only was I so *not* in the mood for another fear-based lecture, but despite the peace and quiet and comfort, something ancient still buzzed in my fingertips. If *I* lost it, influenced by them or my own feelings, I might expose myself more than I already had.

Make my mates question if I was worth the risk—if they wanted to keep this landmine on their territory. One wrong move and *boom*.

I clenched my eyes shut as hard as I could, shoving down the fear and drudging up the anger. If he felt me like I felt him, let Ewan believe I was *furious* that someone had gotten the jump on me.

Just when I noticed him starting to shake, his grip like a snare and his teeth bared, the emergency door flew open again, and out raced a wide-eyed Ethan, his wand drawn, his ridiculous hat forgotten.

His face paint a little smudged…

I guess he and his rosebud had been having a similar sort of night somewhere private and secluded.

"Where are they?" he demanded as Ewan helped me up. I didn't need the support, perfectly capable of standing by myself, but there was something so *nice* about his arm around my shoulders, cradling me into his chest. Clearly, my mate had messaged his warlock buddy about the situation: Ethan stalked back and forth, wand up, searching the shadows—his brown gaze snagging on the weeds I had…

I had…

Done something to.

Yeah, let's go with that.

"No idea," Ewan rumbled, "but I need to find them. Get them the *fuck* out of our territory."

If he was going to chase those walking corpses, then I planned to be right there with him. Had my stupid wrist been fully fixed, I would have sprinted after Lucian and Soren, more than happy to bully any danger to us *and* the humans of Redwood Grove out. "Ewan—"

The emergency door banged open again, and this time Rosa came trundling out, her huge silver dress hiked in one hand, her wand in the other.

"Lyssa!"

Cheeks flushed, emerald eyes panicked, she rushed straight to my side.

"Take her home and stay with her," Ethan ordered—then flinched, the warlock going pale beneath all that face paint when Ewan snarled. Fire surged between us, his grip tightening around my shoulders, and I pushed against the dead center of his chest, willing *my* calm to trickle into him —soothe the inferno, quiet the storm. As if realizing his mistake, Ethan patted the air between us. "No, no, sorry. If…

it's okay, Rosa can protect the house. Make sure they don't, er..."

Much to my surprise, Ewan looked to *me* for an answer one way or another. Head dipped, he tapped the underside of my chin so that our gazes met. No words flowed between us, but the sentiment warmed in my chest. Kira whined, then snorted a response back to our mate, reading him loud and clear.

He wanted my opinion.

My permission, maybe?

No. That was a step too far.

He just needed to know I was okay with that.

Licking my lips, I managed a little half nod, because, yeah, I would go anywhere with Rosa, but I wasn't about to just hide in the house and wait for the males to take care of things.

We were a *pack*, now more than ever before. Mated, fated, we had our own song.

I had a duty to perform for *my* pack and territory.

"Can you spell the gates?" Ewan shifted his attention back to Ethan, his voice just as dangerously low and smoky as Lucian's had been. These vampires had no idea what kind of violent end they were in for, but I wanted to be there when it happened. "Ward the village? *Something?*"

"For sure," Ethan groused back. He shrugged out of his black suit jacket, which he then gently folded and set over the garbage can I'd rustled as he spoke. "Fuck those guys... The Hampton coven *vouched* for them. I didn't want any damn leeches near tonight, and I should have gone with my gut."

"Don't blame yourself," Ewan insisted. "Vamps are slippery assholes." His wolf eyes then narrowed at Ethan. "But let it be clear that I will *not* tolerate them in this territory again."

"Agreed." Ethan jerked up his dress shirt sleeves, wand in hand, his energy... complicated. Just like the witches in the bathroom had changed the air, made it electric and *different*, he and Rosa did too. But Rosa was the cold to his hot, the ice to his fire. She was my honey-and-amber friend, her scent strong and supportive, her physical being radiating the serene majesty of a full moon.

Her husband gave off a strange crackly static that made Kira tense, but from the thin smile he swapped with Ewan, he had already earned the right to be trusted.

The warlock shook his head and swooped a hand over his sweaty dirty-blond hair. "Should have gone with my gut... I'm sorry, but I'll get the village locked down now."

This was all moving too fast without me. Before I could get my two cents in, however, Ewan kissed me—nothing firework-inducing like before, just a firm, hard peck on the lips—and cupped my chin.

"No unnecessary risks, blue eyes," he growled. His arched eyebrow said he wanted me to promise and agree and be a good girl. I briefly clamped down on the insides of my cheeks instead, Kira desperate to hunt vampires.

"I can track them with you—"

"No." Like his word was law, Ewan nudged me toward Rosa—handed me off to the next caretaker. My lips twitched into a snarl, and I grabbed his jacket sleeve, ripping into the fabric and yanking him with me. His eyes flashed dangerously. My teeth bared back.

"Honey..." Rosa's gentle words cut through the mounting tension. If she had *any* sense, she wouldn't put herself between two wolves squaring off, but this witch—the moon to my sun tonight—seemed to trust me as much as I trusted her. She stuck herself right in my narrowed line of sight, not speaking again until we met in a clash of green and gold. "Look, if they were trying to take you... Don't give them

173

what they want. Your home is the heart of the territory, right? You and me are just going to defend it." She rolled her shoulders back and wiggled her red brows. "Seriously. No bloodsucking leeches are getting by us."

Kira grumbled and scratched and paced inside me, her energy trembling through my arms, my legs full of *fight* and ready to run.

But we both knew Rosa had a point.

The house *was* the heart, the throne room, the *whatever* of our territory. I had no idea what those vampires wanted with me besides the fact that I smelled like a dead goddess, but if they were making a play for our land, they'd go for it at some point.

Fine.

I conceded with a stiff nod. Over Rosa's head, Ewan and I traded glances, expressions softened just enough to confirm the fight was over—dead and buried. On to the next issue.

After Ethan kissed Rosa's cheek and reminded her to lock the SUV while we drove, he jogged off with my mate, who seemed to be pacing himself so the warlock could keep up. As soon as they disappeared around the end of the building, I grabbed Rosa's arm and pulled her close.

"One of them said I smell like honey," I whispered, easing up on my grip when pain flashed over her features. "Idunn smells like honey."

Rosa pursed her lips. "Okay, we—"

"And I did that." I motioned to the very alive, very happy trio of thorny weeds growing out the side of the building. "They were dead, and now they aren't, and I don't know what I did, but they—"

"Honey, deep breath." Rosa planted her hands on my shoulders, then sucked down an exaggerated inhale and waited for me to begrudgingly do the same before she exhaled. We repeated that a few times, in and out, in and out, her tone and expression meant for baby Aster, not a grown wolf—but something I appreciated all the same.

Even now, after bullying rival wolves and surviving a vampire kidnapping, this witch was *still* looking after me.

"Tomorrow morning, we're going to tackle this together," she told me, slow and precise—maybe to keep me calm, but maybe because she was still working out my newfound powers for herself. "I've got a few exercises young witches do when their powers start to develop... We'll try them somewhere safe and away from everyone. For now—"

"Home," I finished for her. Rosa let out what I *swore* sounded like a relieved breath, almost like she expected me to fight her on this.

Nope.

Protecting our base made sense—even if unleashing Kira on those vampires would have been more satisfying.

"Home," she whispered back. We then set out together, hand in hand, her wand up and inconspicuous on a night full of magic, danger, and costumes, headed for her and Ethan's SUV parked up the street from the club.

Off to defend my pack's heart—and knowing that if one of those fanged weirdos underestimated us because we were *females*, he was in for one terrible, *awful* night.

13

LYSSA

"Okay…" Rosa closed the driver's-side door as gently as she could. "I think she's actually out this time."

With the SUV rumbling, the windows slowly defogging, Redwood Grove bathed in a bright grey foggy November morning, we both whipped around—and found Aster dead to the world. Tucked into her car seat, fed and fat and swaddled in a pink onesie with squishy little booties and blankets, the tiny witch snoozed away with her head slumped and her lower lip plumped. Adorable. Totally oblivious to the stress hounding me and her mom from the night before, but still very cute.

"Did you leave a note for the guys?" Rosa asked as she buckled herself in, the seat belt's click soft, her effort to keep quiet despite the roaring beast around us almost as adorable as her pup. I shook my head when she glanced up, and she huffed, rolled her eyes, then grabbed her phone from the front console, settled back into the much-too-big driver's seat, and stabbed at the screen. While Ewan was all thumbs on his phone—at some point during my forest exile, the world had evolved from cordless phones being the *height* of communications technology to touchscreen, which, gotta admit, was pretty cool—this witch did everything with her pointer finger and her tongue poking out the side of her mouth.

"I'm letting Ewan know we're going out for breakfast." We both made conspiratorial eye contact as I too slowly and quietly belted myself. The color drained from her cheeks, the same guilt poking at my ribcage. Neither of us wanted to lie to our men, but here we were, sneaking away first thing to practice… magic. Power. *Something*. Ethan had no idea—Rosa promised. My mates were still out hunting vampires, oblivious to the extent of my abilities.

It didn't feel good.

But Rosa had dubbed it a necessary evil for the time being, and I liked that. Not good—but necessary to keep our loved ones safe.

"I'm also telling him to get you a phone already," she added distractedly, brows furrowed deep. "Like, I know you can talk through howls, but it's getting ridiculous that you don't have one yet."

Grinning, I left her to it and watched Aster doze in the rearview mirror, relying on *her* peace to calm my nerves. With Halloween taking a steep nosedive only six hours ago, I should still be in bed sleeping it off. As promised, Rosa had spent the night, but I forced her to get some shut-eye when it became obvious a witch's body couldn't function on fumes like a shifter. Besides, I had it covered without her: no vampire set foot on the main property. I couldn't speak to the rest of the territory, but as soon as the sun's golden rays spilled over the horizon, I did a perimeter sweep of the nearby forest.

Nothing.

No weird smells. No iron. No cold spots. No crunching twigs and rustling leaves that didn't belong.

No Idunn on the wind either, but that was kind of just a small mercy.

Last but not least: no word from my mates. I *had* heard them howling through the early morning hours, coordinating as wolves, their intense focus, their frustration and fury, washing over me in waves—sometimes tidal, sometimes nothing more than a splash.

While I had no idea where they were now, I trusted their abilities.

And, for once, I trusted them to protect each other.

Text sent, Rosa reversed down the driveway and headed out, taking winding roads south. After getting a few hours of sleep, the witch had popped back to her place to relieve the overnight sitter. No Ethan either; we guessed he was part of the vampire hunt, but, really, who knew. With Aster in tow, Rosa had fed her chubby-cheeked pup, breastfeeding at our dining table and demolishing a bowl of cereal I had prepped with my useless kitchen skills while I polished off eight in the time it took her to eat one, and once we tidied up, we hit the road.

The further south we went, the sadder, greyer, and more miserable my territory started to look. Even though most of the autumn canopy had fallen, the Redwood Grove I was starting to know and love was dense. Thick. Packed with tons of trees, foliage, and brush. Game of all kinds. Predators. Bears preparing for hibernation. Reptiles sunning themselves whenever and wherever they could.

Here, the trees turned sparse, and fields of brambles stretched far as the eye could see. Litter peppered the scraggly landscape, the few human towns we skirted sleepy and still on a chilly, cloudy Sunday morning.

Rosa eventually veered off the main two-lane roads, carefully navigating backcountry lanes riddled with potholes, not a house for miles. I had no clue how she decided where to go and when to stop, but she eventually pulled off onto the shoulder, the grass dead and yellow, a whole load of grey nothing ahead. Even the dirt down here had a depressing grimy tinge to it.

I hopped out of the SUV, scanning our surroundings with a frown. My wolf pack had instinctively avoided this as we plodded north, headed for the rich forestry where my mates had originally found us. As Rosa unloaded Aster's car seat, the sleeping pup still buckled in, I prowled into the grey nothingness, runners trampling dead weeds and thorns catching on my sweatpants. Arms crossed, I scoped it out in silence—then tipped my head back and *breathed*.

Kira sucked in a lungful of the almost painfully crisp morning air, both of us scenting out dangers.

No vampires, at least.

No nothing.

Not even my pack. I breathed harder, deeper, really filling my lungs—but they weren't here. And why would they be? Why would they backtrack south where the resources were slim and the ground hurt their paws?

As we did every year, they would have headed west for the winter, then north in the spring.

They... were probably long gone.

They wouldn't wait for me.

Probably wouldn't even look for me.

They were *wolves*. Just wolves. They needed shelter, food, and family. Most of the pack was still there; they'd move on and expect *me* to find *them*, if they spared me a thought at all.

Loss slithered through me like the last rounds of an echo.

Kira howled, calling to her alphas, the yearlings, the pups.

No answer.

We would probably never hear their song again.

But as Rosa's boots tromped closer, I sniffed and wiped

the sadness away, pushing it deep down so she couldn't see it and my mates wouldn't feel it.

In her heels, the curvy witch was roughly my height, but our sense of style couldn't be more opposite. While I left the house this morning in sweats, choosing comfort over style in black sweatpants and a brown hoodie, my running shoes new and *not* something I would actually run in, Rosa somehow found the time to coordinate her look. Black jumpsuit. Faux-leather boots. Long charcoal trench coat. Stylish baby bag in the car. Hair knotted in a ballerina bun with curly red wisps spilling everywhere.

She *looked* ready for breakfast on the town, somewhere posh with all the fancy folk who trekked to Redwood Grove for last night's party.

I... still looked like I lived in the woods.

Whatever.

Today wasn't a day for fashion or guilt.

Together, we meandered toward a clump of grey stones, and I hung back, watching Rosa set Aster's car seat on the least pointy of the bunch. She balanced it, then pulled her wand from her coat and softly muttered an incantation under her breath. White plumed from the end of the polished wood, and she drew a shimmering circle over her sleeping pup, one that flared into an orb. It stayed white for a few moments, then turned transparent with a *slight* rainbow shimmer depending on the angle you looked at it from.

"For protection," Rosa noted, tapping the top of the see-through bubble with her wand. She then perched on the boulder beside her super-safe babe—I would tear *anything's* throat out, here, there, and everywhere if they so much as glanced at Aster wrong—and crossed her legs, wand on her lap, eyes on me. "Okay, so, what happens inside you when the, uh, *power* comes out? Tell me how it manifests and how it makes you feel."

I sucked in my cheeks, heat wending down my body and pooling in my toes, the bottoms of my feet tingling like I was about to *run*. Kira, meanwhile, settled deep within, flopped down, head on her crossed paws, ready to ride this out.

Right.

How did it feel? I shrugged and unloaded everything I could think of—everything I could remember from the last week and a bit of *this*. Buzzing in my fingertips. Heat in my chest. Noise in my skull, the rest of the world muted.

It shook the windows—garbage cans and pens and toothbrushes and coffee mugs placed too close to the edge of the table.

And it made me feel… scared.

Alone.

Terrified, not of *it*, not completely, but of the fact that my mates could take one look at the monster I'd become and toss me aside.

Rosa let me talk uninterrupted, nodding here and there, those bright emeralds radiating empathy and care and motherly love so earnestly that it made my throat thick, the backs of my eyes stinging with tears I refused to shed.

When I finished, she took a beat, twirling her wand between her fingers, one hand to the other, and then nodded.

"Right, so, baby witches go through something similar," she told me, slow and gentle in her delivery—but never patronizing. Never like I was stupid. "It's this scary feeling of being totally out of control. In my experience, it's like you literally have no idea when and where your magic will manifest, how it'll come out… We learn to control it at academies or within our covens, and in time we use incantations to shape it and wands to channel it. Sometimes we use intention, just, uh, the *will* to make something happen, but it's rare." Her eyes swept up and down my figure. "But I think if you were blessed by a goddess, even a dead one, you need to practice intention. Much more like fae magic, you know?"

"Uh-huh." Sure. I knew *exactly* what fae were and how their—I assumed—complex magic system worked. Still, even if her last comment sparked more questions than answers, at least I wasn't a universal oddity. At least this was a *shared* experience and I wasn't some freak.

An outcast, out of control and dangerous.

I mean, I *was* out of control and probably dangerous, but it could be worse. Rosa could have grabbed Aster and booked it, terrified, then pruned our friendship back to the root.

But she was still here.

And she *cared*.

"It seems to happen when you're really emotional," she mused, tapping her lower lip with her wand, "but we want it to happen when *you* want it—not just when your emotions are heightened."

I shrugged. "Yeah, that would be nice."

"Okay…" Rosa clapped her hands and stood, and I found myself wishing the twinkling resolve in her eyes jumped ship and landed here—because she looked, sounded, and, somehow, *felt* much more confident in my abilities than I did. "Let's start with the basics."

I swallowed a groan. Yeah, I knew I'd have to *work* to contain whatever Idunn had given me through the river, but nothing had ever come so hard before. I navigated the separate, equally dangerous worlds of humans and wolves on instinct, trusting my gut, trusting Kira, and making moves as best I could. Sometimes it backfired. Sometimes I failed. But I always got back up, dusted myself off, and *learned*.

This…

This was frustratingly abstract.

The basics involved a lot of vague visualization work, with Rosa walking me through what she likened to a meditation practice, circling me, her voice lulling Kira to sleep. Sure, my hands buzzed and the heat flared in my chest. My senses sharpened. My mind cleared.

But nothing actually happened.

And a million years later, tendrils of dull sunshine fighting through the overcast and a sweaty sheen on my brow, I'd had enough.

I clenched my eyes shut and snarled.

Something clattered at my feet.

"Oh, Lyssa, look!"

A quick glance down showed the pebbles I had been toeing at since we arrived had moved a few inches, presumably bouncing along with my frustration.

"I know," I said tightly. "That's what always happens—"

"Let's capitalize on it." Rosa came in close, *right* up against my back, taking me by the shoulders and urging me to close my eyes. I didn't. She waited. The world went on without us, and Kira finally let out an impatient whine. *Just do it already*. So, I did. With everything dark again, I flinched as Rosa gathered my hair over the opposite shoulder, then positioned her full lips next to my ear. "Okay, Lyssa, imagine a well inside you."

"A well—"

"Like a wishing well," she whispered, "like the kind you read about in fairy tales. Do you see it?"

I crinkled my nose. "Uh…"

"Picture it next to Kira. Deep inside, I know you see her. She's you. You're her. And the well is a part of you now too."

Even with my eyelids shut, I managed to roll my golden orbs skyward with a long, irritated sigh. Still, Rosa had gone out of her way to help me—and pouting, throwing a tantrum like a puppy, was just rude. So, I did my best to imagine the picture she painted: Kira, seated primly as always, with a huge stone well beside her.

My wolf snorted—then nosed at the new addition.

"Is it there?"

"Yes," I whispered.

"Good." Rosa took a beat, her breath soft, her scent overwhelming. "Imagine it full of water—but the water is *different*. It looks like what you saw in the mountain."

"Like diamonds," I muttered, "and starlight. Twinkling. Cold. Fresh."

"Yes, that. *That* is your power, Lyssa. That well holds all the power Idunn gifted you, and it will never run dry."

I cracked an eye open. "How do you know that?"

"A hunch." She tapped my chest with her wand. "Eyes closed, you."

Smirking, I did as I was told.

"When you want to call on your power, you imagine the well. You imagine cupping your hands in that cold starlight, in the diamond water, and you imagine sprinkling it onto the earth."

Lips pursed, I *tried*, but putting myself *with* Kira wasn't natural. I couldn't explain how it felt to have this other half trotting around inside—either my mind, my imagination, my body... No clue how it worked. But climbing in there with her, with the well, felt...

"This is silly."

"It takes practice, honey," Rosa told me gently, "or we could all just do it from the start."

Sighing, I retreated inside as best I could without letting Kira out. I imagined the well, the sparkling water. Imagined my cupped hands scooping some of the freezing liquid out and dumping it on the ground.

Kira seemed just as unimpressed—and unconvinced—about all this as me, her feelings tainting my efforts. I withdrew from the mental picture, coming back to the black and the flashes of color behind my eyelids, to the cool

November breeze and the deathly quiet of our territory's barren southern tip.

Fingertips buzzing, I sifted through my vocabulary for the right words to tell Rosa this felt stupid—

Then she gasped.

Staggered back, her boots marking every frantic step. My eyes shot open.

Between my feet, a dandelion had taken root. Green stem. Bright yellow head. A splotch of color in an otherwise bleak landscape.

Kira snuffled about, her deep breath whooshing around my skull, our disbelief twined. Trembling, I crouched down and stroked the yellow petals.

The very *real* petals—

"No." I shook my head and stumbled away, hands numb, the buzzing between my ears now. Rosa looked so *proud*, her emerald gaze glossy, her mouth lifted in this maternal smile and her hands clasped at her chest, looking at me like she would eventually look at Aster when she, uh, learned to ride a bike or whatever. Pebbles shuddered across the unforgiving ground at our feet as my frustration surged. *Don't look at me like that.* "I-I don't want this."

"Lyssa—"

"*No,*" I barked, shaking my hands out, willing Idunn's touch to just *go* already. The grey day blurred suddenly, and I tugged my hoodie sleeve over my hand, then wiped under my eyes. "I just want to be a wolf shifter. All my life, I thought I was a, a, a *demon*, or a freak, or a mistake. And now I know what I am, and I just want to *enjoy* it." I turned my rage on Rosa, who, despite the gaping distance between us, flinched as if I'd shoved her again. "Is that so much to ask for? That I can finally just *be?*"

Blinking hurriedly, she opened and closed her mouth a few times before her gaze plummeted to the ground.

To the dandelion—now charred and gnarled, black and thin, all the life sucked out of it. An explosion of wispy white seeds littered the ground, but they looked wrong, somehow.

Twisted and warped and dead.

I had done that.

I had made something beautiful, then stomped all over it —without meaning to do either.

What if I did that to a person?

To Rosa?

To Aster—what if *my* power plowed clear through that shimmering bubble around the car seat and hurt her?

What if...

What if, in a fit of emotion, this destructive forest fire inside sizzled along by the invisible strings connecting me and mates—and I did *that* to one of them?

Ewan, Soren, Lucian—in pieces at my feet, their handsome faces contorted, their limbs sucked dry of life, blackened and crooked like the dandelion?

Silent, shoulders rounded and head bowed, Rosa padded over to her stirring pup. She perched on the boulder, lowered whatever she had cast to protect Aster, and then soothed her with kisses and coos and murmurs while I struggled to regain control.

Struggled to keep the dam, well, *dammed*.

"Honey, I know it's scary," the witch admitted sometime later, Aster asleep again and me kicking the ashes of my creation everywhere. "But it's happening. You can't take it back." Sighing, Rosa cast another bubble over her baby and then looked me dead in the eye, her courage back, her presence soothing. "Try to communicate with Idunn in your dreams. See if she can share something with you, and we'll work on controlling it. As long as it takes, I'm here for you, okay?"

Throat too raw with emotion to risk some choked

response, I just nodded, arms crossed, vision swimming again.

"Remember, Idunn is a *nature* goddess," she stressed like I'd somehow forgotten. "Fertility and growth and rejuvenation—that's what she's known for. She represents the cycles of life, and she gave her fellow gods immortality, not asking for anything in return. She's good. She's deeply tied to this world. Don't be scared of her."

I lifted my eyebrows. Don't be scared... of a nature goddess?

A *dead* nature goddess who dumped a bunch of her abilities onto me?

Never mind the absurdity of all that... Nature was terrifying. I might have adjusted to it before I turned ten, two long years already spent in the wilderness with wolves, but even then I knew to respect the natural world.

Or it would kill me.

Nature wasn't sunshine and rainbows, no matter what the Instagram posts said.

It was raw and brutal, domineering and dangerous.

Beautiful and wonderful and amazing to watch, to be a part of—but if you didn't have a healthy dose of genuine fear, Mother Nature would rip you apart.

But I kept all that to myself.

"Okay, okay, got it. I can do this. Let's just try again." Headache brewing, exhaustion settling in, I threw my head side to side and cracked my neck a few times, then rolled my shoulders back. "Ready when you are..."

14

LYSSA

I knew where I was before I opened my eyes.

As soon as alertness trickled in and sleep's deep hold loosened, I came to aware of the tepid air, warm but not too warm, the *perfect* summer day. The muted light behind my lids. The leaves whispering in a gentle breeze. The thick, lush grass at my back, tickling my bare arms.

The orchard.

I ended up here most nights, but for the first time all week, my breath didn't fog with that first deep, annoyed exhale. Slowly, I peeled my lids open to a hazy purply sky, streaks of red and pink and orange putting Idunn's world in a perpetual sunrise.

Or sunset?

No idea.

I had tried to outrun the horizon time and time again, but the goddess seemed content amongst the apple trees.

Clearing my throat, I lifted my head, neck sore like I'd slept at a weird angle, then pushed onto my elbows. Love plumed in my chest, spreading to the heat in my cheeks and the warmth in my toes. There, in a tense *down* just by my feet, was my girl. Kira perked up when our eyes met, hers the same startling bright blue as always, mine the curveball in our life. I grinned and patted my belly.

"Hi, beautiful."

She pounced with a puppyish yip, plowing into me and pinning me to the ground, tail whipping around, her giddiness infectious. Before the darkness followed me here, this was how we greeted each other: playful and happy, two old friends reuniting, rolling around in the grass. Wrestling. Chasing. Once, we howled together—just because.

Today—tonight, this morning, who knew in a place where time stood still—we kept our tussles short. Eventually, I sat cross-legged by her side, Kira sprawled in the grass and sniffing the long blades. Rubbing her belly, I scanned the orchard, the rows upon rows upon rows of lush, full apple trees flourishing under a goddess's care. My sigh forced Kira upright, and after another quick glance, we stood together and set off through the trees.

I didn't need to tell her what we were doing, where we were going.

We ambled along in search of Idunn, Rosa's request still ringing in my ears. Find her. Talk to her. Get some *actual* answers for once.

Kira sniffed her out a few rows over. Draped in white silk, sapphires on her shoulder pads and her feet bare, the goddess had a wicker basket by her side and an apple in each hand. She faced us as soon as the wind shifted, toying with her golden waves, her eyes—my eyes—sweeping over both of us.

"Hello, little wolves." She gently deposited her plucked apples in the basket, then drifted toward Kira as the huge wolf padded over to greet her, head drooped, tail low and wagging. Submissive, she acknowledged the goddess's place in our hierarchy with eager whines and licks, and with a placid smile, Idunn stroked her ears, her neck, then cradled her muzzle, murmuring soft words in a language I didn't understand.

The tone told me the words were kind, at the very least.

I hung back, refusing to crawl on my belly for this woman, this girl who looked a few years younger than me but had eternity in her eyes. Arms crossed, I scrutinized the pair's interactions from a distance, relaxing only when Idunn plucked a ripe green apple from one of the low-hanging boughs and offered it to Kira. My wolf licked her jowls and snatched it up. Her roughness, the lack of finesse, only made Idunn giggle, and she tipped her head to the side, radiating calm as we both watched Kira trot in a circle, then hunker down to gnaw at the gift.

Another *gift* from Idunn.

I cleared my throat, pleased to find Kira's eyes still blue when they flicked my way, the wolf gracelessly munching on her prize.

"Seems like the shadows are gone."

Back to picking, cleaning, and lobbing apples into her basket, Idunn nodded. "Yes. Your mates protected the land from darkness."

"Did you know they were vampires?" My eyes narrowed when she fumbled, her toss a little off this time. The apple bounced off the basket's rim and rolled in Kira's direction. Even though she wasn't finished with the first, she lunged and grabbed this second, then did her usual circling before settling in the grass again. Dressed in the flannel nightshirt I wore to bed, enjoying the soft cotton enough to forgo my usual nakedness, I fiddled with the open sleeve cuffs, picking at the button. "Were they hunting me?"

Her calm mask fell away, replaced with a frown deep enough to cause a wrinkle in her otherwise flawless skin.

Shaking her head, Idunn went back to the apples, back to picking and cleaning and tossing.

"More than vampires," she said—*almost* under her breath, like she was talking to herself, "to touch us here."

Great. I pursed my lips. Someday, it would be *awesome* if she could just answer a question without being so mysterious and otherworldly. After everything, she owed me that much.

But then again, maybe she just wasn't used to talking to people anymore.

Idunn was here alone as far as I could tell, and when *I* spent ages in the forest, far from civilization, months and months walking on four paws instead of stupid human feet... Heck, *my* conversation skills got a little rusty too.

Sighing, I drifted over to Kira, tugging at her ear in passing, and sat between her and the wicker basket. When Idunn turned to toss her next two apples in, I held out my hands. The goddess hesitated, then grinned and passed them over, each one cool and big and smooth to the touch, then went back to picking while I set them with the rest. Wordlessly, we made a little assembly line, with me sneaking Kira a fresh apple as soon as she demolished the one clutched between her paws, core and all.

Let's try this again.

"Did you give me your power when I drank from the river?"

Idunn chuckled, pacing around the tree and squinting into the canopy. "I was wondering when you would finally ask."

"Well?" I rolled an apple between my hands, keeping it in my lap, waiting, staring. Idunn's rosebud mouth quirked, and she stood on her tiptoes to rip an apple from the depths.

"I did."

"All of it?"

"All that I shed, yes." She handed the enormous apple to

me, one that was nothing to her but required both of my hands just to hold. "I took the rest here with me."

Struggling, I dropped the massive green orb and rolled it over to sit beside the basket, worried it would crush its smaller siblings inside. "Why?"

"To keep it safe," the goddess said absently, still scanning the branches.

"From who?"

For the first time since we met in my dreams, Idunn tripped. Her foot snagged on a grasping root, and she crashed into the solid trunk, cheeks pink and hair temporarily disheveled.

Huh.

The winds changed, whipping east suddenly, violent and angry enough that I had to duck and shield my eyes from the debris. The sky darkened. The trees bent. Apples tore free and bounced across the grass.

And then it stopped. Brushing the bits of dust and twigs from my hair, I caught Idunn smoothing her dress, righting her sapphire-studded shoulder pads, and then twisting her hair over one shoulder.

Okay. Not a safe topic, just like me and the wolves. My mates had avoided it for ages, but I knew they'd poke and prod eventually.

I dreaded it.

She probably dreaded whatever made *that* happen.

"I-I don't want your power," I told her, opting to take an adjacent path. Her golden gaze snapped to mine, and I gulped, suddenly feeling very small in her divine presence. "I just want to be a wolf shifter... and be *normal*. I want to mate, make pups, and live in Redwood Grove with Lucian, Soren, and Ewan—"

"That's why you have it, little wolf." Idunn crouched, hastily gathering the fallen apples and tossing them at me, one right after the other, so fast I barely had time to catch them all. Kira helped, shoving into the line of fire and snapping up any strays. When the goddess was finished, the ground cleared and the orchard at peace again, she planted her elbows on her knees and smiled at me. "You have it because you *don't* want it."

"Well, that's..." My mouth went dry, and I focused on getting the last of the apples into the basket. "That's mean of you."

Idunn's laughter tinkled through the orchard like a symphony of Christmas bells.

"No one ever said the gods were *kind*."

Good to know. In no mood to be part of our assembly line anymore, I shuffled back until I hit Kira, then slumped into her massive side like I was cozying into the corner of our giant cinema room couch. The wolf paused her apple feast to look back at me, muzzle stained with sweet juices. She licked at my nose, my forehead, then went back to eating, obviously sensing that I was, in theory, fine. I didn't need to be coddled or babied.

I was just... frustrated.

"Why me?" I muttered, ripping out bits of grass and rolling them into little balls. "How did you... choose me?"

"I knew from the moment you were conceived," Idunn said without missing a beat. My brows shot up.

"Uh, what?"

"The apples started to grow again." She brought one of her harvest to her cheek, cradling it tenderly. "I couldn't make them grow. I designed this world for *me*, for my afterlife, but it wouldn't bear fruit. A barren orchard is so... sad." She wiped the apple on her dress, then scooted back to the foot of the tree and took a huge, crunching bite. The goddess chewed thoughtfully for a moment, then tossed the apple to me. "Then you... They started to grow. I found you in the sky. Or, well…" She licked her lips when I risked a small bite, tastebuds assaulted with the tart sour-sweet tide of a perfect green apple. "I saw your mother, but it was the child in her womb destined to—"

"Did you know my parents?" I blurted, gut dropping. I pawned our shared apple onto Kira, then lurched forward onto my hands and knees. Reed and Nikki didn't even know my parents. I'd pressed them again and again; I called them Mom and Dad for a long time, knowing full well they had only fostered me.

Then adopted me.

Then abandoned me.

No more Mom and Dad for *them*.

Idunn drew her knees up to her chest and planted her sharp chin in the dip. "I know who they are, yes."

"Why did they leave me?"

She looked deep in my eyes, deep enough that my fingers buzzed a warning—*danger, danger!*—and Kira sat upright behind me. The gold in my reflection always gave me pause. It startled strangers and made males *and* females do a double take.

But *her* gold?

It ran so much deeper than mine.

It pulsed with power, streaked with time and wisdom and sunlight. I had her eyes, yes, but mine were a pale imitation, honestly, just a cheap knockoff of the real thing.

"Are you sure you want to know?" Idunn whispered, the breeze dying, the leaves falling silent. Kira sank down at my side with a long, frustrated whine. *Yes.* We had wanted to know from the start. They were Kira's parents too, after all.

I managed to nod, on the verge of being swallowed alive by her unblinking stare.

Idunn's gold brows twitched up. "Are you sure you want *everything*?"

I nodded harder, and then, finally trusting my voice again, I cuddled into Kira's side and choked out, *"Everything..."*

§

I jolted awake in my own bed with a gasp, alone and indoors. No Kira to greet me. No Idunn. No orchard. No purple-pink dawn. Chasing my breath, I rolled onto my side and blinked the world back into focus, staring through the frosty glass balcony doors and adjusting to another grey November day. Yesterday, Rosa and I had spent hours along the southern border of my territory, trying again and again to harness all that Idunn had given me.

When I came home in the afternoon, my mates were there too. Not at work. Not... somewhere else. *Here.* They told me they ran those horrible vampires into Hawthorne territory but would be on constant patrol for the next week, in alternating shifts, to make sure they didn't come back.

Then I'd crashed. Hard. If the smell of fresh bread and all this soft morning light suggested anything, it was that I had slept a good fifteen hours, maybe more. Lucian's scent tickled my nostrils with my next deep breath, rousing a sleepy Kira as well, and I rolled away from the windows, searching for him.

Nope.

Gone.

But he had been here. At some point, my quietest, most reclusive mate had scented up my linens—a theory confirmed when I crawled down the side of my bed, exploring it with my nose, breathing him in with a moan, then a soft, insistent whine.

Why didn't he stay?

Why didn't *any* of them just climb into bed with me?

Ignoring the pang of want, I settled back against the headboard with a huff, surrounded by pillows and clean white sheets...

Thoughts of my history—the real one—on the brain.

Now I knew.

If Idunn had told the truth in my dreams, then my parents...

Well, it wasn't what I had always imagined.

Bloodier.

More violent.

A betrayal to shifter-kind, apparently.

Nikki and Reed would have had no clue. Even if they heard the story—all the gory details—they wouldn't understand. They wouldn't *get* that my mom and dad—both of them, no matter how the story was told—were traitors.

Groaning, I scrubbed at my cheeks, then picked the crusty sleep out from the corner of my eyes.

A lot to digest.

A lot to process.

But in the end, their tragic story made me that much more grateful for *my* mates. Yeah, we weren't a perfect pack —but I knew in my heart none of those alphas would ever do *that*.

I drew my knees up, then winced, bladder telling me, no, that wasn't the ideal position right now. Just as I flung myself over, about to head for the bathroom and ruminate on the toilet over my questionable family history, I noticed it.

Them.

Two gifts on my nightstand.

The first was a box with a sleek rose-gold phone on the cover. It smelled like Ewan when I picked it up, like rosewood bark, sweet and heady and *earthy*. No plastic wrap: he had been in there already, it seemed, and when I carefully lifted the cardboard lid, I found the exact phone inside, so thin and delicate and pink that I was too scared to lift it up and turn it on.

All this time, I'd studied my mates on *their* phones. Soren was careless with his, always twirling it, tossing it between his hands, dropping it and hoping the screen hadn't shattered. Ewan handled his like it was an extension of himself, just another limb, effortless, his fingers so beautifully graceful that just watching him text was another reminder that he could easily pass as an angel.

Then Lucian...

He had a flip phone.

He looked annoyed anytime he had to dig it out.

He told me it was indestructible once, then chucked it against the wall and chuckled when it didn't even dent.

Mine looked and felt like it was made of glass.

Someone else needed to program it for me—teach me how to use it. Before my mates found me, I would have returned it, insisting that I didn't *deserve* something so fancy and delicate.

Now, I knew I just needed to be shown the way. One explanation. One tutorial. I'd pick the rest up on my own.

However, the phone wasn't the only gift waiting for me. No, next to the lamp on the white-wood bedside table was a potted plant.

Not regional. Definitely not local. Setting the phone box aside, I picked up the purple ceramic pot in both hands, then sniffed at the bulbous green leaves.

Succulent.

I'd seen them on Instagram a lot. Soren had made me an account I could look at on the laptop—not that I'd posted anything—and agreed it, like the TV shows I devoured, would make for good research into the modern human world.

It did.

Because I knew this was a succulent.

What kind? No idea, but the fat leaves were cute and smelled pretty safe.

Taped to the bottom—a note.

Don't be afraid.

I didn't need to sniff the yellowing paper to know that was Rosa's handwriting, but I did so anyway, relishing the honey and amber, eyes closed, heart slowing, all thoughts of my past life fading. Kira yipped, missing the witch already, and I tenderly tucked the note under my pillow—then eyed the succulent with a frown.

The gesture was sweet. She must have snuck this in while I was catching up on sleep, my mind static by the time we got back from training and my energy *deep* in the negatives. *Don't be afraid*. Of nature? Of myself? Of the power tingling in my fingertips?

All of it, probably.

Lips pursed, I cradled the purple pot in one hand, then held the other over it, closed my eyes, and went back to the well. This time, Kira had her paws planted on the stone rim, peering into the sparkling water with her head cocked like it was speaking to her. I imagined myself there beside her, just like in the orchard. Pictured scooping the water out and splashing it around. Clenched my eyes tight to block out the real-life hum in my fingertips and palms.

Little spikes poked my skin.

My eyes snapped open—the succulent had doubled in size.

Grown aggressive spikes and two red flowers.

Shoot.

Trembling, I set it back on my nightstand, then stumbled out of bed, a little dizzy, Kira's whimpers making it even harder to refocus. Needing the comfort of a familiar routine, I staggered into the bathroom to pee, wash my face, and rinse the stinky sleep breath away. When I came back, the plant was there, minding its own business, huge and spiky and dangerous—pretty, I guess, in its own way with those flowers.

Don't be afraid.

Excuse you, witch friend.

I *would* be afraid of the natural world because fear meant respect. That was the only way to survive. I wasn't *better* than nature. I couldn't dominate it. I respected it.

Just like I ought to respect Idunn's power.

Because it wasn't sunshine and daisies and twittering songbirds on a spring morning...

This was dangerous, powerful, deadly stuff.

I... could hurt someone with it if I wasn't careful.

Nice sentiment, that note, but, yeesh, maybe a little tone deaf.

After straightening out my flannel nightdress, fixing the collar and sleeves, I grabbed the phone box—something that, while new and flimsy, *wasn't* scary—and headed down to the kitchen, guided by the sounds of cupboards closing and dishware clinking, hoping that whoever was home could teach me how to use this thing without breaking it.

And distract me—*please, just distract me*—from the horrors of my family legacy ringing truer and truer with every shaky step.

15

SOREN

Okay, so…

Eggs, toast, hash browns, pancakes, diced fruit, cereal on the table. Check, check, check, check, *check*.

The only thing missing…

My inner wolf did his derpy little happy dance when I ducked into the fridge and pulled out two packets of the good stuff. Thick cut. Extra fatty. One kilo per packet —*bacon*. In less than a minute, the whole house would smell of it, and if *that* didn't lure her out of bed, nothing would.

As soon as I straightened and slammed the door shut, however, there she was in her adorable red-and-white flannel, sleepy and rumpled, hair like a knotted bronze halo around her head. Lyssa's scent flooded the kitchen, overtaking everything I had prepped so far, and my inner wolf paused, smitten, howling for her like she *and* her wolf could hear, desperate to run despite spending hours in the forest yesterday doing exactly that.

November 2 was supposed to be a pack breakfast. Sure, I hadn't explicitly told the other alpha dicks that, but from the sheer volume of food, I was ready to feed us for the whole day in one meal. Lucian, however, was still on his patrol shift, and Ewan popped in here while I was halfway through the eggs and about to start on the pancakes. Stiff, stern, dressed to the nines in one of his standard pretentious suits, he grabbed some sad protein smoothie from the fridge and bounced, determined to get a few hours of work in before his patrol shift started.

And, I mean, I guess that was fair.

Work was his life—but somehow we had collectively decided that for the next week, patrolling our borders took priority. Yeah, we chased those vampires all over the place on Halloween. All night, right up until sunrise, we hunted them through the mountains, into the western forest, around the lake. At one point, the fanged assholes even tried to hide in a locked Acker cabin; I nearly ripped the thing apart to find them, and Lucian noticed their shadowy silhouettes blitzing into the trees at the last second, three alpha wolves right on their heels.

By the time the sun poked above the horizon, muted behind the thick overcast, we had *finally* pushed them into Hawthorne territory. Let those dicks deal with them.

If those dicks hadn't sent them.

I mean, maybe the leeches went for Lyssa because she smelled good—because she did—but the risk of the Hawthorne alpha stealing her before she had her first pup remained. It wouldn't be the first time a rival alpha stole a breeding female from another pack. An *alpha* she-wolf? A way bigger score, because then he could forcibly build a strong, powerful alpha bloodline from scratch even if he hadn't found *his* fated female yet.

So, maybe the vamps had just happened upon her at the club.

More likely though: someone had hired them to take her.

And if we ever caught the bastards, we'd tear them limb

from limb. Interrogate them along the way. Stuff them full of wooden stakes until we got a name. Introduce them to their first and last sunrise.

Then we'd kill the guy who sent them, on and on until we could guarantee Lyssa's safety.

For now, since we had no dead flesh to stab, we three settled on constant patrols.

Lucian had demanded the lion's share, all amped and anxious and teetering on the brink of wolf madness. Ewan and I managed to talk him down to sharing the responsibility, our patrols split into even shifts, one right after the other, always allowing for someone to be home with our girl.

So, hell *yeah* I took the whole week off. No work. No lake stuff. No check-ins with the franchise owners of the three Farrow's Pubs in the area. No days spent locked in my office surrounded by paperwork.

It wasn't a one-man show in my professional sphere. We had humans heavily involved in managing Acker properties and investments; it was time for them to prove their worth in my absence.

Some of us, meanwhile, struggled to get their priorities in order.

Because Ewan chose to squish in as much work as he could this morning—and missed *this*, our groggy, gorgeous mate sauntering into the kitchen in flannel that cut off around her upper thighs, sleeves hanging loose and open and a little too long, a box tucked under her arm. All that sleep had done her good: gone were the dark shadows around her eyes, the hollowness in her cheeks, the overall pale and sweaty glow.

She looked refreshed, smiling shyly as she approached, my gaze plummeting to those strong, shapely legs.

Ugh. *Perfection.*

"Morning, babe." I kept my eyes on her as I portioned out bacon strips. Eight a piece should do, right? Noticing her nostrils flare, the wolf in her *definitely* tempted by raw meat, I hoisted a handful of fatty pork with a grin. "Bacon?"

"Obviously."

Man, I loved when she *purred* over good food. A she-wolf after my own heart. She headed toward me, then veered away for the island full of food instead—and that wouldn't do. I lunged after her, memories of her helpless cries in that private room making my cock twitch with interest, then gave her neck a sharp, biting kiss that made her squeal and blush and break out in goosebumps. Lyssa scampered away, darting around the island and rounding on me like she wanted to be hunted.

And if my belly wasn't roaring just as loud as hers, I might have.

No one had christened this room yet, right?

However, before I could take one prowling step after her, Lyssa lifted the box and frowned.

"Uh, so, this…?"

"Ewan grabbed it yesterday afternoon," I told her, tossing one portion of bacon onto the cutting board next to the stove, then counting out the next. Okay, *she* could have eight, but for a male—twelve? "Apparently Rosa reamed him out for not getting one yet. What d'you think? Like it?"

Lyssa already had a laptop; it only made sense that she had a phone too. Kind of shitty that it hadn't already occurred to any of us, but I was so close to her most days that it had never crossed my mind. Even when I worked, I just needed to walk the shoreline to check on her.

And Lucian shunned most tech, so of course that weirdo had said nothing.

Seriously though. A pack song, as great as ours was, could only take the modern-day wolf shifter so far.

"Uhm, I like the color." Lyssa set the box on the marble countertop with a huff. "But I don't know how to use it."

"Hold on—lemme see."

Fourteen slices of raw bacon in hand, I sauntered over, sidling right up behind her, then sniped another kiss. This one crash-landed on her temple, which made my mate giggle, and was less teeth, more nibbling peck. Man, she fit so *perfectly*, her back to my chest, the position even better when she scooted backward and nestled under my chin. For a few seconds, I forgot why I'd come over here, safe in a cloud of our mingling scents, everything else background noise so long as she touched me.

I'd wanted to crawl into her bed last night.

Hold her while she slept.

Stand on guard, protecting our mate from the assholes who go bump in the night.

We all did.

For weeks now, one of us would loiter in front of the master suite's door, hesitating, racked with uncertainty, wanting to go in and cuddle with her but unsure if that was what *she* wanted—if that would be okay with the rest of her mates. After marking your fated, sleeping next to them had to be the highest form of intimacy.

But Lyssa had been through the wringer since Gull River. After Halloween, she clearly needed sleep; no one had the heart to wake her yesterday after she crashed in the late afternoon and just slept and slept and slept. *Again*, we had agreed to give her space to process everything—only this time, she set the tone. If she came looking for company, at least one of us had to physically be there for her, a mate always on call for snuggles and comfort and play-fighting in wolf form. We swore it.

And Ewan went to work this morning.

Dick.

As if sensing my distraction, my inner wolf on a Lyssa high and just *begging* me to shove my nose in her hair, my mate tapped the top of the box. Right. Phone.

I squinted at the picture and the name and all the listed features.

Ugh.

Stupid fancy complicated garbage.

Like, if you pressed the screen too hard—common for a shifter—you'd break it.

I should have been in charge of the phone-buying.

"Of course he got you a phone that can launch a freakin' rocket into space," I muttered, glowering at the box like it was *its* fault and not Ewan's. Lyssa tipped her head back, gawking at me with those wide, golden eyes, and I shook my head. Her grasp on common sayings and social norms had improved a *lot* since we found her, but some shit still flew right over her head. "No, sorry, not literally... It's just stupidly complicated."

I mean, I didn't recognize the model number—was it even on the market yet?

Did Ewan have pull in the tech world too?

This guy.

This fucking guy.

"Here." I grabbed Lyssa's wrist, flipped her arm over, and dumped the stack of raw bacon in her palm. "You do bacon. I'll try to set this up."

"But I can't cook," she protested as I eased us around and bumped her toward the stove with my hip.

"Baby, just don't let the meat get black." From the near-invisible waves rising off the pan, it was definitely hot enough to do most of the work for her. I gave her another little push, then patted the perky globes of her bare ass under the flannel, the first light smack making her squeak and skitter forward—but not fast enough. I still managed to cop a feel with my clean hand, then, in an act of restraint that deserved *all* the rewards, headed for the sink to wash up *instead* of prowling after her, ripping that nightdress up, and bending her over the counter.

Instead, I turned on the tap a little too hard, the metal faucet a breath away from flying clean off, my inner wolf still reveling in the taut roundness of her ass cheek. "Just, uh, flip and flip and flip until it's crispy like you like. You'll need to do two or three rounds—just see how many can actually fit in the pan without overcrowding it."

After drying my hands on my sweatpants, I swiped the box off the island, then dipped around it and headed for the dining table. Slouched in my usual seat, I lifted the lid like I was unmasking some ancient, fragile, priceless artifact, the phone inside so damn sleek and thin and clean…

Yeah, I wasn't the right wolf to do this.

I'd broken so many phones over the years, always by accident, usually because my hands liked to keep busy and tossing a phone around was a good way to do that.

This seemed like the screen would fracture if you looked at it wrong.

Oh boy.

"So," I started, needing to put at least a bit of my attention elsewhere or I would *way* overthink this thing, "how are you feeling?"

"Fine."

Phone out and on the table in one piece, I glanced up. Yeah, she said that a little too fast. My inner wolf whined, neither of us buying it. Since Gull River, her emotions had been even more complicated to decipher than this stupid phone. Despite our bond theoretically strengthening every time we mated, I struggled to read the nuances. Sometimes her feelings hit like a hurricane, others a whisper. After mating and marking, suddenly we shared a common dialect, the connection visceral. Invisible, yeah, but so freakin' beautiful and present.

Now it was… complicated.

And getting Ewan and Lucian to admit that they felt the same as me last night had been like pulling teeth.

But they finally did it.

Gull River had changed our girl, and we still weren't sure if it was for the better. All our lives we *starved* for a fated mate connection, and we'd had it so *fleetingly*. It wasn't easy. It never had been—and that created this steep pit in our collective bond, one we needed to fill soon or it would all cave in.

Maybe?

This was uncharted territory for all of us—for three stubborn alphas who each wanted to act like *he* had the strongest bond with the mate we shared.

For the few words he *did* manage to get out, Lucian insisted we wait. Let the water settle. Let nature and Lady Fate find balance again.

Sure.

Alpha males were *awesome* at being patient.

"How are you doing?"

I frowned at Lyssa's back, blinking out of the downward spiral to the hiss of each bacon strip she carefully added to the pan. "Huh?"

Eloquent as always. Seriously, she had to think I was the dumbest of her mates.

She peeked over her shoulder with an arched eyebrow. "You less grumpy now?"

Uh. When had *I* been the grumpy jagweed of this pack? Ewan claimed that title on the daily.

"Er, what?"

Grinning, Lyssa poked at the sizzling strips with a wooden spatula, then sauntered to the island and leaned over the marble. Even though I couldn't see it, it was way too easy to imagine the flannel hiked up, revealing strong, womanly thighs that I suddenly wanted wrapped around my face—

"You've been really grumpy the last little while," Lyssa said as she pointed the greasy-tipped spatula at me. "Like, kind of tantrum-y when we didn't do your fall activities."

What?

Oh. *Oh*.

Oops.

Thought I had kept my shit together a little better than that.

I mean, with everything going on in her world the last couple of weeks, I thought my grump over literally no one listening to me or taking my suggestions for fall fun seriously had slid by unnoticed.

Damn it.

"I... I just wanted to share..." Okay, how to phrase this without sounding like a total pup. "My parents—"

"Soren, we aren't our parents," Lyssa insisted, shockingly firm for a she-wolf who had yet to share a single iota of intel about her past. I sat up straighter as her phone powered onto the home screen, and Lyssa busied herself with the spatula, smearing the grease around its rectangular head. "We have to make our own traditions."

"I know that," I said slowly, hesitant to say anything at all if it cut her off. Was she about to share her past with me? As Lyssa wiped her greasy fingers on her sleeve, I tapped around the phone's main screens absently, getting a half-hearted feel for what came preprogrammed. Right. Not *that* complicated: all looks, no depth. When the silence dragged on, both of us serenaded by the sizzle and crackle of cooking bacon, I cleared my throat and focused on connecting this thing to the internet. "Look, my parents just have a great relationship, and I'm trying to—"

"Copy it?"

I looked up sharply, a little wounded that even my fated mate couldn't see the benefits of carrying forward a tradition of love, mutual respect, and family time. "No. Reproduce it, maybe... Is it so wrong to want to be happy like they are?"

Ewan's pack had a reputation all the way out here, the Quinns known across shifter circles for their heavy hand in the Canadian supernatural *and* human drug trade. He *hated* them; that much was clear anytime the conversation even tiptoed in their direction. Parents, siblings, cousins, whatever —he wanted nothing to do with them. Lucian was a closed book in terms of his past, refusing to even give us his pack name. Clearly, they had both seen and experienced some shit.

Lyssa...

No clue.

But it obviously wasn't a *happy* childhood, right? I mean, someone had dumped her in the woods.

Yet the Acker pack had a history of togetherness and wholesome family moments—cheesy as it sounded—and no one would let me *lead* in an area where I clearly had *some* superiority.

"No..." Lyssa cocked her head, staring through me, probably out to the two-story windows by the soaring stone fireplace. "But we should make our own happiness, right?"

"Yeah, well, this pack kind of sucks at that. It's like those guys *want* to be miserable."

"Right, and some of us get really testy when things don't go our way." She grinned impishly when I glared at her from the dining table. A teasing tongue poke followed, and my mate straightened to stretch out her shoulders. "I mean, it's like *some* of us have never been told *no* in our whole life..."

Ugh.

She had a point.

I'd always gotten away with lots of crap my sisters didn't. I had ignored it until adulthood when hindsight became just a little clearer.

"Look, babe, I get it." I tapped around the phone's app store, selecting the ones Lyssa seemed to enjoy perusing on her computer. No Facebook—she deserved better than that cesspit. "I was being a huge puppy about the pumpkin patch stuff and the horror movies and whatever." As the first of my choices started to download, I leaned back in the chair and folded my arms, locking onto her golden gaze with a huff.

Shit, that gold—so intense. So fiery. So *different* from the grey-blue I had first fallen for.

But...

She could pull it off. Lyssa's olive complexion complemented the warmth, and her hair—a bright caramel brown in the sun, more bronzy and grounded indoors— really suited the change.

Hard to maintain eye contact with though.

Even her wolf had lost the neon, gold inside and out now. My inner wolf couldn't *stop* staring into them whenever he had the chance, and once again, my human side struggled more than the beast.

Unnervingly intense as they were, I needed eye contact for this.

She needed to *feel* my issue.

"But, uh, you need to have my back sometimes too." I scratched at the fresh, rough stubble on my cheek, then up to the shaved side of my head, finding the prickle of that short, coarse hair soothing as I stroked back and forth. "Ewan and Lucian are just two different kinds of hermits. They don't want to do stuff—*we* are the social ones. I promise, anything I suggest is actually really fun."

While still grinning, Lyssa hurled my huff right back at me. "I'm sorry... Horror movies are *fun*?"

"Okay, maybe not." Not to everyone's taste, anyway, especially a she-wolf whose only film experience seemed to be cartoons, romance movies, and reality TV. "I just—" I shot up in a panic. "Shit—flip the bacon."

Lyssa whipped around and scrambled back to the stove, hastily turning strips that had suddenly started to smell a little too toasty for my taste.

"Look, I'm not saying you have to agree with every little thing I suggest," I told her, back to installing all the necessary crap on this much too delicate phone. "You obviously have your own opinion—"

"Sweet of you to notice."

"*But*," I stressed, adding a bit of growl for that snarky tone, "those two will always and forever vote no if it means they have to, you know, miss work or take a night off from patrol or, I dunno, just do something that isn't routine. It really pisses me off. I'm always outvoted because they refuse to try anything new."

"Okay..." She flipped the last bacon strip with some difficulty, then padded back to the island and slumped over it. "Okay, how's this? If *they* don't want to do something, you and me will." Lyssa shrugged, then latched onto a particularly aggressive knot in her mane and ripped into it. "I mean, I think we should all do more pack things together, but maybe Ewan and Lucian just need... time to warm up to that."

My inner wolf and I *both* rolled our eyes, but only my scoff punctuated the bacon-scented air. Eyes sparkling mischievously, Lyssa stopped her hair fussing.

"Is this... another tantrum?" She waggled her finger at me. "Soren, Soren, Soren—"

"It's a tantrum on *your* behalf," I argued lightly, leaning to the side and digging my phone out of my pocket. I then did a deep dive into the contacts page, scrolling through to copy the numbers that mattered for Lyssa so she didn't have to ask everyone separately. "*You* have had to adapt the most out of all of us. You always give in to *our* norms. You're jumping into our lives—" I shot her a cheeky grin. "—and quite flawlessly, I might add. I just think those two assholes..." *Don't pick on her mates in front of her.* "Those *two*... They can step outside of their comfort zones for, like, an afternoon. It's really not that much to ask."

Warmth fluttered in my chest, leaking from her to me in pitter-pattering raindrops for a few seconds—then a whole flood when our eyes met and a smile exploded across her gorgeous features.

"Agreed," she said thickly, and I *swore* her eyes glistened with the light of the pretentious modern chandelier Ewan had insisted be hung over the island. Lyssa then sniffed and went back to the bacon, poking at a few strips with a hand on her hip, for once looking very much at ease in the kitchen. "I'm sorry, Soren—I'll be more open to your suggestions." She fluttered her lashes at me over her shoulder. "Whatcha got for November?"

"Nothing." Stupid boring middle month between fall awesomeness and winter shenanigans. "But December? Hang on to your hat, baby. December is gonna be wild."

Her cheeks flushed a dull pink, the heat in my chest ramping up a notch, and my mate resumed her bacon-poking with a nod. "Can't wait."

As she finished this first round of bacon, then her portion of eight immediately after, I got her phone sorted. Deleted space-wasting apps. Added protective programs to fend off malware and hackers. Gave her all the apps she enjoyed, plus a few my sisters obsessed over. Put our phone numbers, the Perrys, and my family into her contacts list.

"Okay," I said, pushing my chair back and patting my knee when Lyssa dumped a mountain of crispy bacon onto a plate. "Come here, mate, and let me give you a tour."

She practically skipped over and dropped onto my lap like a lead anchor, purposefully throwing herself into it so I grunted. Grinning, smitten with no hopes of ever going back, I wrestled my wriggling, giggling little fated mate up my lap, then tucked my chin into the crook of her shoulder. Once she quieted, I gave her a rundown of her phone, going so far as to turn it off completely and reboot just so she could learn from the start.

Unsurprisingly, she picked up fast. Modern tech was more intuitive than Lucian gave it credit for, and Lyssa was soon tapping, sliding, minimizing, and using dual windows to navigate the digital world.

All while our bellies grumbled and my inner wolf—hers too, probably—drooled over the feast just *sitting* over there on the island, untouched but growing cooler by the second.

"Okay, tech genius." I patted her thighs. "Up. Let's eat."

Lyssa hopped off and tiptoed away, and just as I stood, my phone vibrated across the table. Scowling, I went for it, fully expecting some bullshit comment in the alpha group thread —only to find a message alert from my girl.

Hi.

Nothing more, nothing less—fucking *adorable*.

I looked up and found her beaming on the other side of the island. Lips pursed, I sent a quick reply.

Hello, beautiful.

Her phone dinged. Her eyes lit up. Her smile got wider, and she hugged the fragile rectangle to her chest.

"Now you can *always* reach us... Even Ewan," I mused, more to myself than her—because, *duh*, of course this instant communication made her happy. All she had wanted from the get-go was pack togetherness.

Shit. Should have done this way sooner.

Before I could apologize, however, Lyssa had already abandoned her phone for the bacon, grabbing a handful and shoving it in her mouth, and I raced over to make sure that I actually got a piece of this big, beautiful breakfast I'd made.

One that we demolished together in about five minutes flat, the platters never making it to the dining table.

A meal we then digested down in the cinema room to one of the mildest horror films in my Halloween arsenal at Lyssa's request.

So big, so excessive, so much *food* for just two wolves that we ended up falling asleep before the movie finished the first act, snoozing the day away in each other's arms.

Her emotions clear and strong and happy.

And my heart very much in love.

16

LYSSA

Bare branches rattled in the breeze, the canopy shed and winter on its way. Beneath a cloudy afternoon sky, cool and dry, I trotted across leaf-strewn ground, over valleys and peaks, up and down and around steep drop-offs into the earth. The western wood was quiet today, its critters nesting, preparing for the long, cold months ahead. Pines soared here, more abundant than around Soren's lake, the undergrowth almost too dense to get through in some areas, even as Kira.

Wild. Untamed. Raw wilderness, with bear tracks leading north and remnants of fox dens everywhere. This place felt as ancient as Idunn.

Definitely Lucian's old territory.

I seldom trekked further west than the village. After all, there was more to *do* there—Ewan in particular, but Rosa and Aster were huge reasons for me to stop at Redwood Grove proper and stay awhile. In fact, this was my first solo trip so deep into the western woods, and I made it my mission to *claim* it, brushing on pine boughs and bare trunks alike. I sniffed and sniffed and sniffed, breathing *Lucian* with every breath.

Tracking his old footpaths.

Following where he would have walked before me, stalking along barely visible grooves in the forest floor as Kira, until eventually happening upon the log cabin my other mates had referenced in the past.

And not always nicely either.

Soren and Ewan weren't kind about Lucian's love of quiet solitude. He hid away from the rest of the world for a reason —his scars told that story, I was sure of it—and that spoke to me. My other mates had family. They had a pack. They had a history.

Lucian and I didn't.

And as I crept closer to the cabin, paws soundless, not a twig snapped or leaf crunched, I felt closer to him than I ever had before.

Good thing, too, because two weeks after Halloween and I was starting to feel like we were losing him.

Like... *I* was losing him.

That night had changed him. Lucian had always struck me as a protector, the wolf who hung back and watched from the sidelines. Not showy. Not overly involved in pack activities. But if something went wrong? *Run*, because he'd be there in a second, calm, cool, collected, and about to unleash the killing blow.

Of all my mates, he was the most anxious about territory borders. Always on high alert, always scoping out exits, always mapping the perimeter—even if we were just sitting on the deck of Soren's lakefront pub near the village, enjoying a plate of nachos and a few beers. He didn't *do* fun outings, just like Soren had said.

In the last fourteen days, I'd spent ten with Rosa, down south and practicing my power.

Trying to control it.

Failing to control it, more like.

But my mates had worked out a system, a patrol schedule that Soren stuck to the fridge with magnets so we always knew where each other was and what we were all supposed to be doing. Lucian and Ewan refused to let me tag along with them, but Soren had started bringing me out for a stealthy hike around the Redwood Grove perimeter—if I wasn't passed out by the time his shift started, recovering from Rosa's draining, and still very much secret, lessons.

No vampires had crossed back into our home. Hawthorne wolves howled every night to the east, but none of us had scented so much as a paw over the territory line. Ewan was almost back to his regular work routine, opting for predawn patrol shifts and then heading to the office straight after, and Soren in wolf form was kind of silly on the trail, not taking it as seriously as he probably should.

But Lucian?

Always on guard, even when he *wasn't* on patrol. Always tense and quiet and alert. Thinking. Ruminating. Present but not.

I missed him. I missed his softness, his subdued smiles. I missed feeling small and safe in his big, burly arms. I missed rubbing my face in his beard while he sighed and let me do it. Kind of hard to be around him, to be *mates* just lounging and enjoying each other's company, when he had slowly morphed into a hunk of hyperalert stone. Since the vampire attack, it was like everything that made Lucian *Lucian* had been stripped away, leaving an alpha—*my* alpha—with a one-track mind.

It didn't do him any good—and it made our connection strained. This intense vigilance drained him and kept him away from me, and I just…

No more.

217

Nose to the ground, I sniffed straight to his old cabin, then once around its foundations for good measure. Riddled with dead ivy, it was exactly as I imagined: simple and straightforward. A wooden box with a steepled roof and a chimney that had probably seen countless fires over the years. Tall as the average man in Kira's form, I pressed my snout against a dirty glass window, scoping out the inside with a whine.

Uh-huh, just what I thought.

One room—from the lingering smells, he did his business outside like a wolf—with a wood-burning stove, small tables set up for a kitchen area, a bed *just* big enough for him, an armchair with a sheet over it, and then an empty worktable. Neat and not too showy, just like my Lucian.

I huffed, fogging the glass, and then dropped into a sit. My Lucian was currently on patrol, and given the hour, he ought to be *just* cresting the mountain footpaths, on the cusp of his old territory.

Close enough that when I howled, it probably wouldn't take him long to find me.

Despite it being midafternoon, I unleashed a howl that ripped through the western woods. One that danced over the mountains and skimmed the sapphire lake. I called out to Lucian—the others knew where I was and what I was doing and had told me there was no point in trying to tame that, quote, stubborn old recluse—and I tried to make it flirty.

Sang a range of notes. Really put my heart in it.

When it was over, my song echoed through the trees. With a snort, I padded away from the cabin into the middle of what looked like a man-made clearing where Lucian probably split wood—judging by the old stump and the forgotten stack, anyway—and then waited.

He answered six long beats of my heart later, his howl deep and luxurious.

And, honestly, a little strained.

That hurt to hear.

I called out to him again, harmonizing with his howl, and stayed put so he could find me. After all, the hunt-capture-fuck game I played with Soren wasn't meant for Lucian. We both needed security in this world, so here I'd wait, in this clearing, at his old home, until he arrived.

However long that might take.

Our howls threaded together, warmth unfurling in my belly like wildflower petals under the morning sun. Slowly, the song drifted from *come find me* to… well, just a song. A connection between us, a duet for me and Lucian and no one else. When it eventually tapered off, our harmony still reverberating through the forest, the heat in my belly had made itself at home, this low burn that nestled between my thighs, a cozy reminder of what my mate did to me.

While waiting, I shifted back to two legs and tucked Kira away for a while. As eager as she was to sniff and nuzzle and nip at Lucian's wolf form, she'd have to wait: this was a time for words, my heart exposed to him *again*. In the meantime, I studied the crawling ivy that wove around the cabin, crinkly and brown, the plant withdrawn before winter hit.

Ten afternoons in the last two weeks had been devoted to intention work with Rosa, but my power refused to do what I wanted, when I wanted, always coming too hard, too fast, or not at all. No in the middle. Just… a fire hose on full blast with no handsome firefighters to steady it. Rosa was quick to praise, insisting that I was doing *great* every time I killed something or made it triple in size or turn from harmless to lethal.

I didn't feel great.

Sure, things had stopped shaking on a whim.

But that wasn't enough.

Once again, *I* wasn't enough.

Hot from the shift, the air steaming, I strolled closer to Lucian's cabin, then raised my hand. Felt my fingertips buzz. Felt the pulse in my core where this stupid well was supposed to sit. Felt the *energy* in my palm. Eyes closed, I did the thing. Imagined cupped hands scooping diamond water, Kira watching from behind a nearby tree, *very* aware that I was a mess with all this Idunn stuff. I visualized sprinkling the water onto brown ivy. Not a splash. A misting. Just enough to revive it—bring some green back to those leaves.

Heat scratched at the nape of my neck.

My belly flip-flopped.

My palms broke out in a cold sweat.

And when I opened my eyes, the entire cabin was covered in the stuff. Green ivy, sure, but thorny ivy now, thick and thriving like it had taken on a life of its own.

I clamped down on my cheeks, my snarl muffled, my frustration mounting. Kira nosed at my insides, her soft chuffs supposed to calm me, but it didn't work.

I didn't work.

Teeth gritted, I marched over to investigate, finding thorned ivy covering way more of the cabin than it had before. Coarse and angry, it spiraled all the way up the chimney and strangled the opening.

Like it wanted to keep the smoke in.

Smother the house.

I rubbed my face, groaning. Perfect.

Before I could even try to fix it—or, more likely, make it ten times worse—paws thundered across the forest floor. Leaves crunched. Twigs snapped. Lucian's oakwood scent tinted the air. He made no effort to disguise his approach, and I jogged around to the northeastern corner of the cabin, some of the frustration melting away at the sight of his scarred, grizzled wolf charging through the trees. Brambles and burrs snagged on his fur, his eyes almost as golden as mine in this form, and he skidded to a halt just past the tree line, claws raking up the dirt. In a blink, he shifted back, swapping the huge black wolf for my mountain man.

Tallest of my mates. Thickest. Hardest. Scarred and sweaty, his chest heaved through every strangled breath. Black curly hair dipped down the muscular planes, thickening around his lower abdomen to his shaft. Mossy green appraised me hurriedly, frantically, his body tense, muscles taut—beard long and uncared for these days, lips in a thin line.

"What's wrong?" he demanded, voice all rough and thick, pure wolf. The English accent always tickled between my thighs, but the animalistic *rasp* made my breath hitch and my mouth a little too dry. Even now, his rugged masculinity had me weak in the knees. Would it always be this way? Would they *always* stun me with their beauty? In my appreciative silence, Lucian scanned the clearing with a growl. "What is it?"

Naked and hulking, he prowled straight for me—then stopped, gaze lifted over and beyond me.

Oh. *No.* He'd seen the ivy.

Kind of hard to miss.

His frown deepened, taking on a slightly different air. No longer panicked, his expression twisted to outright confusion, the emotion zinging down my spine all itchy and uncomfortable. My mate then pointed at his cabin, opening and closing his mouth a few times.

"Right, what…?"

"Nothing's wrong," I told him as I strolled closer, adding an extra sway into everything that jiggled in a sad attempt to distract him. Somehow it worked: Lucian's layered greens plunged to my breasts, then my hips, then slowly—so slow I felt the burn over every *inch* of skin—up my center to my lips. "I just miss you."

He let out a brisk breath and scratched at the back of his neck. For a few seconds, everything about him relaxed—then tightened again, as if realizing he had let his guard down—when my hands smoothed up his burly chest. Kira whimpered at his frown, and a small part of me hated that he didn't immediately stroke my arms or cup my backside or sling his arm around my waist. Instead, he just stood there, staring down at me and looking as tired as I'd felt after my first lesson with Rosa. "Little mate..." Some of the velvet was back, his voice a salve that could fix the world. "We saw each other at breakfast, and—"

Whatever else he had to say went away as soon as I hugged him. Clinging to his sculpted torso, I held tight, hands locked behind his back, and closed my eyes. His heart beat so *hard*, so fast and firm, and not like it did with the effort it took to shift. This was something more. The heat radiating off his body—*more* than that of a shifter.

Fear. Stress. I felt it in my teeth the longer I embraced him, the weight he had been carrying the last two weeks trickling into me, the dams barely holding. He was still my mountain man, strong and solid, but he had lost some muscle.

Probably because he ate less lately.

So focused on *us* eating, on minding the pack and watching for predators in the dark, that he forgot about himself. Pair that with being constantly on the move—it was a recipe for disaster.

I squeezed tighter. Clenched my eyes harder, stemming the tears.

What are you doing to yourself, mate?

Finally, after what felt like hours of him just standing there, Lucian hugged me back. Draped his strong arms around me, but not as firm as I wanted.

"You've been so busy," I mumbled into his chest, Kira's

pitchy whine-growl telling me we were definitely on the same page about him, "and when you're home, you're not… home."

All my mates were busy, Ewan most of all, but this was different. Lucian had no obligations outside of patrol duty, but lately he was a million miles away, and nothing we did could bring him back to earth.

Another rough exhale tickled the top of my bare shoulder, and Lucian snuggled into my hair, his dick perking up against my thigh.

I kissed the dip between his hard pecs with a grin. "I see you missed me too?"

"Lyssa…" He said my name like it *hurt* him. "I swear it isn't purposeful—"

Once again, I cut off whatever he had to say, head tipped back as I cupped his strong jawline. Strands of grey and white streaked his unkept beard today, oddly bright in the afternoon light. His eyes, my favorite shade of green, were hollow and ringed in shadow.

Sacrificing his personal well-being for me—for my safety, for the territory, for the pack…

"It's enough now," I murmured, steering him back to me when he tried to look away. "*Enough.* You're more than enough as you are, Lucian." I stroked his cheekbones, only just noticing the way his cheeks curved inward, hidden from a distance by the beard. "We protect each other, and you need to let go a little." He reared back, but I followed, gripping hard, fingertips gritting into his face. "*I* need you to come home."

From the look in his eyes, the argument already at a simmer in our fated bond, Lucian had no *idea* how much I needed him these days.

I needed his calm.

I needed his strength.

I needed his quiet and his support.

I needed *him*—sprawled out on the deck beside me, like before, both of us soaking up the afternoon sunshine as wolves. I needed to be a wolf with him, because of all my mates, *he* was the most wild. I needed walks in the forest and rabbit hunting and drinks in the stream. I needed him grooming my ears and rough play that *didn't* lead to mating—just play. Just fun on four legs.

Idunn's power terrified me. Even with Rosa's support, the energy inside was scary and dangerous. I turned innocent greenery savage and mean. I couldn't control it.

And I just… needed to feel his arms around me.

Needed to feel *safe* again.

Him patrolling and working himself to the bone? It didn't make me feel safe.

Not even close.

Having him so *close*, his breath warming my lips, his eyes locked on mine—it all went quiet. The storm raging inside, Idunn's power churning with my own warring feelings… Gone. Silent. It was just me and Lucian, alone in the forest, surrounded by the nature we so loved and the peace we both deserved. Swallowing hard, I stood up on my toes to kiss him. Softly, gently, our lips *just* touching. He was so warm.

So warm and gentle and *mine*.

His beard tickled my chin, my cheeks, and his hands finally curved possessively over my backside, hoisting me higher as the kiss deepened. Even with our lips parted, tongues caressing one another like old friends, nothing turned frantic. With Ewan and Soren, the chaos came so fast, the want and need and desperation driving us to madness in seconds.

With Lucian, it was like we needed to *savor* each other. Reconnect with each other's taste, scent, and touch.

Still so quiet and calm. He made the frantic merry-go-round in my brain, the one I couldn't get off and glittered like diamonds and whizzed so fast it made it sick—Lucian made it stop.

I closed my eyes and speared my fingers into his hair. He clutched me tighter, lifting me off the ground. His arm slipped under me like a muscly seat while his other hand cradled the back of my head, tipping me back—*dipping* me, just like in the movies—to taste so deep we both moaned. Always harmonized, me and Lucian, our sounds music to my ears.

His desire suddenly nudged harder into my belly, his shaft a thick, solid line of want trapped between us. With a protesting whine, I wiggled out of his hold to stand on my own two feet, never once breaking the kiss, and caressed his shaft with both hands. My mate rumbled appreciatively with the first stroke. Not too hard. Not too rough. The skin there for males was so tender and sensitive; I just ghosted over it, the smear of damp at the tip not enough to turn the whole thing silky.

Nipples pebbled painfully, I snapped at his lower lip, ready to take this from a gentle hello to a desperate *I want you*. Lucian nipped back, his bite fiercer and catching me off guard. Pain tingled in my lip. Want flared in my belly, the air scented with my womanly musk, and through the crack of one eye, I caught his nostrils flare with his next impossibly deep breath, like he was breathing in the rush of wet between my thighs.

"I learned something recently," I murmured into his mouth. My mate snarled, his grip tightening in my hair the lighter I stroked him.

"What's that?"

Ugh. Hard to be the seductress with all the power when he sounded like *that*, velvety yet dark, dangerous and powerful and all *man*.

225

"I learned—" I eased away from his lips, fluttering my lashes and grinning. "—that I'm *very* good with my mouth…"

As soon as I started to sink, about to fall to my knees before him and take that impressive—and kind of intimidating—dick in my mouth, determined to give it my best try despite the size, Lucian caught me by my upper arms.

Stopped me.

"Little mate, wait—"

"No." I pouted up at him, at his wolf eyes blazing gold just like mine, at the tense line his mouth made as if deep down he didn't *want* me to stop. "Let me. Please… I want to make you feel as good as you make *me* feel."

"But *I* want to use my mouth on *you*," Lucian rumbled. His wicked smirk nearly dropped me to my knees for all the wrong reasons, the teasing lift of his lips an incantation all its own.

"Oh." How did that work? Who went first? Me? Him? "Uh, okay, but—"

"Here." My mate withdrew completely, and panic lanced through me at the thought of him *leaving*. His gaze snapped sharply to mine, and while he didn't say anything, he didn't go far either, settling on the ground at my feet, sprawled on his back. He then patted his chest and motioned up to his devilish smile. "Bring your dripping cunt right *here*, little mate. Let me taste you while you taste me."

Oh. My eyes widened. *Oh.*

Fire ripped through me from top to bottom, and I took a few seconds to process, then consider my options. He seemed to want me to sit down right on his face, arms outstretched and ready to guide me, but squatting on top of him like I was about to pee next to a tree wasn't sexy…

Was it?

Pushing through the fog, desire and primal need making

226

it hard to think, I stepped over him, then slowly lowered myself down to his chest.

"The other way, little mate."

I frowned. What? The other—

Oh. Right. Blushing up a storm, I turned around to face away from him, then perched on his broad chest, a muscular plane capable of supporting ten of me. Then, before I could figure out where to put everything, Lucian grabbed my hips and scooped me up, then literally *lifted* me over his face.

"Go on, then," he growled with a front-row seat to my swollen, aching sex. "Show me what I've been missing…"

Lucian then arched up and *licked* me, and, *oh*, now it was even *harder* to think. The first sweep of his tongue stoked the fires burning within, and I stumbled forward, bracing on his taut abs, thighs already quivering. His dick stood tall at the helm of his tree trunk thighs, and while it would have been so easy, so *good*, to get lost in what he was doing to me, I refused to submit.

No surrender.

Not when images of Ewan's submission danced across my mind, this angelic, sharply beautiful alpha male totally in my thrall.

All because my tongue did that *thing* he seemed to really like.

Shoulders back, I sank over his huge frame, then fisted the base of his shaft and flicked my tongue over the tender tip. Lucian bucked, his thrusts into my body with his powerful tongue faltering for a second. Right. Okay. Two could play at this game. Grinning, I took him as deep as I could, then licked the rest, spreading my saliva to make each pump of my hands smooth as silk.

Despite that skilled tongue being wholly occupied, Lucian's teeth, tongue, and lips *very* dedicated to the task of making me squirm and mewl and *squeal* when he teased the sensitive bundle of nerves I now knew to be my clitoris, he wasn't quiet about it. He devoured me like I was his favorite meal, moaning and groaning and lapping me up with such ferocity that I struggled to keep pace. Still, I could throw him when I swirled my tongue or cupped his balls. He loved the slow, torturous pumping of my hands, but his noises turned tortured when I went faster.

We knew how to undo each other.

How to make the other stumble and fall into our control.

Not a word shared, just an inferno brewing between us, within us, hearts connected. His want swelled through me, punctuated by regret, the emotion plunging in cold icy drops down my spine. Lucian's feelings were just as messy as mine, just as complicated, flowing back and forth, the two of us connected by more than just the physical.

I lost it first.

Quite unfairly, too, because as soon as he slipped two rough fingers in me to stroke my inner walls, his mouth dedicated to only my clitoris, I was *done*. The explosion came hard and fast, furious and fiery as pleasure tore through my limbs. Even with his shaft halfway in my mouth, I howled through the sensation, one hand raking up his thigh, the other gripping him maybe a little *too* tight from his next choked breath.

But that seemed to do it for him, the painful slash of my nails jumping from his thigh to mine, the sensations shared —including his climax. *Orgasm*. I'd added more terms to my vocabulary during my blowjob research, and his hit like a detonation, like a building demolition. *Boom*, pleasure shooting you sky-high, then the fall of *everything* crashing back down.

It touched me too.

Heightened my own bliss, upped it to unsafe levels so that

I sobbed into his thigh, barely able to take it, as he spilled himself in thick, hot bursts all over my fist.

But when it faded away and I sat up, it was like I could draw a deep, full breath for the first time in weeks.

Like that first gasp after cracking through the ice, no longer at the river's cruel mercy.

As I shimmied down his body, struggling to spread my legs around his massive shoulders, all I wanted now was to waste the day away here, on the forest floor, cuddled against my Lucian and all the peace he offered. My mate had other ideas, however, and just as I started to climb off, ready to tuck myself under his wing, he caught me by the hips and rolled me. Pinned me to the ground. Climbed up and prowled over so that he blanketed my body with unstoppable muscle and raw masculinity. I spread my thighs for him, happy to let him settle there, and he filled me with a single thrust, already hard again, already wanting for my body. It took me by surprise, so relaxed and hazy one moment, stretched and taken the next. My lips tumbled open in a soundless cry, and I arched up and into him, letting him claim me.

And claiming him in turn.

Lucian bundled me up as best he could. While my back took the brunt of the ground's harsh bite, he blunted it here and there, arms under me, head cradled. After stealing another slow, toe-curling kiss, my mate nestled into the crook of my neck, nibbling along my skin, licking over the scar he had left with his bite. His mark tingled, made me shudder with featherlight waves of pleasure, and I hooked my legs around him, *barely* able to lock my ankles, then dug into his hair for support.

We rocked together, slow and steady. No merciless pounding into the dirt. No biting kisses and brutal hands. It wasn't like I didn't *enjoy* what I had with Soren, nor did I only crave Ewan's intense, passionate lovemaking that always ended with the most delicious aches.

With Lucian, it was just different.

Not better, not worse. Different and sublime and *deep*, our gazes frequently crashing together, locking, gold on gold with his wolf eyes *right* at the surface. Emotion thickened in my throat the deeper I lost myself in his gold. Tears stung the backs of my eyes. I'd needed this, *him*, for so long.

A quiet moment.

A soul connection.

No words. No declarations. Just—*this*.

I closed my eyes and burrowed into him, hiding my face against his shoulder and hearing a declaration with his every thrust. *Need you. Need you. Need. You. Needyouneedyouneedyou.* Because he felt it too, the ropes binding us together thick and sturdy and a little scary. Dangerous, to be so *open* to each other but suddenly so closed off from everything else.

This climax broke me. The pleasure tore me to pieces and scattered me on the wind, the emotional bond my undoing, the closeness my downfall, the *connection* my salvation. I came apart in his arms, pleasure burning white-hot, sobbing again. Too intense. Too much. Eyes squeezed shut, I rocked and bucked and drove it harder, *taking* all of it even if it terrified me.

My fingertips buzzed.

Diamonds sparkled behind my closed lids, exploding, turning into starlight that went on forever and ever, just like the orchard—to the horizon and beyond. I choked his name, and Lucian stabbed into me one last time, hard and possessive, his breath ragged and his voice rough as he snarled *little mate* back like the burn of a branding.

We held each other tight in the aftermath, almost like if we let go, the other would slip away, sand falling through our fingers and disappearing on the breeze. In time, the starlight faded behind my eyelids, the pinwheels of color dying, leaving only a heavy darkness. It threatened to lull me to sleep, knock me out right here on the forest floor, in Lucian's arms—and I would have let it.

But Lucian stirred, rumbling as he dragged his open mouth up my neck and along my jaw, breathing life back into the fire between us. His interest zinged through me, swelling between my legs again, and I arched into him with a moan, lifting off the dirt and leaves, smoothing my feet down the backs of his strong thighs. Slowly, my eyes fluttered open and met with his mossy greens, his golden wolf gaze tucked away for now.

I stroked his cheek, his untidy beard, missing the gold already.

Resting on his elbows so he didn't crush me, my mate grinned, the feeling of his open affection like a cozy blanket wrapped around us both. His lips parted. He inhaled softly, about to say something—

Then his gaze snagged somewhere else.

All around us.

His smile vanished. He pushed up with a harsh breath, ripping the affection away with him, stealing the blanket that kept us warm and safe and together.

"What…?"

Oh.

Oh *no*.

Fear welled in my throat, nearly closing it for good.

All around us—a field of wildflowers.

Spring wildflowers, mostly white and yellow with the odd stamp of red. Scentless.

Evidence of Idunn's gifts, her power in *my* veins, bloomed as far as the eye could see, dominating Lucian's clearing, surrounding his cabin, flourishing at the deadbolted door.

Lucian pushed to his knees, taking it all in with wide eyes, jaw set and lips in a thin, horrifying line again. All the post-mating looseness—gone. Suspicion panged from him to me, tearing up and down my spine, making my belly loop and bile sizzle in my throat.

"Lyssa—"

"P-please *don't*—"

"Lyssa," he growled, reaching cautiously for the nearest yellow bloom, "what just happened?"

My mind went blank.

Kira fell silent.

I couldn't *lie* to him—not to any of my mates, but especially not Lucian.

But how could I tell him the truth?

He always made a face when Rosa or Ethan came up in conversation, clearly not the biggest fan of magic, so how could I—

Lucian hissed, pain stabbing in *my* fingertip, the very same finger on his hand that had just stroked the flower's stem. While thin and green, innocent from a distance, up close I realized every single one of these stupid wildflowers… had thorns.

Tiny, angry, violent little knives on their stems—and one had just ripped Lucian's finger open. He withdrew and glowered at the pluming red dot at the tip. It healed in seconds, but the dull ache lingered, like a whisper of a childhood wound echoing in me.

No. No, no, no, *no*. I buried my face in my hands, smothering the hot, wet panic before he saw, then rolled over and curled in on myself.

Why was it always thorns?

Why couldn't I make something *nice*?

"Lyssa?" His knuckles ghosted along my arm, and I shook my head, swallowing an agonized wail, *fighting* for just a speck of my mate's effortless calm.

I mean, what if this had been something *worse* than thorny wildflowers? It had happened without my consent—and it was big. The whole clearing this time. The ivy on his cabin. Thorns, thorns, thorns. Dangerous. Unpredictable. What if ivy had, I don't know, *snaked* around his neck, thorns and all?

What if, in a haze of bliss, lost in our connection, I accidentally smothered him?

Or stabbed him?

Or, or, or, *or…*

Rosa had put so much time and effort into helping me the last two weeks.

And now *this*.

It didn't matter.

I was hopeless—and one day, I might accidentally do something to my mates.

Something I couldn't take back.

Something even shifters couldn't heal from.

"I-I can't control it," I blubbered, coiling into a ball as the floodgates burst. Kira finally nosed at me, whining, panicked but trying her best to be supportive. She was all I had in this mess, and—

"Little mate, please don't cry."

Suddenly, Lucian's enormous body nudged up behind mine. He curled around me, folded over me, protecting me from the world and all its problems with his rough hands and fiery skin and raw *strength*. Sniffling, hiccupping, snotty and wet, I lowered my hands just enough to blink at the ocean of wildflowers, then twist back to him. He… He was still here. I'd expected him to run. To pick through the clearing, demanding answers, furious that I had so *obviously* kept something from him.

"Can't you feel how it *pains* me when you cry?" he whispered when I faced forward again. My mate swept me closer, my hunched back to his scarred chest, and I soon felt his breath on my neck, on my shoulder where he had once marked me. Shoving the fear aside, I tried to just listen to his breathing, to count the even exhales.

"I-I'm not ready to explain yet."

"Why?" he rumbled.

"Because you'll leave." *You'll all leave.*

"Never forget, little mate," Lucian whispered, lips brushing his mark with every word, "you don't scare me."

My chest squeezed, both from my own emotional turmoil *and* his. So tight I could barely breathe.

"No," I murmured, "but the world does."

Lucian stiffened at my back.

He patrolled relentlessly because everything else scared him. His past must have brutalized him—and my mate wouldn't let that happen again. Not to him. Not to his pack. Not to his mate. The world was a bad place for my Lucian...

But maybe now *I* was bad in his eyes. When he realized what had happened, the depths of what I'd become, the weight of all the secrets I had kept, I might eventually scare him too.

And then he would run me out of here, just like those vampires, hell-bent on protecting his territory from a monster.

"I'm here, Lyssa." Lucian cuddled me to him harder now, like that would drive the point home, a powerful declaration that he was *here* for me, by my side, at my back, no matter what. His resolve scorched through me like a forest fire, so hot and insistent that sweat broke out across my brow. Of all my mates, I felt Lucian the deepest, our connection almost soul-level. He readjusted his arm, cutting across my chest, between my breasts, like he *needed* to feel my thundering heart. I closed my eyes tight. He breathed me in deep. When I stole a peek at the wildflowers, the thorns had grown to about an inch.

My eyes dropped to my curled fingers.

Belatedly, I felt the buzz of power.

Driven by *feeling*.

By a depressing resolve.

"I'm not going anywhere," Lucian growled. "I swear it. We'll get through this together, little mate."

I closed my eyes again, squeezing out a few tears.

No.

Not together.

Clearly, I needed more help than even Rosa could give. This might be beyond her skill.

Or *I* might be beyond help.

One day, I could kill the wolf at my back without meaning to.

Nature *wasn't* nice. It wasn't carefree and gentle. It was violent and cruel and unpredictable, and that... was what Idunn had turned me into.

Lucian might not be going anywhere, his promise resonating through me, but Kira howled desperately inside, calling to her mate—like she wanted to *snitch* on me.

Like she wanted to warn him...

He might be here to stay, but after today, I wasn't.

I couldn't.

I had to save Lucian, Ewan, and Soren... from myself. From a cursed she-wolf with no control. From a monster, a freak, an abomination.

And to walk away, to *run* fast and far—that would kill me.

But, in the end... better *me* than them.

EWAN

...So, this isnt goodbye forevr.

But it is goodbye for now. It has to be. I hope you all undrstand.

L

The *fuck?*

Naked and sweaty from my recent shift, weighed down by a pleasant full-body soreness after my daytime territory patrol, I shook out the small slip of lined paper, then read it again. Brows furrowed, I squinted at Lyssa's chicken scratch, her misspelled words, and hoped that I had missed something the first time around.

But nope. The bullet points remained the same.

She cared very deeply for all of us.

She was so grateful *we* were her mates.

She looked forward to one day starting a bloodline—but was scared she would hurt us.

And for now, needed to leave.

What.

The actual.

Fucking.

Fuck?

I'd returned to a quiet house, Lucian napping on the back deck beneath a foggy sunset and Soren rustling around the kitchen having just returned from *his* full day at work. Slated for an evening patrol, I figured the blond alpha was about to start dinner—and that Lyssa, her musky rose scent faint in the air, was still with Rosa.

She had told us this morning…

Something about a movie with Aster, a mom-and-baby showing at a cinema in Hampton, the lights kept on in the theater, the sound lowered, the flick decidedly *chick*.

And now this.

Crumpling the note in my fist, I stalked out of my bedroom, cock swinging, naked and grimy and in desperate need of a shower, and barreled through Lyssa's half-closed door.

Empty bedroom.

Made bed.

Lights off and too quiet.

Scowling, I ripped open her walk-in closet door and noted a few key items missing: winter jacket we had recently ordered her for the sake of appearances, some jeans and T-shirts, her underwear and sock drawers completely pilfered.

No laptop anywhere. I reread the note one more time, hoping that maybe I had *dreamed* its contents. Nope. Same shit. I went for her bedside table—no phone either, the charging cord gone. If I called it, she probably wouldn't answer.

"Fuck."

Inner wolf on high alert, sniffing deeply, our hearts pounding as one and his concerned whines melding with the high-pitched screech between my ears, I barreled downstairs and plowed straight into Soren as he left the kitchen, a chilled beer in hand.

"Shit, sorry, man—"

"What the *fuck* have you done now?" I snarled. My alpha counterpart staggered back with his bottle of Belgian brew, and then cocked his head to the side. His wolf eyes flared—and so did mine.

"Uh, what?"

I shoved the note at him, hating the way my whole arm trembled, rage and fear turning foul in my chest. "What—did—you—*do*?"

Soren flashed his teeth as he snatched the crinkly paper, shock pinging briefly through our bond, followed by a thunderclap of fury. We had been getting along better lately, connecting through this more evenly divided patrol schedule. For once, we three males had been a *team*; it wasn't just Lucian shouldering the burden of protecting our territory, but all of us, myself included.

It nuked some of the simmering tension, being a team.

But that flew out the window as I gnashed my teeth and glowered at the fucking *cocksucker* in front of me as he read Lyssa's note.

Because obviously he had done something.

Wasn't it always him?

First Gull River, and now this?

Gone.

"I-I thought she was with Rosa," Soren stammered as soon as his wolf eyes touched the bottom of the paper and snapped back to the top, skimming it a second time, faster, his mounting anxiety buzzing in the nape of my neck. I swatted at it like I'd picked up a bunch of mosquitos and growled when Soren shook his head, both arms suddenly limp at his sides, his eyes blue again—and a million miles away. "She told me this morning… They were… The movie, right?"

Behind him, the sliding glass door separating the living room from the back deck whizzed open, then thunked shut, followed by Lucian's slow, firm prowl across the hardwood. Clearly the flash-bang in our bond woke him, and if he had slept through Lyssa sneaking away—I'd kill him.

Or, you know…

Just punch him, really, really hard in the face.

For now, I centered my wrath on Soren. "Again—what the *fuck* did you do?"

Because I sure as shit hadn't done anything. The two and a half weeks since Halloween had been oddly peaceful. No vampires in our territory—not a whiff of danger around our mate. No Hawthorne wolves testing our borders. Ethan had set up charms and spells and whatever else warlocks did around the village to ensure our humans didn't become prey during some fucked-up leech open season. The guys and I got along better. Lyssa seemed happy to have us all home, cycling in and out but sharing more meals as a pack. Beyond us, she had Rosa, spending plenty of afternoons with the sweet witch, something we all agreed was key for our mate while she developed her sense of self as a shifter.

She deserved—and, frankly, *needed*—at least one friend outside of the pack. Wolves who got too into their own dynamics were just… weird.

Desperate as *I* still was to hoard our mate, I let go—just a little—so she could foster a social sphere outside of *us*.

And I hadn't said anything hurtful lately.

I'd been *very* careful about that, watching my manners, minding my words, a lot of the beef between me and Soren quashed after our Halloween threesome. Things had been going well; with patrol and work and house stuff, I hadn't been this tired in for-fucking-ever, but I liked it. Staying busy like this, balancing the impending Redwood Grove winter chaos, the many, many, *many* events we had planned for residents and tourists alike, with pack duties—it was *good*.

Made me feel... connected, to her, to them, to my inner animal, who got to stretch his legs daily now.

All this made me a more balanced wolf.

And that was... a good thing.

Until now.

Until *this*.

"I don't get it," Soren muttered, beer tucked under his arm as he smoothed out the note. "What does this even *mean*?"

"It clearly means she *left*," I snarled, temper spiking, my inner wolf right there with me and ready for a fight, "you fucking shit for brains—"

"Why would you assume *I* did something?"

"Because it wasn't *him*." I shoved a finger in Lucian's direction as the hulking alpha lumbered up behind Soren, a few inches taller, a great deal wider, and looking annoyed as fuck. "This fucker doesn't talk enough to send her running—"

"That's not fair," Soren growled, eyes narrowed and amber again, all canines as he sprinted to Lucian's defense. The enormous Brit behind him merely looked between us, a strange calm washing through the bond—frosty and dangerous. I swallowed hard, my inner wolf on edge at the sensation, and shrugged.

"Well—"

"What's this?" Lucian rumbled. The air went deadly still, Soren and I holding our breaths, the gravelly, demonic timbre of his tone fucking terrifying. "Lyssa *isn't* with that bloody witch?"

Despite the brewing brawl, I swapped glances with Soren, both of us unnerved by whatever the hell *that* was—some fucked-up monster in Lucian form—and he shuffled out of the doorway and into the foyer, near me but out of arm's reach so neither of us could fling a sucker punch. Quick as he and I had been to fight in the past, we had an unspoken truce to try harder, be *better*, for Lyssa's sake.

Only Lyssa wasn't here, so...

My inner wolf's lips peeled back, ready for a fight with *anyone* right now as a storm of feeling hammered our alpha bond.

Lucian sauntered into the doorway, filling it, glaring between us and demanding answers. That icy calm turned to steel, his resolve to assign someone the blame setting my teeth on edge.

"Look, if anyone scared her away, it's *you*," Soren insisted. While he sounded less confrontational now, those were fucking *fighting* words and he knew it. The blond shrugged when our gazes clashed again, his righteousness undercutting Lucian's steel. "I mean, *you* are the one who runs his damn mouth whenever you're stressed... Any more speeches about bloodlines lately that we should know about?"

"Says the douchebag who let her drink from Gull River—"

"If Lyssa's gone," Lucian interjected, "she scared herself away. It has nothing to do with us."

I rounded on him with a snarl. Had he read the note already? No, it was still in Soren's hand—but he spoke with such confidence, such calm certainty, that it made me want to straight-up attack him. Triggered as I might be, my emotions bleeding into the bond unchecked now, Lucian radiated pure, uncut *alpha*, his energy smothering, his stance tall and strong. His voice's guttural rasp had softened, but he sounded perfectly in control.

"*What?*" I'd kill for control right now. What I got instead was fear and panic and anger, all bundled into some ugly, nauseating brew. Bile sizzled up my throat. My jaw ached from clenching. My nails, trimmed and neat for my mate's comfort, gritted so deep into my palms that a droplet of steaming red *plopped* onto the tile at my feet.

She was gone.

And I was fucking losing it.

And it pissed me the fuck off that I seemed like the only one in a kamikaze tailspin.

Wordlessly, Soren offered me his beer. Still full—one of the Belgian whites he so loved.

Rather than downing it, I hurled it at the wall.

No one moved.

No one acknowledged the glass shattering and the beer streaking.

My inner wolf whined—and I felt even worse.

"Ewan..." Out of the corner of my eye, Soren reached out for me, then quickly dropped his arm. "Take a breath, okay? We're all worried—"

"Shut the fuck up, Soren," I growled back. At no point did I need his *pity*, and the warmth rippling from him to me through our bond only made me even more uncomfortable in my own fucking skin. Quinn wolves had never been touchy-feely. My pack lacked transparent communication and logical discussions and understanding and looking at things from each other's perspective.

Lyssa did that.

Soren too—to a degree.

And it made me feel about two inches tall. I pinched the bridge of my nose, my inner wolf equally unsettled by the olive branch. "Just let me—"

"Gull River changed her," Lucian announced, deftly changing the subject, not an ounce of pity lobbed my way. I glanced up appreciatively, but something told me he didn't do it for me, even if it was a flawless redirect, checking all our aggression and feelings back where they belonged. "She's scared she'll hurt us."

"I..." Soren held up the note with a frown. "What the hell does that even mean?"

It was then that Lucian finally decided to share a few crucial details about *our* mate.

Because—fucking *apparently*—not only could our brave little she-wolf rattle the windows and make grown humans cower with a glimpse of her golden gaze...

But she could summon wildflowers from the earth.

Make them grow strong and tall and spiky.

Breathe life back into ivy that had already retreated for the winter—then double its size.

Rage detonated through the pack bond, Soren and I suddenly on the same murderous wavelength.

All this... had happened *yesterday*.

"And did that not seem like something worth *fucking* mentioning?" I bellowed. This time, I took on the demon's fury, my voice harsh and low. The surge of adrenaline was dangerous, pounding from me to them, adding fuel to a fire that shouldn't get any bigger.

"She's struggling," Lucian countered with a flash of teeth. Stoic as his exterior might seem, there was no way he could take the brunt of two packmates seething at him, raging, absolutely furious that he had kept this fucking secret to himself. His cheek twitched, and the alpha suddenly rolled his head side to side, searching for that satisfying *crack*. "And I respect Lyssa enough to let her share what's happening when she's ready—"

"And now she's gone." Soren threw his hands up, terse exasperation oozing from his every pore, then tossed the note at Lucian's feet. "We could have avoided this, Lucian. You aren't an island unto yourself anymore—we're a goddamn *team*."

"I'm well aware of that—"

"Obviously the gold wasn't the only thing she picked up from the river," Soren ranted on, blowing by Lucian's objections as I started to pace, needing to put this adrenaline to use before my wolf forced a shift and we did something we might regret. The blond alpha stabbed a hand through his hair with a low growl. "She's stopped making stuff shake, so I just thought—"

"We all *just thought*," I snarled. That was the fucking problem: we as a pack had let too much slide. And brutal as it was to admit, we were *all* at fault here. We thought our connections ran deeper than they did, like the thickening bond between us was enough to manage a pack. "We babied her feelings and her, her, her *experience* when we should have gotten to the root of the issue."

"She said we would leave her if we knew the truth."

I wheeled around on Lucian with a scoff. Leave her? Fucking ridiculous. Now that I'd found her, I would *never* abandon my mate—even if something were wrong with her. When we first dragged that wild woman out of the woods, kicking and screaming and slashing her claws, sure, I had my doubts.

But Lyssa was meant for me—and me for her. She was strong, brave, and adaptable. Tough. Brash. Independent. Eager to learn and grow and explore. Impulsive. She needed guidance, needed a mate who would pump the brakes when necessary, just as much as I needed a fated who would put me in my place and drag my ass out of the office every once in a while.

Remind me what *should* matter in life.

And together, we needed time to create that dynamic.

To forge that connection with *all* of us. Unified alphas meant an unbreakable pack—our bloodline would rule Redwood Grove like fucking royalty.

We had been making huge strides lately...

Now this.

"So, what, reject us before we can reject her?" Soren kicked at the note on the floor. "I don't get it—"

"She's not rejecting us," Lucian argued roughly. "She—"

"She's not going *anywhere*," I snapped, then motioned stiffly to the front door. "We're going to bring her home and figure this bullshit out."

"Agreed."

The fuck? Soren and I slowly turned on Lucian, who was already yanking off his T-shirt and tossing it aside, preparing for the shift. Slow to agree to *anything*, this bearded fuck was usually the first to press pause and demand a thorough investigation—know absolutely everything about a situation before diving in.

"Those leech *cunts* are still out there," he growled, tugging his sweats down and booting them off. "I smell them sometimes just over the border... They're hunting her, either for themselves or for another."

"Maybe the Hawthorne alpha," Soren muttered, more to himself than us, but anxiety throbbed through the pack bond all the same, each of us radiating the stuff, muddying the waters and clouding our minds. The blond scratched at the back of his neck roughly, the sensation buzzing in the exact same spot on me, and then bared his teeth. "Lyssa is marked, but she hasn't had a pup yet. In theory, he could still take her... *breed* her for himself..."

Nope. My inner wolf, normally so calm and collected, stoic and standoffish, lost it at the thought. We had no idea who the vicious Hawthorne pack alpha was, but I'd never wanted to find out: I had no time in my hectic life for scum like that, some piece-of-shit drug runner and pimp, all too reminiscent of the old Quinn legacy.

And in my old pack, the gilded shithole I'd been born into

—males would have plucked a delectable peach like Lyssa and destroyed her. Not right away. No, they'd break her over time, chaining her with silver like monsters, breeding her again and again to make a stronger army.

I'd seen it happen.

Never been a participant in my cousins' fucked-up games, but the gory details were forever burned into the darkest pits of my soul.

Nope. Nope, not *fucking* happening to my mate.

I stalked for the front door, heart in my throat, inner wolf losing his mind. "We'll bring her back *tonight* and make her talk. Then we'll figure this shit out as a fucking pack."

"Ewan—"

"*No.*" I whipped around and bared my canines, wolf eyes blazing, muscles taut and sweaty, *ready* to state my case with brute strength if I had to. "No more feelings and letting her take her time... We find out the *truth*, and we fucking deal with it, or fix it, or whatever."

The house fell silent.

I straightened, arms falling limp at the assault through our pack bond—this strange, cohesive *whumping*, blood beating, war drums pounding.

A heartbeat.

Our heartbeat.

Soren's cheeks flushed a dull pink. Lucian rolled his shoulders back, eyes closed, one hand flexing in and out of a fist in time with that pulsing rhythm.

This...

We...

I blinked, swapping glances with Soren, then Lucian when he finally came back to us.

Us.

United.

Together.

Emotion stung the backs of my eyes—made my throat raw.

"Okay, okay, no sappy shit," I grumbled before ripping the front door open and barreling outside, the others at my heels. By the time we all trundled down the porch steps to the gravel drive, we were three naked alphas on the cusp of a shift, the air thick, my wolf calmed by the heartbeat of our pack—quieter now, just background noise, constant and reassuring.

A little past the midway point of November and the sun set early. Barely six o'clock and darkness blanketed the landscape, the porch lights activated by our presence, the lake still, the forest unnervingly silent. Bare branches. Birds migrated south. Game big and small already tucked in for the chilly night ahead. Frost tinted the windshields of all three vehicles in the driveway, and our breaths fogged, the ice on the breeze beyond invigorating.

Just the kind of shit to put you in the mood for the most important hunt of your entire fucking life.

"Me and Soren should track her scent," I insisted. The others fanned out on either side of me, wolf eyes reflecting the light, nostrils flared as they familiarized themselves with the natural world. "Lucian—border patrol." The alpha arched a thick dark brow at me. "Just keep circling. We'll cover ground faster apart, and you know our borders best. If something seems off, you'll see it first."

Difficult as it was to give him a compliment for his intense, almost obsessive patrol habits, it wasn't *as* difficult as usual. For once, the Brit's anal-retentive paranoia about safety and borders was about to be a serious asset.

"East," Lucian said in a caveman grunt. "I'll start east." He veered away from us, headed right to the scraggly yellowing grass along the side of the driveway, then paused and glared over his shoulder at me. Those golden wolf eyes—so like

Lyssa's, just a few shades duller. Soren inhaled sharply, almost like this was the first time he'd realized it, same as me, and I stood taller when the gold narrowed. "Be gentle when you find her."

I blinked back at him, waiting for the punchline, then remembered that the fucker didn't *joke* about this shit. When I glanced at Soren to help, he just raised his eyebrows and crossed his arms.

Did they seriously think…?

For fuck's sake.

"You assholes really think I'm heartless, don't you?" My inner wolf's snarl tainted every word, the syllables coarse and brutish. "I'm pissed because of the circumstances, not *her*."

I mean, a little bit at her—and I didn't deserve any shit for that. Lyssa was the one who pushed for conversation, open and honest communication, the *truth* at every turn. And here she was, fleeing into the night without so much as a proper goodbye, just some horseshit note left on my fucking pillow.

When no one said anything, the pair just staring, waiting for me to out myself as the insensitive bastard they had seen a few times already, I growled low and threw my hands up.

"*Obviously* I'll be gentle with her. I…" *Love her?*

No. Not quite. It was… too soon. It had to be too soon.

Logically—

My inner wolf snarled, and I culled the internal debate before it gained traction.

Fate was more intoxicating than I'd anticipated, nudging me deeper and deeper into a love-drunk stupor from the moment I first saw my she-wolf emerge from the shadows.

"If not," Soren mused, cracking his knuckles as if to intimidate me, "I'll rip you apart."

I flipped him off.

He growled.

Lucian... smirked.

The fucker actually *grinned*, like he possessed a *speck* of humor, then shifted and trotted along the eastern shoreline. Soren and I mirrored him, paws on the ground in seconds, greeting each other briefly—nosing at each other's snouts, scent-marking our fellow alpha as we never had before—then set out together. I hung back, letting Soren lead; he had spent more time with Lyssa's wolf form, hunting her through the mountain range, which meant he ought to take point.

But that only mattered *if* she was in wolf form.

I scanned the dark, barren tree line as we approached, sniffing deep, my wolf side hyperaware of every little detail.

About ten feet into the forest, Soren with his nose to the ground, his wolf side unnaturally focused and *barely* bouncy, a howl split the night.

Long, loud, and mournful, Lucian's call to our mate stilled my thundering heart. Made Soren shoot upright. Ears perked, hackles high, we both listened to his desperate song. Stiffened during the fading echoes. *Waited* for our mate to answer.

Nothing.

He tried again, longing slicing through our bond like razor wire, his heartbreak so visceral and *real* that it knocked the wind out of me.

Soren dropped into a sit and threw his head back, joining the howl. I added a third voice to the chorus, our tones varied and fluid, the perfect harmony, our message clear...

Please come home.

Our song would carry for miles and miles, rippling through the territory. No telling when she had left or how much of a head start she had on us, but Lyssa would hear the echoes. She'd *feel* this, us, her pack unified and searching.

When the icy breeze eventually carried the last of our howls away, silence answered us.

Lyssa had a beautiful song, high and clear and sweet, the perfect soprano to our range of baritones and altos.

Nothing.

Anxiety plucked at the bond again, like some aggressive asshole pulling a guitar string as far out as possible, *just* on the verge of breaking it, before letting it *twang* back into place.

I snarled and bulldozed into a still-seated Soren, forcing him to move. He smoothed his muzzle down my body from tip to tail, a brief moment of seeking comfort in my fur, my scent, then scampered around me and straight ahead. Nose to the ground, he sniffed furiously, searching for her, then veered sharply to the left.

After a quick glance back toward the house, I followed in his pawprints, praying to Lady Fate that we hadn't lost her tonight for good.

18

LYSSA

I knew exactly where our territory ended.

No fence, no marker, no lines in the sand—the scent of my mates just stopped. That was enough to tell me I had come to the northwestern border of the Redwood Grove territory...

I was supposed to be over it and gone ages ago.

But I couldn't bring myself to do it.

Seated on the edge of a rocky cliff jutting out from the forest, the mountain range at my back, the sun set and the nighttime chill settling on my skin, I hugged my knees to my chest and sighed. The city of Hampton glittered in the distance, slowly coming alive after sundown, lit up like a great neon jewel in a sea of darkness. Forest on all sides, it was a beacon, a spotlight—a guiding North Star, showing me exactly where I needed to go.

According to Rosa, Hampton was witch central for the region. About a forty-minute drive north of Redwood Grove, it was the last real metropolis before the province's northern nothingness. It had a human university *and* a supernatural academy, a ginormous shopping mall—all the modern amenities. I'd ambled around it once when the pack settled somewhere nearby, maybe six, seven years back. Clueless. Totally unaware that there were shifters one town over and that many of the people with strange energies and stunning eyes were probably witches and warlocks.

One of them *had* to be able to help me. Rosa had done her best the last two weeks, but her best wasn't enough—not when I was such an unpredictable disaster. Idunn's magic needed taming. It needed a teacher with more knowledge. We couldn't stumble around in the dark anymore.

I couldn't...

I couldn't hurt my mates by accident.

I couldn't maim them, scar them, *kill* them.

Yeah, we shifters healed in seconds, our bodies resilient and strong, but at the end of the day, none of us understood this gift—this curse. What if a dead goddess's power went above and beyond what we could handle? What if, in the middle of a heated argument, I sprouted thorny vines and smothered my mates?

What if, what if, what if, what if?

All the *what-ifs* forced my hand.

No more what-ifs. *Control.* I was an alpha wolf, sure, but I needed to be alpha of *everything* within me. The power buzzing in my fingertips—it had to know who was boss. It had to come and go when *I* ordered it.

Not on a whim.

Not when I was distracted.

Not when I was emotional.

No.

If Hampton had its own private academy for witches and warlocks like Rosa said, then, yeah, I bet someone there could help me.

Lucian's howl suddenly shattered the night. My head shot

up. My heart leapt into my throat. So sorrowful. So desperate. A cry *just* for me.

Come home.

Where are you, little mate?

Kira answered, her howl just as frantic, just as devoted.

I stayed quiet. Buried my face in my knees. Plugged my ears when Ewan and Soren joined in, our pack's chorus so beautiful and layered and deep, beckoning to my *soul*. Not only that, but their emotions ripped through me like a hurricane. Confusion. Loss. Anger. Fear. My note hadn't been enough, but I knew that when I wrote it. If I talked this out with them, they wouldn't let me go.

I knew that too.

This was for the best. It felt heartless, even now, but the blowup would have been much more devastating if I had rounded my mates up and told them I had to leave—but then couldn't tell them *why*.

Our pack song struck deeper, whittling into my marrow, tattooing itself on my ribs. I threw my arms over my head and balled up tighter, fighting it, resisting that sweet, sweet call to just come home. Shivers tore through me, head to toe and back again, and didn't stop even as the howls tapered off, their final echoes rippling across the starry sky.

Kira's frustration blurred my vision when I straightened. Sniffling, eyes watery and throat sore, I zeroed in on Hampton, on the bright lights of the city. The plan had been to get there by nightfall. I mean, I left the house this morning. Hiking out there, even on two legs, should have been a breeze.

But I'd stopped here, hunkered down, butt cheeks asleep, and couldn't move—for hours.

Kira had left me to my thoughts all that time, maybe because she thought I would change my mind. However, as I stood and sighed, dusting my hands on my never-before-worn pants, she let me have it. Snarled and snapped. Ripped up my insides so that my next swallow had a painful metallic thickness to it.

"Stop that," I muttered, emotionally drained and confused as heck. Sometimes this felt like the right decision. Sometimes, like when I grabbed my backpack and slung it over my shoulders, it felt like the biggest mistake of my life.

But I wanted to keep my mates safe.

If we were going to have pups and raise a pack, I *couldn't* be this unstable. I needed to be better.

And I could do that.

I'd done it before.

Changed. Grown. Adjusted to new circumstances—new problems and roadblocks and fears.

I could *do* this.

So, why did every step across the cliff face feel like I was wading through quicksand?

Despite wearing them all day, these hiking boots were more annoying than helpful. They felt awkward and too big, my bare feet better for this kind of journey, but I had prepared for my mates to follow me. Track me. *Hunt* me. These boots? Never worn them before. The jeans, sweatshirt, and winter jacket with its faux-fur-lined hood? New. Scentless. Purposeful. I zigzagged through the territory, crossing streams and marking where I shouldn't—hopefully just enough to lead my mates south.

They were strong wolves. Powerful alphas. Masterful and beautiful and *perfect* for me...

But this was my domain.

And I'd use that to my advantage.

Phone off so they couldn't even track that, I already had a motel in mind, a little dive on the outskirts of Hampton that I had passed with my wolf pack more times than I could count in the last ten years. Pretty sure I'd robbed the housekeeping cart once or twice, maybe even the odd room if I wanted to go into the city. It was cheap and dirty, which meant the handful of cash I'd saved from whatever my mates handed me for lunches with Rosa would go far, but it was also quiet and out of the way. Once I had a room, I'd let them know I was safe.

Hopefully talk to Lucian first, *maybe* Soren...

Ewan would just freak out on me, his anxiety a standout, dancing like electricity through the invisible live wire that bonded all of us.

So long as they knew I was okay and that I *would* come home soon—hopefully—that might curb their efforts to drag me back themselves.

This hurt everyone, but I hadn't *asked* for Idunn's power. I didn't even want it.

I couldn't risk my pack's safety anymore. I wouldn't do it.

This was for the best. Had to move. Had to leave the territory. Get out and find a mentor.

I closed my eyes and took a deep breath, boots on the brink of our territory line. *Just do it. This is for the best.*

Right?

Emotion hammered me the second I put a foot over the territory line. It snowballed fast, just an avalanche of *feelings* as I brought the other foot over too. I swallowed hard, vision blurring, Kira snarling, and sucked down a ragged sob.

This was it.

Outside a territory that I had no idea existed just a little while ago.

Now, leaving it like this was *painful*.

A knife in the back, stabbing over and over and over again with every step. Arms crossed and head down, I stumbled into the ravine and didn't hold back. Tears slicked my cheeks. Sobs bounced off the trees. Kira eased up a little, my distress infecting her, wounding her just as deeply as it did me.

The boots did me some good here, durable and tough, made for the terrain. I felt every step in these stupid things, separate from the natural order, and for now, that was good. Instead of spiraling inward, I focused on the *clomp* of the soles over the forest floor, counting the footfalls and just letting the tears flow.

Get it all out.

My fingertips buzzed.

Dead foliage coiled back to life around me, greenery trailing behind, tree roots nudging out of the ground ahead like they were waiting for me to dust them with... whatever came out in these moments. I pushed harder. Walked faster. Tried to get my breathing under control—if only to stop the thorns and vines twining up the surrounding trees, an ocean of thickets rising on all sides.

A twig snapped.

I stilled. Kira stopped whining and whimpering and growling, her alertness melding with mine.

The forest had been so quiet today, on the decline to winter, animals fattening up and plants retreating, preparing themselves for the snow that would hit any day now.

That *snap*... had been intentional.

And it came from behind me.

With a deep breath, I peered back, scanning the shadows, the foliage, the savage underbrush of my own design.

Nothing.

Shoot.

This was how it had started last time, noises herding me through the village.

Ewan had interrupted the vampires' hunt before, but I didn't scent my mates anywhere. Judging from their howls, they were still back at the house, just a little east of central Redwood Grove.

I was on my own out here.

Alone—yet not.

Tears dried, I started up again, slow and meticulous, the buzz in my fingertips sharpening…

But the plants had stopped growing.

Like Kira, it seemed the magic in my veins was on the lookout, waiting for danger to reveal itself before the next explosion.

Another *snap*, still behind but more to the left this time. An owl hooted somewhere close, the sound followed by the flutter of wings. A beat later, an enormous silhouette zipped above the canopy, my winged friend getting out of here before trouble started.

Right.

Good enough for me.

I shrugged out of my backpack and tossed it aside, followed by my jacket, and then pushed my sleeves up.

"Come on, then," I barked, flexing my hands, finding a strange comfort in the tingling heat gathering in my palms. My vision sharpened, Kira poking through, and it leapt from tree to tree, stone to stone, just waiting for one of those pale, dead jerks to show his face again.

Vampires were predators—and Redwood Grove, with its abundance of humans and wild game, was the perfect hunting ground.

Of course they wouldn't leave for good.

Another *snap*, narrowing my search to a few old maples to my immediate right.

"Show your *face*! I'm not scared of you," I shouted, trembling with the effort it took to keep Kira contained. Meanwhile, about two dozen daisies soared from the frost-hardened ground.

Which was... kind of useless.

I snarled as the wind shifted, preparing for their cold, iron scent to wash over me.

But I was struck by something else.

Something so familiar that it made my knees buckle. Dirt and moss and forest. Wilderness. Blood from a recent kill. *Fur.*

I sucked in a harsh breath, shock coursing my veins, and Kira whined—

A wolf face poked around a nearby maple.

I recognized her right away.

Mama.

She had aged a decade since I'd last seen her, her yellow eyes cloudy, her muzzle sunken, her fur patchy.

But there she was—the wolf who had found me in the forest, abandoned and wailing and so, so lost.

The wolf who, like her mate, had outlived the life span of wild wolves.

The internet told me that.

Wolves had *maybe* fifteen years, but she was pushing twenty.

I blinked back at her, stunned. She limped out from behind the tree, revealing herself, her body frail, her head cocked.

Kira lost it, wailing and screeching and baying for her.

I crashed to my knees with a sob, tears watering the field of flowers around me.

With a low whine, my alpha hobbled forward, and a beat later, her mate followed. He had also seen better days, aged years in just a few months. Tails tentatively wagging, they clambered over the rocky terrain with some difficulty, and I folded over, clutching at my chest, *aching* for them when the rest of the pack made their way out too.

They all slowed, however, when Mama stopped. She

eyed me warily, the grey in her pupils a sign that she couldn't see as well as she used to. Shivering, I wiped my face dry and held out my hand for her to scent me better. Kira settled somewhat, but she vibrated with the effort it took to be patient, to let my *real* mama approach in her own time.

She padded forward, then stopped to stretch for me, sniffing my fingertips from a distance.

"I'm sorry I went away," I croaked. We rarely interacted like this, wolf and woman, but she had licked my tears dry enough over the last eighteen years to *know* me. Was she upset I left? Or did she understand, somehow, that my time had finally come to start a pack of my own?

Mama sniffed hesitantly, then retreated. Sniffed and retreated, stretching as far as her long, lean legs would allow each time.

And I waited.

Kira held her breath.

Please remember me.

Finally, her bushy grey tail started to wag again. Slow at first, then faster, recognition sparking in her cloudy eyes, and she limp-bounced toward me with a cry. Gasping, I lunged for her too, desperate to hug her, hold on, and never let go. Instead, I let her lick my face and inside my mouth, nose around my neck and in my hair, learning about this new me, where I had been all this time, through her strong sense of smell.

Since Mama said it was okay, the whole pack followed. Papa whined and snorted and slammed into me, his eagerness to get just a little of my attention all too familiar— exactly the same moves I'd pulled as a pup, just the three of us against the wilderness alone. Soon, the yearlings squished in to greet me, my field of wildflowers trampled, thorns be damned, the whole pack whimpering and barking, peeing and scent-marking, turning their heightened emotions onto each other.

In this form, even wild wolves were huge, which made the greeting rough and a little dangerous—if I were human. But I took every jostle, every accidental snap of teeth, every growl and rumble and claw swipe with a smile, happy tears streaming down my cheeks.

It soon became obvious that the pack had a new mating alpha pair, one of the stronger greyish-white females, just a pup four summers ago, finding herself a mate from a different pack at some point in the last month and a half. The others submitted to them, tails tucked, ears flush—even Mama and Papa. But they didn't demand the same obedience from me. Didn't pull rank. Didn't try to force my submission.

Because I was an alpha too.

And even if shifters and wolves were *different*, they must have sensed it.

Kira burst free the second I let my guard down. She tore through my clothes and sent my old pack scattering, some even disappearing into the trees. Once I shook off the tattered fabric and kicked aside my boots, they swarmed, slamming into Kira's massive body, the pups from this past spring keening for attention, *this* version of me way more recognizable.

They were so big now.

Plump and well-fed, Redwood Grove beyond kind.

Finally on four paws, I got in on the play. I wrestled with my kin, nuzzled my wolf parents—more parent to me than Reed and Nikki, and definitely more deserving of the title than the *actual* alpha and she-wolf shifters who created me. I greeted the new alphas cordially at first, until we all remembered that the female had been raised by my side. Then it was business as usual, playing, wrestling, bouncing around the trees.

Eventually, we all ended up in a dogpile, spent and sleepy, wolves scattered around the valley clearing that I'd accidentally overwhelmed with greenery. Sandwiched between my dozing wolf parents, the pair dwarfed beside me, I snuggled in, belly to the forest floor, limbs stretched way out in the front and back, muzzle nestled between my front legs. A long, luxurious sigh roused a pair of nearby puppies, and they went back to play-wrestling, boxing each other with their paws, nipping at ears, snapping their sharp little teeth without ever actually biting.

It felt so *good* to be home.

And yet...

Something was missing.

I couldn't feel them—any of them. No shared emotions. No *feelings*. No pain, no pleasure, no hunger. The connection between bonded shifters ran so much deeper, and as I scanned the subdued wolf pack, everyone clumped together and happy, I knew I couldn't do it again.

Couldn't go back to this—to feeling so *separate* from my loved ones.

Snuggled between Mama and Papa, the pair so much older now, weak and frail, like a waning moon...

I ought to be with *my* mates. These two had had each other for way longer than wild wolves usually did. They had a lifetime of togetherness, memories and love and pups.

"Why me? How did you... choose me?"

"I knew from the moment you were conceived."

"Uh, what?"

"The apples started to grow again."

Was it all because of me?

Had I been *more* than a shifter all my life?

And when I left, they aged—turned grey and white along the snout. On the decline.

I whimpered, nosing into Mama's thinning coat, and closed my eyes.

Being here with them now, sleeping and snuggling like we used to, reminded me of how it felt to be with a pack.

And I had my own pack now.

I *wasn't* a wolf, as much as I loved them.

Maybe I wasn't *just* a shifter anymore either, but I belonged with my mates.

Mama and Papa did everything together. He roamed sometimes, but we always expected him to crest the horizon within a few days after scent-marking our territory.

Lucian was Papa.

Soren had the energy and spirit and earnestness of the yearlings, of every new spring litter.

Ewan was the invisible backbone, the strength, the nose-to-the-grind spirit that kept the pack afloat in a human world.

And I…

I made the apples grow.

I made flowers bloom.

I would start a bloodline, a legacy, and make Redwood Grove *ours*.

I have to go back.

This… had been a mistake.

What I was looking for, what I *needed*, wasn't in Hampton.

It was behind me, with them.

This power was still dangerous, unpredictable, and wild as nature herself, but once the secret disappeared, we could figure it out together.

As a pack.

As fated mates.

As a real *family*.

How could I ever turn my back on them?

Fear didn't get to rule my life anymore.

Not now, not ever again.

Careful not to jostle anyone too much, I slowly stood and stretched, toes splayed, butt way up and tail curled. As soon as I'd had my fill, I shook out my fur, then stepped over Mama and padded back toward my territory. No goodbyes. Wolves didn't *do* goodbye.

Halfway up the rocky hillside, however, my ears twitched, clued in to the sounds at my back.

They… followed me.

The entire pack, right at my heels. Alphas at the front, then the yearlings and the pups. Mama and Papa at the rear, slow but steady as they scaled the rough forest terrain, made tougher and less walkable by my burst of raw goddess power earlier.

I waited for them to catch up, the rest of the pack scattered around me, then carried on, leading my family back into my territory. As soon as we crossed the border, I breathed easier again, Lucian's scent ripening, a few tree trunks neatly clawed by Ewan, Soren's burrowing in the dirt deep enough to make trenches. I nosed at the marks, pointing them out to my old pack's alphas, soundless, making direct eye contact with each one.

Look.

Mine.

The pair sniffed and rubbed their scent glands here and there, the male urinating on a few bushes.

They weren't shifters, but they were pack.

And if they stayed, I knew, deep in my heart, that they would defend this territory too.

Weaving through the western woods, I kept an eye out for a good spot for them to settle. Lucian's cabin made the most sense: tucked away from civilization, no humans dared hike the terrain. No bear dens. No nosy foxes. No snakes. No danger around, his alpha presence warding them all away.

Halfway there, that ivy-covered log cabin soaring in the distance, a howl split the night again.

But not a howl I recognized.

I stilled, ears up, every muscle tensed.

The alphas paused too, flanked by me on either side.

A second howl joined the first.

Another stranger.

Then a third.

A fourth.

A fifth, sixth, and seventh.

Head tipped and senses straining, I clocked their location. *East.*

My nostrils flared. My claws gritted into the forest floor. *Hawthorne pack.*

Snarling, I charged into the night—then lilted hard into a birch when *agony* ripped through my side. A sharp, fiery sting sliced from my shoulder to my left hind leg, so powerful, so *real*, that it took my breath away.

Only a quick glance back confirmed the pain wasn't mine.

It belonged to a mate.

I whimpered, stuck shuffling until the pain lessened. More howls erupted after the last song tapered off, new voices—so many voices.

Another burst of pain, this time across my belly. Sharp and messy like barbed wire.

I zeroed in on this new song, snarling, flashing my teeth.

Ahead, the forest came back to life. Ivy and vines and flowers, leaves unfurling on barren branches. The *power* that usually buzzed in my fingertips hummed now in my chest, Kira's strength *there*—her heart. Her spirit. Her *soul.*

"She's a part of you. She's you, Lyssa."

I sprinted into the shadows, headed east without delay, several of my old pack at my heels.

264

Determined to punish whoever was hurting one of my mates.

Make *them* hurt just like he did.

Make them suffer.

Make them remember once and for all...

Redwood Grove was spoken for, and to challenge us... was to challenge *death*.

19

LYSSA

I found them in the same clearing as last time, right along our eastern border.

But not just four wolves testing our defenses, tentative and uncertain and probably young.

No, twenty at least—full-grown men *and* wolves, some shifted on four legs, others brooding and naked on two. They didn't bother to hide downwind, to mask their scents billowing into our territory, but why would they? Those howls, their violent pack song, had summoned me here.

This wasn't a secret.

I skittered to a halt, claws gritting into the frostbitten ground, pain slicing across my chest, over my belly, around my neck. My old packmates had already peeled away, bolting back to the western woods when we first smelled the chaotic mishmash of rival scents.

Not that I blamed them.

This was more than they could handle.

This wasn't some lone wolf tiptoeing around looking for a mate or to scavenge from our kill.

This was an army of shifters, big as bears when they turned.

And they had brought their alpha this time.

An icy calm slithered through me when I met his eyes, this huge man at the front of the group. His pack loitered behind him, some snickering, others watching on, assessing me from top to bottom. Tall as Soren. *Almost* as broad as Lucian. Salt-and-pepper hair, short and stylish like Ewan, and some rough facial stubble. Tattoos snaked up and down both arms, across his chest, religious symbols Nikki and Reed would have loved and hated, appreciative of the meaning but not the medium.

At his feet…

My mate.

Lucian, kneeling, naked and in chains.

Silver.

I smelled it in the air, the scent cold like those vampires, but it was the seared flesh that stood head and shoulders above that.

The metal sizzled into Lucian's skin, draped around his neck, his wrists, his abdomen, blood weeping down his torso and painting his thighs. I swallowed hard, muffling the whine, then stood taller, hackles up, posture confident.

Not scared.

I stared the alpha dead in the eye, his a startling neon green, practically glowing in the darkness. Moonlight spilled through the bare canopy, a spotlight on the unfolding horror. He quirked an eyebrow, daring me to attack.

I held my ground and ignored Lucian's growls, his grunts, his barely contained whimpers at the way his skin hissed and oozed and blistered beneath the silver restraints.

I'm not afraid of you.

"Hello, little alpha." The male tipped his head side to side, appraising me with a sharper scrutiny than the rest of his pack. Behind him, wolves snorted and huffed, pawing at the ground, while the Hawthorne shifters in human form crossed their arms—tried to make their muscles bulge. They all paled next to Lucian.

Lucian in pain.

Lucian *suffering*.

Lucian terrified, his fear slicing through my belly sharp as any knife—

No.

I bared my canines and focused on the alpha. Losing myself in my mate, distracted by his agony, was exactly what they wanted.

"I was hoping you'd get here first," the Hawthorne alpha admitted, his voice low and tinged with a smoker's rasp, cigarette smoke on his breath.

"Lyssa, get—" Lucian erupted in a fit of coughing and hacking and wheezing. He folded into the silver with a muffled snarl and heaved a mouthful of blood, then straightened—with *such* difficulty, the weight of those chains tearing through me too—and flashed his teeth. "Get the *fuck* out of here."

The alpha jerked my mate's restraints, burying the silver deeper into Lucian's flesh, and I only then realized he was wearing a black leather glove on that one hand—and clenched a gun in the other. How had that escaped me?

"Let the girl talk, *boy*," he snarled. Another blunt tug had the silver coiling tighter around Lucian's neck, unleashing a fresh wave of steaming red over his shoulders. I gulped down yet another whine, rage nudging aside the terror in my bones, *fury* thawing the ice in my veins.

How dare they come into *our* territory...

Torture one of *our* alphas...

Make demands and orders and *smile* like this was *funny*?

Idunn's power bloomed in my chest, soft and subtle this time.

Just a reminder that it was there.

Unable to articulate *my* authority on this land in Kira's form, I shifted back.

"L-Lyssa," Lucian rasped, arms limp and pale hands curled over the forest floor. "*Go.*"

I ignored him completely.

Of course he would tell me to leave.

Abandon him to his fate.

Save myself while they ripped him apart.

Not happening.

"You're prettier than I expected," the Hawthorne alpha drawled, that unnaturally bright green gaze sweeping my figure slowly as steam spiraled all around me. "Shame Lady Fate paired you with three failures."

"What do you want?" A few of the sniveling chuckles died. Eyebrows lifted on the men behind him, and the alpha stood straighter—like none of them expected my calm, assertive tone.

Real alphas were exactly this.

We weren't the fire in our blood—not until we gave our enemies the chance to flee, to scamper into the night before we *ended* them.

Looping the excess silver links around his gloved hand, this naked alpha gestured to our surroundings with the tip of his gun.

Handgun.

Smaller than you'd expect for a man his size.

And that was about the extent of my gun knowledge: handgun or shotgun. One was a little cleaner than the other. One filled you with neat holes—the other split your chest wide open.

"My wants are simple." He lazily pointed the gun at

Lucian's temple, and my heart skipped a beat. "I just want a piece of the pie, sweetheart."

Land. Territory. Money. *Possession*.

Of course.

Disgust dribbled through me with his next leer of my naked body, Lucian snarling at his feet. Kira, meanwhile, remained silent. Still. Calculating every risk, every reward, of every option—totally on my side. Our hearts beat as one. Now wasn't the time to split the difference; we had to *trust* each other.

My words were hers. Her strength was mine. Our resilience came from each other.

"No." No discussion. No snarky pet names. No clever back-and-forth. I wasn't here for a game of wits. No negotiation. *Get out*.

The Hawthorne alpha ripped Lucian to the ground, the silver down to bone at his ribs, the air thick with blood and burnt skin. Again, the silver touched me through our bond, caressed me like a fiery ghost. Behind him, wolves licked their lips and men eyed the red pools around Lucian's crumpled figure, scenting a wounded predator and ready to make the killing blow.

I held strong on the outside.

Dying on the inside for my mate.

"You seem to forget, *Lyssa*," the alpha sneered before kneeing Lucian's face, bone *crunching*, nose breaking, "that I have all the leverage here."

"Your vampires weren't leverage enough?"

It was just a working theory that those bloodsuckers came from the Hawthorne territory, sent in to disrupt our pack's growth, but from the way this alpha's face twisted in disgust, *warped* with rage, his pack twitching and flinching and clearing their throats awkwardly—that theory hadn't exactly panned out.

"What the *fuck* did you just say?" Another blow to Lucian's face, this time with the butt end of the gun. Pain flared in my cheek, and I bit the fleshy insides, fighting it, whimpers caught in my throat. "You think I deal with filthy fucking *leeches*?" His wrath spread like wildfire, the shifters behind him suddenly furious, hackles up and an army of bright wolf eyes blazing in the darkness. "Watch your tongue, pup."

All I wanted to do was fall to my knees and crawl to Lucian. Peel that horrible silver off and cradle him in my lap while he healed. Kiss the pain away.

I held my ground instead, battling back tears, shoving down a lifetime of my own pain and suffering—drawing on it instead.

Power hummed in my fingertips.

"Look, you're not getting so much as a blade of grass from this territory," I said frankly. I kept my inflection minimal, giving nothing away, like we were making small talk at a crosswalk before the light turned green. "So, let him go and leave—before things take a turn."

The alpha glowered at me for a beat, eyes narrowing, narrowing, narrowing, *clenching* shut with laughter. Great hooting howls echoed through the clearing from him *and* his pack, and I folded my arms, hating the way my already stiff nipples pebbled even tighter.

"You smell like honey and luxury, she-wolf," he sneered with another dismissive once-over. "I bet you've never tasted *blood* before."

Fine.

Let him think that.

I lifted an eyebrow, daring him to underestimate me.

I'd killed bigger, smellier, fouler beasts than him before—all by myself, thank you very much.

We squared off for ages, each waiting for the other to

break first. The temperature continued its nightly plunge, our breaths fogging, the Hawthorne pack getting antsy.

Lucian bleeding everywhere.

Suffering.

Surviving.

"Counteroffer." He blinked first, gaze landing on my breasts. "Mate with a *real* alpha in exchange for your mate's safe—"

My snarl cut him off, contempt overwhelming the forced calm. Even Kira bared her teeth, the thought of another *male* touching us, rutting into us, biting us and spilling his seed—

I'd rather die.

His laughter lacked humor this time, cold and cruel, the males behind him smirking, his dick hard.

"Fine. So be it."

"Lyssa," Lucian bellowed, seeming to muster the last of his strength to shout at me, "run *now*!"

The Hawthorne alpha lifted his gun—and fired four shots, *bam, bam, bam, bam*, into my chest.

It happened so fast. Too fast. So much—*agony*. Kira yelped over and over and over again. I collapsed and squealed and arched on the ground, pain beyond any I'd ever experienced ripping me apart.

"Silver bullets." Vaguely, over Lucian's roars and the pack's laughter, I heard the Hawthorne alpha call out to me. "Heal from that, bitch."

Hellfire blazed in my chest, the scent of sizzling flesh so much closer now. Eyes wide, mouth locked in a silent scream, I twisted down for a look. Four clean wounds—oozing, my blood darker than usual.

And glittery like Gull River.

My ears filled with cotton, slowly blotting out the chaos. Lucian's pain paled compared to my own, and every breath became a struggle, harder and harder to take. My eyelids refused to stay open. The world went fuzzy and soft—black.

And then it was just me and the well.

No Hawthorne pack. No *crack* of gunfire. No Lucian howling.

Silence.

And *pain*. Gasping, I staggered toward the stone wall, crashing into it with a wail. This dream world, this imaginary place inside of me, shifted in and out of focus, the water twinkling like starlight, filled *right* to the top.

Hurts.

So.

Bad.

It would be easy to just collapse. Let my knees buckle like they desperately wanted—fall to the ground and close my eyes and wait for it to be over.

I gripped the stone with both hands, glaring into the water.

I should be dead.

A soft whine forced my head up. There, across the well, sat Kira—Idunn by her side. Unlike our encounters in the orchard, the dead goddess was all wispy and hollow, transparent, the sapphires stitched into her shoulder pads dull, her eyes a muted gold.

Kira huffed and snorted.

I dipped one cupped hand into the well.

My grip went slack, and my elbow folded. I buckled onto the grey stone, teeth gritted against the agony.

"Be brave, Lyssa."

Kira slunk to my side and propped me up, using her powerful body to support my hips and back.

Blinking hard, I brought the dreamscape into focus and tried again. Scooped the water—dumped it on my chest.

Massaged it into the wounds, even though it set my skin on fire. Made me woozy and weak and oh, *no, don't faint.*

My wail echoed through the darkness, a strange fog creeping across this world.

"I know it hurts," Idunn whispered, her voice so very far away as I went for another scoop. "I know, little wolf." She braced against my next sob, her hands flying to her ears, then falling back to smooth over the well wall. "I'm here with you."

Trembling, panting, sweaty and sore, I washed the wounds on my chest. Cleaned the torn, blistered skin. Stuck my fingers inside and scooped out the silver bullets. Flushed the holes. Kira held me the entire time. Idunn watched and nodded and encouraged me to keep going—to *drink* when the agony dulled to a whisper.

And I did.

She had tricked me before with a drink, but this time I gulped it down greedily, dunking my face in the well and taking my fill.

When I pushed up, my arms didn't shake this time.

I could *breathe*.

Best of all, the fog had lifted.

And Idunn was gone.

Kira had stopped whimpering—

One blink and I was back in the clearing. On the ground, on my side, four crushed silver bullets there to greet me. Every shallow breath ached with the dull reminder of pain— but it got easier by the second. Kira huffed inside me, nosing around, poking me, demanding I get up and throw myself back in the ring.

Give me a second.

I needed to just… breathe.

Across the clearing, the Hawthorne pack had been whipped into a frenzy since I last saw them, wolves jumping about and snapping at each other, men hooting and shouting and pumping their fists. The alpha kept his back to me, even more religious tattoos smeared down the rigid line of his spine. He was talking—stoking the pack fire—but I couldn't make out the words. Even as the world came back to me, I struggled to be present.

Until one of the males stalked forward with a lumber saw.

Gave it to his alpha.

Who relinquished his hold on the silver chains snaked around Lucian's bloody frame. He shoved them at another gloved male—then fisted my mate's hair.

Wrenched his head back and spat at his snarling mouth.

Bared his throat.

And started to saw.

Agony ripped through my neck with every strike, and I shot up in a panic, the whole world on fire again.

"Stop! Leave him alone!"

A few of the Hawthorne wolves stilled, surprise flashing from male to male; they thought the silver had killed me.

It should have.

But I wasn't a shifter anymore. I wasn't like *them*.

And I never would be.

The alpha continued hacking through Lucian's throat, his naked body blocking me from my mate, from the gruesome *horror* happening some fifteen feet away.

I leapt to my feet with a terrified snarl. A few of the Hawthorne wolves backed away. The alpha kept sawing.

Pain and terror and heartache exploded through me, twisting and coiling and weaving into one, and I finally just let go.

"Get your hands off of him!"

It wasn't only my voice that clawed through the clearing. No, it was a dozen screams, including mine and Idunn and what Kira might have sounded like if she could talk. All

275

pitches and volumes, demonic and angelic. I lunged forward, arms out, fingers reaching, *power* flooding from them. Tornado-strength winds slammed into the trees and lifted a few of the wolves clear off their paws. Trunks snapped. Debris spiraled. Thunder *boomed* and lightning seared the sky. Thorny vines shot from the earth and wound around legs and necks.

The Hawthorne pack bolted, all twenty-plus of them, screeching and shouting and scampering over the territory line.

I let them go.

I only had eyes for *him*.

The alpha whipped around just as my feet left the ground. I slammed into him like the bullets he fired at me, so fast, *too* fast, tackling his much bigger body, snarling and screaming and cursing him in a language that wasn't mine.

No control.

No stopping it.

The world bled red. Kira's howls faded. Idunn's whispers disappeared on the wind. It was just me and him. Fear flashed in the neon green, and he tried to swing that bloody saw over—maybe stick it in my back.

I ripped his throat clean open with my bare hands.

I didn't *need* a weapon.

I am the weapon.

I then plunged my fingers into his chest. Shredded skin and muscle and tendons. Cracked his rib cage. Dug deeper and harder, ferocious, screaming, my mate's agony turning my throat bloody.

Didn't stop until I reached his heart.

Pulled it out for this alpha to see.

Watched the light leave his eyes.

"Heal from that," I sneered in just the one voice this time, all me but more animal, more savage, "*bitch*."

Heaving, seething, I lobbed the useless hunk of bloody muscle toward the territory line, dismissive, like tearing out a male's heart was an everyday thing. From the shadows, hunkered down beneath wind-bent trees, the Hawthorne pack watched on—and then slunk away into the darkness.

Silent.

A wave of light-headedness crashed over me, and I frantically blinked the red mist away—left instead with literal red, the alpha's blood splashed in my eyes and across my face. Up my arms and over my breasts. Between my thighs lay a male with his chest ripped open, his insides on the outside. Trembling, too *hot*, I scrambled off his body, falling, collapsing onto my elbow as the inner war drums went quiet.

A beat later, the earth took him.

My fingertips buzzed. My mind went blank—then the ground opened and swallowed this alpha wolf whole.

A gurgle dragged me out of my stupor.

Wet and strained and, *oh*, Lucian—

My mate sprawled on his side, throat slit deep, chains sizzling into his flesh. Tears streaked my cheeks as I crawled to his side, fingers clumsy and burning when I wrenched the silver off. Threw it as far as I could.

"I'm h-here, Lucian," I told him, all the calm, confident bravery from before gone. In its place: the pup abandoned in the forest. Lost. Confused. Terrified. Kneeling at his head, I hauled his limp body into my lap, then clapped both hands over the gaping neck wound, his skin ragged and frayed, his body struggling to heal itself. Snot and spit and blood and tears soaked my face, but I pushed it all down, crouching to nuzzle his sweat-slick forehead. "I'm right here w-with you."

His chest *barely* rose and fell with every hollow breath.

Blood watered the ground.

Scented the air.

Broke my heart.

Eyes shut tight, I went back to the well. No fog this time, my inner world crisp and clear and in focus. No Idunn either, just me and Kira—and then Lucian. My mate at my feet, his faint, fading heartbeat pumping all around us.

I splashed him with diamond well water. Fed it to him. Washed his body clean.

But when we snapped back to the clearing, he was still filthy. Still cold. Still *barely* with me—

"Oh, *good*." I folded over with a sob after peeking under my hands.

The wound had closed.

His chest moved with more purpose now, up and down, up and down. My fingertips buzzed almost painfully as the color trickled into his cheeks, his beard caked in dirt and blood.

The silver had left grooves in his flesh.

More scars for his collection.

No, no, no, *no*.

Weeping, I tenderly smoothed my hands over all the dips, *trying* to fix them like I did his neck, but that just set off a headache like a hundred wasp stings behind my eyes.

Kira whined softly. I ignored her.

She whimpered *louder*, her cry rattling my teeth, prompting me to look up...

Across the clearing, safe on our side of the territory line, stood Ewan and Soren.

Naked. Sweaty. Splashed with dirt and smelling of the southern wastes.

Staring at me.

Gawking at me.

Horrified.

A numb, staticky hum resonated between us—almost like our bond was so overloaded it had no idea what to make of everything. Lucian sucked down a deep breath, his eyes closed, his lips in a thin line, then groaned.

Tears squished out from behind his lids.

His consciousness, his agony, suddenly exploded through our shared connection.

I opened and closed my mouth a few times, torn between him and my other mates, looking back and forth.

"I-I'm sorry."

What else was there to say? All of this… was my fault. They were out here for *me*. They… I… If I hadn't…

I smeared the Hawthorne alpha's blood from my cheeks, weak and drained and on the verge of collapse. For a moment, I tried to keep it together, tried to reclaim the power and control I had shown our enemies.

But under their wide, frightened eyes, I fell apart. Came undone. Sobbed hideously.

"Ewan, Soren, I…" *Please don't hate me.* "I… I'm so *sorry*."

TO BE CONCLUDED IN
LOVED BY WOLVES
AUGUST 2021

ACKNOWLEDGMENTS

Shout-out to Amanda, my editorial queen! You pick through my first drafts without question, always there to support and uplift. No one gets my work like you do. Every author also needs a phenomenal, supportive, sweet proofreader, and I'm so grateful to have found that in Sandra at One Love Editing. Sometimes typos slip by all the professionals AND multiple rounds of editing, which means my incredible ARC typo-checker Linda is a LIFESAVER. You ladies rock my world!!

Big love to my fantastic ARC Squad!! I'm always humbled that I actually have readers... excited to read my final drafts? Who want this? Who squee and support and go nuts right alongside me?? It's bonkers and it makes me really emotional. I'm bad at emails, but big on love.

Thank you to all the readers who fell in love with my brand of wolf shifters in *Raised by Wolves*, and here's to the exciting end of Lyssa's journey with her stubborn mates!

Huuuuuge props to my GORGEOUS reader group on Facebook!! I have so much fun with you pretties, and even when I'm totally wiped out, you always make me smile. xoxo

To my Sun and Stars, you're my everything. Thank you

for your kindness and support throughout this crazy author journey.

Shout out to my mom, my #1 fan.

If you enjoyed *Hunted by Wolves*, feel free to leave a review on Amazon or Goodreads. Reviews help indies thrive, and we appreciate every single one of them.

See you very, very soon in *Loved by Wolves*!!

xoxoxoxo
Rhea

ABOUT THE AUTHOR

Rhea Watson is a Canadian reverse harem author who loves a good paranormal romance. She writes layered alpha heroes with rough exteriors who melt for their strong, independent soulmates.

In her spare time, Rhea babies her herb garden, bows to her cat's every whim, and flies through Netflix shows like it's her day job.

Want to keep in touch with Rhea about her life, writing cave shenanigans, and upcoming releases? Opt into her monthly newsletter here.

FACEBOOK READER GROUP
WEBSITE

Also by Rhea:

ALL THE QUEEN'S MEN SERIES
(Paranormal Romance RH Standalones, Same Universe)
Reaper's Pack
Caged Kitten
Root Rot Academy: The Complete Trilogy

ROOT ROT
(Professors-Only Academy Reverse Harem Trilogy)
Term 1
Term 2

Term 3

BLOODLINE TRILOGY
(Wolf Shifters & Fated Mates)
Raised by Wolves (#1)
Hunted by Wolves (#2)
Loved by Wolves (#3 - August 2021)

❧

RHEA WATSON WRITING AS EVIE KENT:
(Dark-ish M/F Paranormal Romances, Same World Standalones)
To Love a God
In the Demon's Debt (Spring/Summer 2022)
Surrender: A Lily of the Valley Novella

❧

RHEA WATSON & EVIE KENT
(One author, two pen names — darker content with multiple heroes)

BIRDS OF A FEATHER SERIES
(Standalone, Same Universe, Menage Paranormal Romances)
Shrike (Winter 2021)

www.ingramcontent.com/pod-product-compliance
Lightning Source LLC
Chambersburg PA
CBHW020303200626
46814CB00006BA/2059